I0678888

Jewel

A Rory Mack Steele Novel, Volume 6

Eugene Lloyd MacRae

Published by CreateSpace, 2013.

This is a work of fiction. Similarities to real people, places, or events are entirely coincidental.

JEWEL

First edition. August 5, 2013.

ISBN: 139781927767009

Written by Eugene Lloyd MacRae.

Chapter 1

"I BELIEVE JEWEL IS GOING TO KILL ME!"

Alton Fitzhum thought he heard a sound. His hands shook. Slowly turning his head, he took a peek over his shoulder at the bank of computers behind him. Could she hear him? Everything was quiet and dead still in the room. Slowly turning back to the WebCam, he leaned in a little closer, lowering his voice, "I'm positive she knows I was spying. I know it was wrong, but I was in love. And I guess it's true what they say, you do stupid things when you're in love."

There was a musical tinkling from the bank of computers behind him.

The coldness of fear surged through Alton Fitzhum's body. He closed his eyes for a moment, then nervously looked around at the bank of computers again. The monitors were all in hibernation and black. But that didn't mean anything. She could still be listening. He strained to hear the slightest indication she was getting ready to act. But the only sound in the room was his ragged breathing. After a few moments, he turned back to the WebCam, "I'm probably just being paranoid. But I also know that Jewel has already killed a number of other hackers. Maybe up to 25. Maybe a lot more. I know, I know, I should have called the police but

I thought I could patch things. I was wrong. I was so wrong. That's why I'm making this video for my video blog. I'm going to try once more to make things right. But if I can't, and something happens to me, someone has to stop her." He ran his fingers through his long black hair in anguish, "I swear to you, I never expected it to turn out this way. I didn't realize how my actions would turn out."

Chapter 2

ALTON FITZHUM PACKED in a hurry and left his apartment, heading on foot for the cab company three blocks away. He knew if he called for a cab, Jewel might hear it. Walking had its own dangers though. He nervously watched every vehicle that went by. Who knew when or how she could strike. And when he finally got into a cab heading to LaGuardia Airport, he thought he would feel better. But he didn't. Sitting in the back seat was just as nerve-racking as the walk. No matter how he tried to think positive thoughts, he imagined all the scenarios of how she might kill him. Every car that passed, every pedestrian, every stop at a red light had its own perils.

The arrival at the LaGuardia terminal was no better. Alton told himself she couldn't do anything at this point but he felt so exposed as he got out of the cab. He realized how little he really knew about Jewel at this point. He really wasn't sure if she was capable of killing him here on the spot or not. His nerves stayed on edge as he walked into the terminal and headed for the ticket line. He normally would have bought his ticket online. Or used the computer kiosk just a few steps away from where he now stood at the end of the line. But he was so afraid she was monitoring him that he had decided against it. Wasn't that a delicious irony? The great Alton Fitzhum, computer whiz, and Internet guru, at the mercy of someone else's computer abilities. As the line snaked slowly ahead, Alton glanced up nervously to the surveillance cameras. Was she watching? Did she know he was here? No, he was pretty sure he had left his apartment without her knowing. He had shut down all of his computers and disconnected each of the WebCams to make sure.

"Are you all right, sir?"

Alton's heart leaped into his throat. He was ready to run as he looked to his left. It was just one of the airlines terminal employees, there to assist passengers. Or was she? His mouth opened but he couldn't talk.

"Sir?" asked the lady again in concern as she put her hand on his forearm.

Could Jewel hire someone to kill him? No, that was ludicrous. But Alton wondered for a moment if she was going to stick a poison needle in his arm. Then he saw a couple of security guards just beyond the lady, looking at him in concern as well. Alton realized he may look like a nervous bomber to them. He had to get a hold of himself or he would never be able to get on the plane. Who knew what Jewel could do to him if he was held in custody? He finally was able to nod his head and spoke in a ragged voice. "Yeah...just...just afraid of flying."

The lady just nodded her head in sympathy and smiled, "There's no need to worry sir. Everything will be fine. You can move ahead."

Alton looked ahead and realized that there was no one left in front of him. The lady at one of the wickets was waiting for him patiently.

"Let me take that and we'll get you booked in," said the lady as she slipped Alton's duffel bag off his shoulder. She took his arm to guide him to the wicket. Alton didn't protest. He noticed the lady slip the bag to one of the security guards behind her as they walked forward. The guard unzipped the bag quickly, taking a look inside as Alton stepped up to the counter. Alton paid for his ticket in cash and was relieved when his duffel bag was tagged and returned to him.

The lady attendant guided him over to the waiting area, telling him about little techniques he could use to relax. Alton really wasn't listening. He watched each and every passenger they walked past. He was led to a seat next to the flight counter and the flight attendants were told about his nervousness. They kept encouraging him to be calm but the wait for boarding to be called was nerve-racking to Alton. His clutched his duffel bag as if it would offer protection. His knees bounced up and down as he watched everyone around him.

Chapter 3

ONCE HE WAS SITTING in his window seat on American Airlines Flight 4516, Alton Fitzhum finally felt some relief. He had made it this far. And in an hour or so he would land at Boston Logan International Airport and head over to see his childhood friend Calvin Sergent at the Massachusetts Institute of Technology. They had grown up together, built and programmed computers, hacked into school records to give themselves better marks and then went to MIT together. Whenever they had a problem beyond computers, Calvin was the one who usually had a good idea on how to solve it. He hoped he would know how to solve this one as well.

Alton's dug his fingers into the armrest and held his breath as the plane taxied into position for takeoff. Despite what he had said to the attendant, flying was the easy part. Takeoffs were another matter. He was always nervous on takeoff. The landing wasn't that great either. He always remembered the statistic that showed most plane crashes took place at takeoff or landing. And who knew what Jewel might do at those critical times?

The engines rose in pitch as the power was applied. The cabin shook as they were propelled down the tarmac - the shaking stopped the second they left the ground but Alton closed his eyes tightly. Would it happen now? A few minutes later, as the plane began to level off, he opened his eyes and let out his breath. He turned his head and watched the terrain below, still unsure.

Ten minutes into the flight, Alton began to relax a little. So far, so good. He wondered when the flight attendants would bring around the drink cart. He could use a real stiff drink right now. In fact, he could use several. He unbuckled his seatbelt and tilted the seat back a notch. Closing his eyes, he concentrated on relaxing his body. He concentrated on slowing his breathing. A moment later, his concentration was broken when the plane engines began to whine a little louder. The plane leveled out and the engine noise rose higher. Alton could feel an increase in vibrations through the body of the plane. He wondered if that was normal. He realized the passengers around him were talking loudly and he opened his eyes. He stretched his neck a little to look around, wondering what was happening. From his seat a little further back in the plane, Alton could see the passengers, sitting over the wings, beginning to get concerned. One of them called a flight attendant. She assured them everything was fine. But when she headed for the flight deck, her face definitely showed concern. That made Alton return his seat to the upright position. He looked at the passengers around him. Everyone was talking and nervously looking out the windows. The plane engines began screaming loudly. The body of the plane began to shake violently. Alton gripped the armrest tightly. This had never happened before when he took a flight between New York and Boston. His thoughts went to Jewel. Was it possible? Could she reach him at 30,000 feet? An instant later, American Airlines Flight 4516 dipped down at a 45° angle. Everyone around him began to scream. Alton realized he was screaming as well. His thoughts went to Jewel Tanya Afterburn. He wished he had told her how much he loved her. Maybe he wouldn't have been spying. Maybe this whole thing would have never happened. Woulda coulda shoulda. All because he never had the courage to tell a woman how he felt. In 20 seconds it didn't matter. Impact buried them all in a temporary grave.

Chapter 4

U.S. DISTRICT COURT, Pearl Street, New York

JEWEL TANYA AFTERBURN looked every inch the bad girl as she was led into the courtroom. A spiky, red and black hairstyle, heavy black eye makeup and bright red lipstick made the spectators nod. She must have done it. Her handcuffs seemed an appropriate fashion statement that went along with the small pins that sliced through her eyebrows and the black metal studs that ringed the outside of her ears. A buzz rose louder in the courtroom.

"Quiet. Or I'll clear the court," the judge said sternly.

Jewel was shaking with fear and could barely walk. The handcuffs were hurting her wrists severely. One of the arresting officers had squeezed them tighter, right after he called her a killer of young children. None of this made any sense. She glanced at the courtroom spectators. They were definitely there just to see her. Along with a number of the media. But why? Why was this happening? She was led to stand by her lawyer. The judge pounded her gavel again and Jewel jumped.

The judge spoke louder, "Quiet. Last warning."

A court official stood up and read from a piece of paper, "Case Number 166346, the people vs Jewel Tanya Afterburn, charges are murder in the 1st degree."

Jewel's knees nearly buckled. That's what the arresting officers had said she was being charged with. She had refused to believe it. Someone at some time would say it was a mistake. But now it was out there in actual words in court.

"How does the defendant plead, guilty or not guilty?" asked the judge.

Jewel was so scared she could barely get the words out.

"Speak up clearly," instructed the judge.

"N-not guilty, your honor," Jewel finally answered.

Jewel's lawyer spoke up," Your honor, Jonathan Benson of the public defender's office. These charges against my client are ridiculous. The state has no actual evidence to charge my client–"

"We have a video made by the victim that identifies his killer, your Honor," said the Assistant District Attorney to their left.

"No, your honor," replied the public defender, "all they have is a video placed on a website *before* the death of Alton Fitzhum where Mr. Fitzhum speculates on someone trying to kill him."

The Assistant District Attorney shot back, "The victim specifically named Jewel Afterburn–"

"No," interrupted the public defender in a firm voice. "Your Honor, Mr. Fitzhum only said the name Jewel. There was nothing to indicate it *was* a first name. And *if* it was, there was no mention of a middle name or a last name."

"Is that true counselor?" the judge asked as he looked at the tall slender woman to his right.

"Your Honor, the defendant is the only person named Jewel in the victim's life," the Assistant District Attorney stated emphatically. "This is a very specific and unique name and serves as very strong circumstantial evidence against the defendant–"

Jewel's public defender interrupted, "Your Honor, according to the 1990 U.S. Census, out of 4,276 names recorded, Jewel was at number 522 in popularity." He turned and addressed the Assistant District Attorney, "Are you going to arrest all 22,383 women in the United States of America who have the same first name?"

"He has a point, Ms. Terry," the judge said to the Assistant District Attorney.

"We believe Ms. Afterburn took down a whole plane, your honor," the Assistant District Attorney replied. She was ramping up her judicial outrage. "She attended the prestigious Massachusetts Institute of technology. She has the computer skills to do it remotely. There are 73 other people dead because Ms. Afterburn ignored the lives of others in order to kill her intended target–"

"Then why aren't you charging her with 74 deaths?" shot back the public defender.

Jewel's mind swirled as she listened to them argue about her. About her killing people. Lots of people. How was this happening?

The judge interrupted the arguing lawyers, "Ms. Terry, I would suggest you bring more evidence before the court before you bring these charges again. There is no way I can allow you to proceed with only a first name."

"Your Honor, we request remand in this case while we work to bring you more evidence and for public safety," the Assistant District Attorney insisted. "Ms. Afterburn is a danger to society–"

"You can't hold someone just because you *think* they're a danger to society," rebutted the public defender.

"He's right Ms. Terry. Remand is denied," ruled the judge.

The public defender nodded to Jewel and gave her a smile of assurance. The crowd in the courtroom broke out in excited chatter. The judge banged her gavel, asking for order again.

A wave of relief washed over Jewel. A tall officer stepped up beside her and produced a key. As the cuffs dropped away, Jewel rubbed her sore wrists. She couldn't wait to just go home and–

"Your Honor, may I approach the bench?" Everyone turned to look at a man who was standing in the front row with the courtroom spectators. He buttoned his suit jacket.

"Who are you?" questioned the judge.

The man stepped forward to stand beside the public defender, "Your Honor, I'm Carl Speller with Homeland Security. If you don't have any objection, we would like to take custody of Ms. Afterburn." He held his credentials out towards the judge.

Jewel looked up at her lawyer. He looked as confused as she felt.

The judge motioned for the man to come forward, "And what is your interest in this case?"

"It has to do with cyber security and terrorism your honor," said Speller as the judge examined his credentials.

The courtroom exploded with excited chatter. The judge pounded her gavel, calling for order again.

Jewel couldn't believe what she was hearing. Cyber security and terrorism?

The courtroom quieted again. The Homeland Security officer accepted his credentials back from the judge, "There is some evidence that links this person, Jewel Tanya Afterburn, to the deaths of several government employees."

Jewel was stunned. What in the world was happening? Her public defender looked at her, a stunned look on his face as well. Then he addressed the judge, "Your Honor, we have no knowledge of any evidence regarding–"

Carl Speller simply stepped around the public defender and took Jewel by the arm, "If you have no objection, Your Honor, I would like to take her into custody under the Patriot Act."

The judge could only shrug as the public defender and the assistant district attorney both objected. "I have nothing to hold her on relating to the charges brought before this court," she said. "As for the rest...you can take it up with Homeland Security," she said to the public defender.

A woman quickly moved forward from the courtroom spectators who were in a buzz and took Jewel's other arm. "Let's go," she said as she pulled Jewel away from her lawyer. The two Homeland Security officers marched their prisoner, Jewel Tanya Afterburn, towards the back of the courtroom.

Jewel looked back at her lawyer and the judge, "Help me. Please. I didn't do anything. I didn't murder anybody. Why won't you believe me?"

But not one single person moved to assist her. She was on her own.

The two officers led their prisoner through the swinging doors to exit the courtroom, leaving the buzz of voices behind them. Speller passed a pair of handcuffs over to the woman.

Jewel winced in pain as the handcuffs tightened on her already chafed wrists. "Why are you doing this to me?" she asked weakly.

But the two Homeland Security officers ignored her question and began marching Jewel swiftly through the busy hallways of the courthouse.

"Where are you taking me?" Jewel asked as they moved down a set of stairs.

The two government officials stayed silent. A moment later they were on the ground floor and heading for the front doors of the courthouse.

Chapter 5

JEWEL WAS SHAKING with fright. She had no idea what was happening or where she was going. She asked a couple of people to help her but her pleas went unheeded. No one in the judicial building was the least bit concerned with another handcuffed criminal being ushered through the building. Jewel desperately looked for a way out of this nightmare. They were passing a ladies washroom. She had been in this building a few times on an assignment and there was one possibility. Jewel leaned her head closer to the woman beside her and whispered loud enough for the man to hear, "Can I at least go pee and...?"

The woman looked at her.

"Please," pleaded Jewel, "I was so nervous this morning that I couldn't even..."

The woman looked across at Speller who rolled his eyes then nodded his head. He let go of Jewel's arm and the woman turned her towards the ladies washroom.

But Jewel held her ground and held up her cuffed hands to Speller, "How do you expect me to wipe myself?"

Carl Speller turned red as he pulled out the handcuff key and unlocked the cuffs, "Okay, but no funny stuff. Don't make us chase you."

"Thank you," Jewel said as she rubbed her wrists.

The woman led her towards the ladies washroom, where she stopped and pushed open the door, checking inside. It was empty. "No funny business," she said sternly as she led Jewel inside. There were four stalls. The first two were occupied and Jewel was led to the third.

Jewel went inside the stall and closed the door behind her, sliding the lock softly closed. She lifted the toilet seat up and then let it bang back down. Turning her backside to the toilet seat, she stood there for a moment before peeking through the crack of the door.

The Homeland security officer turned to a sink and began to wash her hands.

Jewel held her breath for a moment, then quickly got down on her back. Her hands shook as she gripped the bottom edge of the partition. Careful to keep noise to a minimum, Jewel slithered and pulled herself into the next stall. Once inside, she carefully got to her feet and looked up at the small window. It was open! She stepped onto the toilet seat, careful not to make any noise. She placed her hands on the top of the stall and pulled herself up. Glancing to her right, she saw the woman still washing her hands. The wall partition shook as Jewel got one foot up on top - then the other one. Rising slowly to finally stand up on the wall of the stall, Jewel was now able to push the window fully open. It was still going to be a tight fit though. But Jewel was determined. She grabbed the window frame and slowly pulled her head through the opening. She pushed the toes of her shoes hard against the wall, trying to get more leverage. There was a scraping noise on the wall.

"Hey!"

It was now or never. Jewel pushed hard with her toes and pulled hard with her arms. Her shoulders went through the window...and suddenly she fell forward. She hadn't thought about this part. She felt herself falling. He legs flipped forward and she landed hard on her back, on a number of garbage cans. They softened the blow but she still felt the breath knocked out of her. She rolled around, flailing her arms, trying to get to her feet. Despite the racket of the tumbling garbage cans, she could hear someone swearing back inside the washroom, yelling for Speller. Jewel struggled to her feet, only slightly aware of some startled people standing a few feet away from her. Finally up and running, Jewel began moving away from the front of the courthouse as fast as her legs could carry her. She wanted desperately to leave the nightmare far behind her.

Chapter 6

CARAVAGGIO RISTORANTE, New York

RORY MACK STEELE wondered what had happened to his client. He stepped out of the Caravaggio Ristorante and stood on 23 East 74th Street. He had flown into New York from Toronto this morning on a red-eye. The New York offices of Highland Investigative Services said a client had asked to meet him here. He was asked for specifically, but no one had shown up. Avis said the woman had sounded desperate. That worried him. He stood under the short green canopy covering the entrance and wondered if he should continue to wait. The Polletto Arrosto Su Crema Di Carote had been good but he had only picked at it, wondering where his client was. After a few more minutes of waiting, Rory turned right and walked along the sidewalk towards his Jaguar XK R-S parked just down the street. There were a few people on the sidewalk but no one he recognized and they didn't even look at him. He detected some furtive movement up ahead on the right. He remembered a concealed doorway but it didn't worry him. At 6'-2" tall, with ten years of Canadian military service, that included six years with the Canadian Special Operations Regiment, he could handle himself. As he approached his car, a woman in a gray sweatshirt and blue jeans stepped out from the doorway. She looked extremely nervous as if she was expecting someone to pounce on her at any moment.

The woman's eyebrows pulled in, uncertain, "Mr. Steele?"

"Yes."

"My name is Jewel Afterburn and I need your help."

Rory narrowed his eyes and looked at her closely. She was about 5 ft 7 inches tall and somewhere in her mid-20s. Her blonde eyebrows told him the red and black spiky hair was a definite dye job. The heavy black eye makeup made her blue eyes pop. Rory had the impression the bright red lipstick, the small pins slicing through her eyebrows, and the studs ringing the outside of her perfect ears were all an outside affectation. There was more to this young woman than met the eye. And one other thing was evident to Rory. Through all that heavy makeup, Rory could see she was very beautiful - not that it mattered in the scheme of things.

"You helped the step-sister of a school friend of mine some years ago. Her name is Annie Rowbottom, I reached out to her and she said you could be trusted," she added as she glanced nervously at people walking on the other side of the street.

Rory nodded his head in recognition. As a private investigator for the family business, Rory had helped a lot of people. But Annie Rowbottom was only 12 when she approached Rory with $9.82 to hire him to prove she had been kidnapped as a baby. Her family was high profile and politically powerful and no one would believe or help her. It turned out to be true. The wife was schizophrenic and the husband had covered up the crime. The Rowbottom's had adopted Annie not long after. "I remember her. How can I help you?"

"The police said I killed someone, but I didn't," Jewel said. She was very fidgety and kept looking up and down the street.

"Okay. Who do they say you killed?" Rory asked. He wondered if someone was following her. Was this a boyfriend-girlfriend thing?

"Alton Fitzhum. But I swear to you, I didn't do it," she insisted.

Rory's eyes narrowed, "That name sounds familiar."

"He was one of the people killed in that plane crash to Boston," Jewel explained.

It finally came to Rory. He snapped his fingers."American Airlines Flight 4516," he said. "No survivors."

"That's the one," Jewel said as she crossed her arms, "they think I crashed it somehow."

"If I recall correctly, there was no evidence of a bomb," Rory said.

She hugged herself tighter, "Well, however it happened, I didn't do it. They arrested me but the judge said they didn't have enough proof. But that didn't stop Homeland Security from taking me into custody–"

"Homeland Security? Why would they be involved?" Rory asked in astonishment.

"They spouted some nonsense about cyber security. Apparently, they think I killed some government workers as well. Which makes me some type of a serial killer I guess."

He considered her story for a moment. "How did you get here?"

"I walked," she said. "I've been hiding in shelters–"

"Okay," Rory said. "Let's take my car." He indicated the Jaguar just behind her. "We can go somewhere and talk."

"You won't turn me into the police?" she asked warily.

"If I find out you *did* do it, I will," Rory said as he stepped past her to the car. He clicked the button on his keychain, unlocking the door and got in.

Jewel hesitated for a moment and then went around to the passenger side and climbed into Rory's Jaguar.

Without a single word passing between the two of them, Rory drove them to the Loeb Boathouse Lakeside Restaurant in nearby Central Park for seclusion. He led her inside and asked for a table away from other people. Jewel said she wasn't hungry as they were seated. But Rory figured, if she was staying in shelters, that might not be the case. He ordered two of the filet mignon with all the trimmings and he was right. She dug into hers and wolfed it down. Rory slowly ate his own meal, watching the young woman, trying to ferret out information about her. Despite her appearance and overwhelming hunger, she exhibited good table manners. She knew which knife and fork to use and she placed a napkin on her lap. Rory had the impression she was well-educated. That didn't rule out her being a killer but the contrast of the appearance and manners were an odd contradiction. Rory ordered coffees after they were finished.

"So...why do they think you killed this Fitzhum?" Rory asked, finally getting into the meat of her story.

"He left a video on his blog saying he thought I was going to kill him," she answered as she added cream and sugar to her coffee.

"Why would he say that?" Rory asked.

She shook her head, "I have no idea. It doesn't make any sense. I barely knew him."

Chapter 7

RORY COCKED HIS HEAD, "He left a video blog saying he thought you were going to kill him...but you say you barely knew him?"

"Uh, huh."

"So...how *did* you know him?"

She took a sip of coffee as she thought, "I met him at the Massachusetts Institute of Technology. We were both studying for a degree in computer science. I left in my second year and took journalism courses at Columbia University instead."

"That's quite a switch," Rory observed.

Jewel nodded her head, "I became more of an activist once I got to MIT and began to move away from the pure techie stuff. After I graduated, I created my own job using the combined skills I had developed at MIT and Columbia. I started a blog called The Cyberspace Sleuth. And I started publishing investigative reports about how governments and the authorities misuse the Internet to spy on us. It's become quite successful and pays the bills. I even did exposés for a number of large print magazines. Anyway, it turned out Alton Fitzhum lived in the same neighborhood down in Greenwich Village. An uncle had an apartment in Washington Square Village and Alton moved in to help him when he took sick. After his uncle died, Alton inherited the apartment. He had also started his own Internet business. He and I would bump into each other when we were picking up our coffees in the morning but that was it."

"You didn't date? No other contact?" Rory asked.

"No. We never dated and we never saw each other except in the morning," stated Jewel. "Back at MIT, a bunch of us students used to get together at one of the pubs but Alton and I were never alone. We were never in any personal relationship."

"And you have no idea why he would feel you were going to kill him?" Rory asked.

Jewel shook her head in utter bewilderment. "No. I have absolutely no idea why he would say that. He must've meant someone else."

"But he used your name in the video, correct?" Rory asked.

"Yes. But he must've meant another Jewel. Maybe this is payback for all my investigations and exposés I've done." She was becoming agitated, "I know a lot of politicians were not happy with me over the years. Maybe they set me up for this"

"It's okay," Rory said in a calming voice. "It's okay, we're going to figure this out. Did this Alton have any friends? Is there anyone we can talk to who might know something more?"

Jewel slowed her breathing and tried to relax, "You...you said 'we will figure it out'...does that mean you'll help me, Mr. Steele?"

"Call me Rory," He said. He looked at her for another heartbeat, then nodded his head, "I'll help. Now, tell me about Alton's friends."

Jewel took a deep breath, "Like I said, we didn't see each other that much. And we weren't in the same circle of friends. I really don't know of anyone down in the Village who would know anything."

Rory nodded, thinking, "Was there anyone you saw him hanging around with? Was he with anyone in particular when you bumped into him at the coffee shop?"

Jewel shook her head, "No. Not that I can remember. He was always alone. There was only one person I ever remember seeing Alton pal around with. But that was at MIT a long time ago. His name was Calvin Sergent. He and Alton were always together. Maybe he might know something. But I don't even know if they were still in touch. Or even where Calvin is."

"It's a start. I'll phone my office and have them do a search for this Calvin Sergent," Rory said as he pulled out his cell phone. "And I'll have them find a place for you to stay while I figure this out."

"I'd like to help," Jewel said. "I'm not too good at sitting on the sidelines, letting someone else do all the investigating."

"No offense, but I think you'd stand out a little bit too much when we start talking to people," Rory said with a twinkle in his eye.

Jewel opened her mouth and then shut it. "You're right. I'll just have to go undercover." She began pulling off the studs ringing her ears. "These are just slip-ons," she said, "and the pins in my eyebrows come right out."

Rory watched in fascination as she began to drop all the bits of metal from her body on the table.

Chapter 8

RORY HAD DECIDED a visit to Alton Fitzhum's condominium would be in order. Deciding to stay close to the neighborhood as well, he set himself and Jewel up in a two-bedroom penthouse suite at the Trump Soho on Spring Street for the night. This would also serve as their base of operation for the time being.

In the morning, Rory was having a coffee, waiting for a report from his office on this Calvin Sergent character. Jewel came padding out of her bathroom, toweling her wet hair. Rory's coffee stopped halfway to his lips. All the pins and studs were gone and so was the heavy eye makeup. Interestingly, the more professional eye makeup enhanced her blue eyes even more. She had asked for blond hair dye and the black and red hair was gone. The young woman was now a platinum blonde with a slightly less spiky hairstyle. The yellow dress she wore settled just below her knees. Ms. Afterburn was very beautiful. And very shapely.

"What's wrong?" Jewel asked as she stopped dead in her tracks.

"You clean up real good," Rory said as his eyes traveled down her long legs.

"Oh," she said. Jewel actually blushed. "I'm used to the stares, just not *those* kinds of stares."

"I don't see any tattoos. Doesn't that go with the pins and studs?" Rory asked.

"Well, I do have *one* tattoo. But it will take more than one steak and one breakfast to see that." Jewel gave him a wink.

"Interesting. I thought buying you breakfast in the penthouse suite would mean I've already seen it," countered Rory.

Jewel blushed again

Rory changed the subject to avoid further embarrassment for her. "I ordered us breakfast," he said as he indicated a large cart in the center of the living room.

Jewel padded over to the cart and lifted the lid off a large plate and the scent of crepes filled the air, "Mmmm. Smells good."

Taking the lid off two other plates, Rory said, "I also ordered toast, coffee, and some bacon as well."

Eagerly grabbing a large fork, Jewel said, "Grab a plate and I'll serve."

A few minutes later, they both moved with their breakfast and coffee to a small table where they both ate, staying silent as they looked out over the New York skyline.

"Did you find out anything about Alton's friend?" Jewel asked finally as she pushed her plate aside.

"Good question. Let's see if we have an email on that yet." Rory pulled out his cell phone and checked. "Here we go. Apparently, Calvin Sergent is still at MIT. He is actually a member of the faculty. And he's living at The Greenhouse Apartments, 150 Huntington Avenue in Boston."

"Are you going to contact him?" Jewel asked as she sipped her coffee.

Rory did some thinking as he nursed his own coffee. "I thought we would slip over to Alton Fitzhum's condo first."

Jewel pursed her lips as she did some thinking of her own. "Do you think his stuff is still there? It's been a week. His family has taken probably everything out of there by now."

"Possibly," Rory answered. "But it's worth a look."

"But how do we get in?" Jewel asked.

"We'll find a way," Rory said confidently. "We don't really have much to go on right now. Even some small piece of information might help us to figure out why this is happening to you. And why he named you in that video." Rory watched as Jewel lowered her head at the comment. She was obviously affected by the fact someone she knew had named her as a killer. That had to be difficult. Or she was good at play acting. Rory had to keep his guard up, just in case.

RORY PARKED HIS JAGUAR half a block away from Alton Fitzhum's condo apartment in Washington Square Village. He and Jewel got out and walked towards the apartment complex. Rory noticed Jewel's pace starting to get ahead of his.

"You seem a lot more upbeat than when I first met you," remarked Rory.

Jewel looked over at Rory and slowed down. She nodded sheepishly, "That's just me. I feel so much more in control when I can do something. I feel so much better going on the attack then the defensive—" She cut herself off and looked up at Rory, "That doesn't mean... I didn't..."

Rory just nodded, "I know what you mean. But let's just take our time okay? Fools rush in and all that."

Jewel nodded in return.

As they drew closer to the building, Rory stopped in his tracks. Jewel stopped next to him. They watched as a man punched a code into a keypad at the front doors. "I didn't expect that. It looks like we're going to need a password to get inside," Rory said. He looked up at the gray building with the vertical panels of bold, primary-colored glazed bricks and terraces. Fitzhum's apartment was on the 17th floor. Climbing up and breaking in would be difficult if they couldn't get through that front door.

Jewel didn't hesitate. "I think I can handle that with my new disguise." Before Rory could stop her, she jogged ahead and called out to the man, "Could you hold the door for me, please." The man turned and smiled as he kept the door open for her. "Thank you," Jewel said. She gave the man a big smile, "I'm so dumb when it comes to numbers. You saved me having to dig into my purse." The man smiled and continued into the lobby.

Rory walked up to Jewel as she held the door open for him, "You do realize you don't have a purse?"

Jewel shrugged, "What can I say. Even punk girls know men never look past your smile." She batted her eyelashes at him.

"I think you're enjoying your new disguise a little too much. Let's go, Mata Hari," Rory said as he brushed past her into the lobby.

Jewel let the door close behind her. She followed Rory down the lobby towards the elevator. The elevator dinged and the doors opened as soon as Rory pushed the button. The ride up to the 17th floor with smooth and quiet. The elevator stopped, the doors opened and Rory took a step into the hallway. And he turned back into the elevator so quickly Jewel bumped into him.

"What's wrong–" Jewel asked.

Rory held a finger up to his lips to shush her.

Jewel's eyes opened up wide and she whispered as she took a step back into the elevator, "What's wrong?"

Rory held the elevator door open and peeked back around the corner. Then he said in a low voice, "There are a couple of men in suits standing guard in front of the door to Alton Fitzhum's condo unit."

"Standing on guard? Why?" Jewel asked in a louder voice.

Rory put his finger to his lips to quiet her again. "That's a very good question," he said quietly. Rory stepped back and let the elevator doors close. He pushed the button for the ground floor. "Why would someone want to put a pair of guards on a *victim's* condominium?"

"Do you think it's Homeland Security?" Jewel asked.

"Probably, since they were the ones involved in your case." Rory stared at the floor of the elevator, trying to make sense of it.

"This is getting crazy," Jewel said. She crossed her arms as if she was holding herself together.

"I agree," Rory said as the elevator opened up on the ground floor. "Since we can't get into Alton Fitzhum's apartment, maybe we should go visit that friend of his at MIT. Since Alton Fitzhum was flying to Boston when he was killed, maybe he was going to see Sergent. Maybe Sergent knows something."

"And if he doesn't?" Jewel asked.

Rory didn't have an answer. And his mind whirled with other questions that had no answers. What was Fitzhum into? What would attract the interests of Homeland Security? And did it have anything to do with this new client beside him?

In a moment, he and Jewel got back into the Jaguar and drove off.

Chapter 9

FIVE HOURS LATER, Rory steered the Jaguar off the Massachusetts Turnpike onto Beacon Street. Rory looked over at his passenger. Jewel had fallen asleep on the drive up to Boston and the yellow dress had ridden high up her shapely legs.

The change in acceleration woke her up. Jewel stretched, sat up and looked out the side window. "Are we there?" she asked in a groggy voice.

"Yeah. My office tried to make contact with Sergent but nothing so far. It will probably have to wait until morning. Are you hungry?" Rory asked.

"Famished," Jewel said. She realized the yellow dress was high up her legs and she pushed it down, clearing her throat as she glanced at Rory.

"I wasn't looking," Rory said.

"Yeah, right," Jewel said with a smirk.

"The office made us a reservation for the Cloud Nine Penthouse at the Nine Zero Hotel. They have a great Sous Chef and they offer 24-hour in-room dining."

"Really? I hope you're not charging me for this, cause your gonna be disappointed," Jewel said.

"No. But I figure one more penthouse suite and maybe I get to see that tattoo," Rory answered.

Jewel giggled.

IN THE MORNING, RORY and Jewel left the Nine Zero Hotel and drove over to Calvin Sergent's apartment. Rory's office had made contact with Sergent and it turned out it was a day off from MIT for him. However, he had agreed to meet with Rory. The Jaguar's GPS made the trip quick and easy and soon the seventeen-story, brown brick apartment building came up on the right. Rory turned into the parking lot and left the Jaguar in a visitor's space close to the building. They followed a young couple inside. After a quick elevator ride to the sixth floor, Rory knocked on Calvin Sergent's door.

A moment later the door opened a crack. A young man with brown shaggy hair and wearing black wire-rimmed glasses peered out, "Yes?"

"Mr. Sergent? I'm Rory Mack Steele, my office talked to you on the phone earlier."

"Oh right, you're the one who is looking into Alton's death." The door swung wide open. "Come in," Sergent said.

Rory and Jewel walked into the apartment. The apartment was sparsely decorated with mismatched furniture. A large flat screen television mounted on the far wall dominated the room. On each side of the flat screen were tall bookcases. Both sides were filled with DVDs for Doctor Who, Star Trek, Star Wars, the Big Bang theory and others Rory had never heard of. Rory couldn't see any sign of an actual book in either bookcase. The smell of coffee, eggs, and toast lingered in the air.

Sergent himself was dressed in blue jeans, a baggy sweatshirt, and loafers. Rory had the impression that in thirty years, this guy would be the prototypical absent-minded professor.

Sergent closed the door and crossed his arms, "Why are you looking into Alton's death? Is this some kind of insurance thing?"

"Something like that," Rory said. "We understand that you were good friends with Alton Fitzhum."

Sergent nodded, "We grew up together. Did Alton leave me some money? Or is this just insurance money for his family?"

Rory ignored the question. "I'm wondering about this video that he made before he died. Do you have any idea why he would say this Jewel wanted to kill him?"

Shrugging, Sergent said, "I dunno. He was in love with her–"

An astonished Jewel straightened up, "He what!"

Sergent's eyes went big in astonishment. "It's her!" he yelled and pointed at Jewel in terror. "It's her," he yelled again as he ran across the room. He ran into a bathroom, slamming the door shut and yelling, "Call the police. Call 911. Hurry up before she kills me too."

Rory looked at Jewel and then strode over to the bathroom door, "Mr. Sergent, it's all right. She's not here to do you any harm. We're just trying to figure out–"

"That's Jewel Afterburn, you idiot," he yelled through the door. "She's in disguise and she's here to kill me. She'll probably kill you too now that you know."

"Why would she want to kill you?" Rory asked. He looked back at Jewel, wondering where this was going.

"Because I'm the one who got the video from Alton. I'm the one who called the police," yelled Sergent. "I turned her in and she's here for revenge. Call 911. Now!"

Rory continued looking at Jewel and did some thinking. Then he turned back and spoke through the bathroom door, "Mr. Sergent, did you call Homeland Security?"

There was a brief moment of silence, "No. I called the local police to have them take care of it. Why would I call Homeland Security?" Sergent asked through the door.

"Because the police couldn't hold her. The judge ordered the District Attorney to let Jewel Afterburn go. They didn't have enough evidence. Actually, they didn't have any evidence at all to convict. It was Homeland Security who took her into custody when the judge said she was free to go," Rory answered.

There was more silence. Then the bathroom door opened a crack, "That doesn't make any sense." Sergent stuck his head out and looked at Rory, "If Homeland Security is involved..."

Rory nodded, "Maybe we're both just paranoid. Then again..."

Calvin Sergent came out of the bathroom and looked over at Jewel, "You sure she won't try anything?"

"You know me, Calvin," Jewel said as she crossed her arms.

"Not that well, apparently," Calvin answered.

"The plane wasn't brought down by a bomb. Do you really think I have the engineering skills to manage taking down an American Airlines flight just to kill one person?" Jewel asked.

Sergent was silent as he considered what she was saying.

"There's more," Rory said. "We went by Alton's apartment yesterday. Do you have any idea why Homeland Security would have two men guarding his front door? A full week after he died?"

That caught Sergent's attention.

"You look like you know something," Rory said. "Do you mind opening up to us? Homeland security is trying to pin Alton's death, as well as the death of several government employees, on Jewel. Do you have any idea why they would do that?"

Sergent shook his head no. He looked confused by the news. "I only thought it was about the video. There was nothing about government people."

Rory walked over to the sofa in the living room, leaving Sergent by the bathroom door. "Do you mind if we talk about this?" he said as he sat on the sofa. He patted the seat beside him to get Jewel sitting down. She did, sitting like a very prim and proper young lady.

Calvin Sergent slowly walked back into the living room. He looked at what Jewel was wearing. "I never saw you wearing a dress before," said Calvin in a quiet voice as he looked down at her legs.

Jewel self-consciously pressed her yellow dress down against her knees as Sergent sat in the easy chair across from them.

"You said Alton had feelings for Jewel?" Rory asked. "Strong feelings?"

Jewel fidgeted beside him.

Sergent nodded, "He was–" He stopped himself and looked at Jewel with a little fear in his eyes.

Jewel blushed, "He never said anything to me about it."

"I can believe that. He was never any good with girls. We were just a couple of typical nerds. Watch the girls from far away but too scared to get close. All our relationships were in our heads. I thought maybe he was making some headway because he said he saw you every day–"

Jewel frowned, "We bumped into each other for coffee every morning. That was *it*."

Sergent held his hands out defensively, "Okay, okay..."

Jewel looked at Rory for a moment. Then she looked back to Calvin, "Is that why he moved into my neighborhood with his uncle in the first place? Because he was...?"

Calvin Sergent nodded.

Jewel Afterburn put a hand to her mouth in shock.

Chapter 10

RORY COULD SEE the genuine shock in Jewel's eye and her manner suggested it was real. But there was a question he had to ask Sergent, "If he was in love with her, why would he say she was going to kill him?"

Calvin Sergent shrugged, "I don't know. He never really said a lot to me about it once we both graduated from MIT. He went on to Columbia for a PhD in software engineering. When I saw the video I just thought things went bad after he told her."

"Do you really think I'd kill somebody because they came onto me?" Jewel said sternly.

Calvin blinked his eyes, "Once you went Goth—"

"Punk," she shot back.

"Okay, punk," corrected Sergent. "You became a rebel—"

"Because I wore pins and studs?" exclaimed Jewel.

Rory put his hand on Jewel's knee to calm her down, "This is not getting us anywhere. Calvin, why would Homeland Security be guarding Alton's apartment? That isn't normal protocol for the authorities to take charge of a victim's home. You definitely reacted when I said they were there."

Calvin Sergent did some thinking. Then he took a deep breath, "Alton and I grew up together as I said. We were always working with computers, programming them, trying to come up with new ways to do things. Truthfully, Alton was much smarter than I was when it came to programming computers. He just had a natural knack for working with software. After he left Columbia he started his own business. He was doing a lot of cyber-security programming for various companies, protecting their computers and networks from attacks over the Internet. He was way ahead of everybody else. I'm just afraid Homeland Security has found something there they can use in one of their schemes to rule the world."

"You think they found something on his computer?" Rory asked.

Calvin Sergent laughed, "Computer? Alton didn't just have one computer, he had dozens of them. They were all hooked together in one room. I don't know how he did it, but he had a number of monitors and several racks of motherboards and hard drives chained together."

"He made a supercomputer?" Jewel asked.

"More like a super-supercomputer," answered Sergent. "He was one brilliant dude. I just wish you two could have gotten together and you got to know him like I do," he said to Jewel. "Like I did," he corrected himself, looking sad.

Jewel seemed very embarrassed by that thought. "I'm not very good one-on-one with people either," was all she said.

Rory did some thinking. "None of this answers why he Jewel said was going to kill him. Or why Homeland Security thinks she killed some government employees. Or what evidence they have."

"Maybe they brainwashed Alton or something," Sergent said. "Or maybe they killed him to get his work and they are setting

Jewel up to take the fall. I never looked to see if that video was cobbled together from other pieces."

"And since we can't get in his apartment to see what's there—" Rory said.

"We don't have to," Sergent said confidently, "we can do it from here."

"What do you mean?" Rory asked.

Calvin Sergent stood up, "I can access his computer setup from here. We used to do it all the time." He turned and headed across the living room for a door on the far side.

Rory and Jewel got up and followed Calvin Sergent into the other room. As soon as he passed through the doorway, Rory was astonished at the bank of hard drives he saw on racks lining the walls. There were several large LCD monitors on the walls as well. In the center of the room was a massive desk with an extra-large computer monitor on it. Rory had the feeling this was the epitome of a real geek's computer paradise.

Sergent sat down on a chair in front of the extra large computer monitor and began keyboarding. Lines of code began to fill the computer screen as Calvin Sergent typed on the keyboard. Rory rolled two other chairs over next to Sergent. Jewel took the seat on Sergent's left and Rory took the one on the right. Electrical whirring noises came from the computer beneath the desk and suddenly the large computer screen was filled with an image of several men inside a room.

"What are we looking at?" Rory asked.

"I'm using Alton's WebCam to look inside his computer room," Sergent explained.

Rory leaned forward to take a closer look at the image, "It looks like there are three men inside that room. And you can see somebody outside that open door."

"That would be Alton's living room," Sergent said. "I assume they're all Homeland Security government flunkies," he added.

"That would be my bet," Rory said. One of the men they were watching got up and sat in the chair in front of the WebCam. Rory sat back in concern, "Can they tell we're looking at them?"

Shaking his head, Sergent said, "No. Alton built his own WebCam. He didn't bother putting an indicator light on it so they don't know we're watching."

"This is kind of creepy," Jewel muttered.

Sergent typed on the keyboard and the image disappeared, "Let's see if we can figure out what Alton had on his computer that they're so interested in." He brought up a screen that showed a long list of hard drive letters.

"He had all those hard drives hooked together?" whispered an astonished Jewel.

"Yep." Sergent gestured with his hand around the room to indicate the racks of hard drives he also had, "I've tried it but I haven't come close to what he was doing." Sergent double clicked on the first hard drive letter on the LCD screen, opened it up and began examining the files on it. He shook his head, "There's nothing special that I can see with just a quick look." He brought the view back to the screen with the long list and clicked on another hard drive. He looked at it for a few minutes and then clicked back to the listing and clicked on the first drive.

"What's wrong?" Rory asked. "You look like something is bothering you."

Rubbing his forehead for a moment, Sergent clicked back to the second hard drive he had been looking at, "It's just...it looks like he has access to his WebCam at two different points."

"Why would he do that?" Rory asked.

Sergent shook his head, "I have no idea. It doesn't make any sense." He clicked on an icon and another image came up on the screen. Sergent shook his head again, "That's not his computer room. It must be another room in his apartment–"

"Son of a bitch!" It was Jewel. She sat up straighter, her fists clenched.

Both Calvin and Rory were startled by her outburst. Rory leaned forward, looking across at her, "What's wrong?"

Jewel stood up - the chair she had been sitting on crashed to the floor as she backed away from the image on the LCD screen - her voice was filled with rage and betrayal, "That's my apartment. In fact, *that's my bedroom*. Alton Fitzhum, you son of a bitch. You were spying on me!"

Chapter 11

JEWEL WAS LIVID. "Did you know about this Sergent?" she yelled. "Were you two pervs exchanging pictures of me?"

"I swear to you, Jewel," pleaded Sergent, "I didn't know he was doing this. Honest–"

"Yea, right. Am I gonna find nude pictures of myself all over the Internet now? Or whatever you assholes do with them, you creep!"

Rory stood up to calm her down, "I know you're mad and I don't blame you. But you do realize - if there *are* nude pictures of you on his computer - they have a motive for your murdering Alton Fitzhum?"

Jewel looked shocked, "But...I didn't know anything about it. I swear to you–"

"And he swears he didn't know about it either," Rory said. "If you don't believe him, why should I believe you?"

Jewel opened her mouth and then shut it.

Rory turned and looked hard at Calvin Sergent, "On the other hand, if I find out you *did* know about this Sergent, you'll be doing all your computing at Attica prison. And somebody there will be playing with *your* mouse."

"I swear," Sergent said as he held his hands up, "I didn't know he was doing this. On my mother's grave."

Rory looked back and forth between the two. Both of them were silent. "Okay then," he said finally. "I will promise you one thing Jewel, if there are any pictures of you on that computer, they'll be wiped out later."

"But why not now–" she protested.

"Because they didn't give this evidence to the District Attorney to help convict you. That doesn't make any sense. They could have easily tied the video Alton Fitzhum made to this information and you would have been convicted on a strong circumstantial case. But they didn't. Think about it, Jewel. They didn't share this information. You're an investigative journalist. Why wouldn't they do that?"

Jewel looked at him for a few minutes, considering all the possibilities. Then the realization hit her. "Because there's something else at play."

Rory nodded. "There's something else happening here and we have to figure out what it is. There has to be some reason for them not cooperating with the District Attorney. By not sharing the information, they made sure the judge would release you. So they could take you into custody themselves."

"Maybe you know something," Sergent said. "Something real important. And they were going to make you disappear." He snapped his fingers, "Or maybe they water-board you to find out–"

Jewel looked at him with a raised eyebrow, "What in the world would I know that they would want?"

Sergent shrugged, "I don't know. I'm just sayin'...."

Jewel crossed her arms over her chest, "That's just ridiculous–"

Rory spoke up, "He could be right, Jewel."

"You too with the ridiculous?"

He shrugged, "Maybe you know something but don't realize it. Or they just *think* you know something." He looked at Sergent, "And there must be something on Fitzhum's computers that they want. That seems to be where they're focusing their attention. We can't change anything on the system in case we alert them. But you need to keep digging, Calvin. Can you do that without them knowing?"

Calvin Sergent thought about it for a few moments. Finally, he nodded, "I think so. As long as we keep an eye on them." He turned his attention back to the keyboard, typing in commands. After a few moments, the image looking into Fitzhum's computer room popped up on the monitor again. Calvin made the image smaller and moved it to the top right-hand corner of the screen. "Just keep an eye on the WebCam image on that monitor. If anybody approaches any of the computers, let me know and I'll back out."

Rory picked up the fallen chair up and placed it back beside Sergent.

Jewel sat down in the chair again and spoke softly, "I'll keep an eye on the WebCam."

Rory massaged the tension out of her shoulders for a few moments, "Don't worry. We'll figure this out yet."

"I know," Jewel said. She didn't sound entirely convinced.

Chapter 12

CALVIN SERGENT CONTINUED to sort through the files on the various hard drives. Rory kept an eye over his shoulder. Files came and went on the monitor. Nothing seemed to be relevant. Half an hour later, Rory was sitting to the left of Sergent, watching as he filtered through the different files on another hard drive. When nothing of interest popped up, Sergent closed it and moved on to the next hard drive. But this time, when Sergent tried to open the hard drive, it stayed shut and there was a beep.

"What's that?" Rory asked as he went on alert.

"It's an encrypted hard drive," answered Sergent. "This is one that Alton definitely wanted to keep someone from accessing." He reached into a pocket of his jeans and pulled out a thumb drive. He inserted it into a USB slot in the computer under his desk and the contents appeared on the monitor. Sergent double-clicked on an icon and a program began running.

"What are you doing?" Rory asked.

"Alton and I devised various algorithms to encrypt our hard drives from the time we were kids," replied Sergent. "And we developed this program to unlock our own hard drives instead of having to remember passwords. It has all the algorithms and the specific keys we developed over the years. Software programmers also create back doors and we developed a number of different ones to use when we set up our hard drives. This thumb drive also goes through all of those different methods and locations normally used in the software or hardware code."

Rory and Jewel watched in fascination as numbers and symbols scrolled across the screen. Then the hard drive suddenly opened up and listed all the files it contained on the screen. Sergent began to go through each one. Several were scrambled to hide their information and Sergent unscrambled them. One file caught his attention and he sat up a little straighter.

Rory moved in closer to have a look, "What did you find?"

Sergent seemed reluctant to talk. He closed the file.

"That was a list of names," Rory said. "Do you know what they're for?" When Sergent just sat there, Rory stood up, put a hand on his shoulder and spoke sternly, "Bring it back up Calvin."

Calvin Sergent nodded and brought the file back up and unscrambled it.

Rory bent over and read the heading but it was still scrambled. "Come on Sergent, unscramble that heading as well."

He did. Rory read it and stood up straight.

Jewel noticed the two were just staring at the screen, "What is it? What did you find?" When she didn't see anything, she moved her chair closer and looked at the screen. She read what was there and straightened up herself "What the–!"

The heading read: 'List of names of people killed by Jewel.'

Chapter 13

"**DID YOU PLANT THAT** while we weren't looking?" Jewel yelled. she sprang from her chair and began attacking Calvin Sergent with her balled fists.

Rory an arm around her waist and pulled her away from Sergent. She continued swinging her arms, "You son of a bitch. You were in this with Alton from the beginning. First, you spy on me and then you try to frame me!"

Sergent swiveled in his chair and pushed himself away from the shrieking, attacking blonde, "I swear I didn't do it. It was just there."

"He's right," Rory said as he held her thrashing body. "I kept a close eye on him. The file was there just as he says."

Jewel's arms slowly stopped swinging and she began to cry. Rory gently set her feet on the ground as she broke down. She turned towards him. He put his arms around her as she cried against his chest. "Why? Why is this happening to me?" she kept asking.

After a few moments, Rory looked towards Calvin. "Can you print that list out for me?" he asked quietly.

Calvin Sergent nodded. He wheeled his chair back to the keyboard and hit a button. A printer over on the right went to work and spit out a piece of paper.

As Jewel regained her composure, Rory went over and picked up the paper. He looked down the list of names for a brief moment and then turned back to Sergent, "Keep digging. There must be a reason why he had this list. And why Jewel's name is on it."

Sergent nodded. He looked at Jewel and spoke in a soft voice, "I know this is hard to believe after all this. But Alton really was in love with you, Jewel. And I don't think he would have ever meant to hurt you like this."

"Then why would he put her name on the top of a list like this?" Rory asked sternly as he approached Calvin.

Calvin Sergent took a deep breath and let it out. He shook his head in frustration, "I don't know. I know he wouldn't try to frame Jewel, no matter what. Even when bullies picked on us as kids, he never tried to get any kind of revenge. That just wasn't him." He scratched his head, thinking, "Maybe it's code."

"What do you mean?" Rory asked.

"Well, when Alton and I were kids and we didn't want people to know what we were talking about, we made everything into a code. We did the same thing when we were at MIT. Maybe Jewel is some kind of code and it stands for something else. Do you see what I mean?"

Rory nodded, "Possible. But a list of names is still a list of names, isn't it?"

Sergent reluctantly nodded his head in agreement.

Rory took a deep breath and let it out, "Okay. So, if it is a code, how do we figure it out?"

Calvin Sergent shook his head slowly, "I'm not sure. In all honesty, Alton was really a lot smarter than me when it came to this stuff. I'm not sure if I *can* figure it out. Unless he left the key behind..."

"Maybe there's something else on the computer that could help us to crack it," Rory reasoned.

Sergent nodded his head slowly as he did some thinking. He turned his head and looked at the computer monitor, "There are still a lot of hard drives to go through. Maybe we'll find something." He turned back to the keyboard and began typing again. He tried to open up another hard drive and the beep occurred again. He brought up the cracking program from the thumb drive again and began to run it.

Jewel walked back to her chair, dabbing at her eyes with a tissue, "I'll keep watch on the WebCam again while he searches."

A small white square flashed in the middle of the monitor Calvin Sergent was working at. A beam of light shot out like a sharp searchlight and focused on Calvin Sergent's face.

Nanoseconds later, a second beam of light shot out and illuminated Rory's face.

Then a third light beam shot out and highlighted Jewel's face as she stood beside the chair.

For a few seconds, all three beams danced around each person's face and then disappeared.

Calvin Sergent yelped as he pushed himself away from the computer and nearly rolled over Rory's foot.

Jewel stood stock-still.

Rory looked at Calvin, "What the h - e - double-hockey-sticks was that?"

Chapter 14

CALVIN SERGENT HAD an astonished look on his face, "I have no idea. I've never seen that before. As far as I know, none of my computer monitors has that capability." He slowly began to walk his chair back towards the monitor.

"What computer monitor *can* do that?" Jewel asked as she remained frozen on the spot.

His voice was distant as Sergent shrugged, "I'm not sure" He looked back over his shoulder at Jewel, "Maybe something set up for holograms?"

"Maybe," Jewel said, "but a hologram wasn't created. This was like a laser used as a search beam. Did anybody get a pain in the eye? Or hear a clicking or popping sound from your eyeballs?"

Both Rory and Calvin shook their head no. Rory looked at Jewel, "What would a clicking or popping sound mean?"

"It would mean you have retinal damage. The laser would cook spots in your eyeball at 100 °C. That would mean blind spots in your eyeball."

Rory frowned, "That doesn't sound good."

"No," Sergent agreed as he wheeled back a foot.

Jewel pursed her lips and nodded, "Yeah. But - if we don't have blind spots - there's no pain - no clicking or popping - that means it was probably a white laser."

Sergent scratched one cheek softly, then the other, "I would say you're right. It could be a white laser. But...."

"But what? What else could it be?"

"I have no idea. I just know my monitors *and* my computers aren't set up for *any* kind of laser effect."

"Oh."

Rory gestured to the screen, "Maybe it came from Alton Fitzhum's computer?"

Sergent stared at the computer screen for a moment. Then he shook his head, "No - well - maybe - but I'm not sure how that would happen without my systems not being equipped–"

Jewel jumped forward, yelling as she pointed towards the WebCam image, "Someone is sitting down on the computer!"

Two of the men in Alton's condo could be seen sitting down side-by-side at his computer.

"Pull the plug," Rory instructed urgently.

Calvin Sergent went to work on the keyboard and quickly broke the connection between the two computers. Everyone was quiet for a moment. "I don't think they were aware of us," Sergent said finally.

"How would we know for sure?" Rory asked.

Sergent shrugged, "Probably when they break down my door–"

"Oh great," Jewel said. She looked ready to run.

"I'm pretty sure they didn't," Sergent said in an attempt to calm her down.

"What do we do now?" Jewel asked as she looked at Rory.

Rory thought for a few minutes. "Do you think they've been able to get into that last hard drive? The one that hit us with the laser beams?"

Sergent looked at him, "I don't think they were lasers—"

"Whatever. Do you think they were able to break into it?"

Shaking his head with conviction, Sergent said, "No. I know Alton's work. It would take them a hundred years because they don't have the algorithms and keys like I do. And I still hadn't found the combination of keys and algorithms to open the drive before that beam thingy happened."

"Do you think those beams were a security device?" Rory asked.

"I'm not sure what they were," Sergent admitted. "It may have been just to scare somebody. But it would definitely take me a while to get into that hard drive. And I have the algorithms and keys to work with."

"Unless he invented a new algorithm and a new key," Jewel said.

Sergent nodded, "That's possible."

"Well, we're going to have to wait until they get off that computer before we can try again," Rory said.

"Maybe not," Sergent said.

"Why not?

"This is underground knowledge so you can't repeat it," Sergent said in a conspiratorial voice. "But some of the students at MIT have created a computer program they use to break through the Internet censorship in the People's Republic of China. The communist government there blocks websites and monitors the Internet access of the individual citizen. We call it breaking through the Chinese firewall. It's part of a plan to bring democracy to the Chinese peasants there."

"How does that help us?" Rory asked.

"The program virtually makes you invisible and untraceable on the Internet. And it makes it impossible for the Chinese government to track you even if they do find you on their government computers. We can go to MIT and use their system to go back into Alton's computers. It's highly unlikely they would know we were there. And even if they did see us, they couldn't track us down and prosecute or arrest us."

"Okay, that sounds good. Let' get going. We can take my car." Rory headed for the door, Jewel right behind him.

Sergent jumped up and followed them, grabbing a set of keys off a small table near the door, "Actually, I have some equipment in my truck that we'll need. Rather than take the time to transfer it, you can follow me over there."

Chapter 15

IT WAS RAINING LIGHTLY when Rory drove his Jaguar XK S from the apartment parking lot onto the street behind Sergent's Ford Ranger pickup truck. The street lights danced off the wet pavement as they drove towards the Massachusetts Institute of Technology campus. Their speed picked up as the traffic thinned out. Jewel was quiet as she sat in the passenger seat beside Rory. She genuinely seemed to be in shock over the invasion of her privacy and the list they had found on Alton Fitzhum's computer. Rory was beginning to wonder if he wasn't being scammed by her. But the involvement and actions of Homeland Security were even more troubling. Why were they searching Alton Fitzhum's computer system? Why were they guarding his apartment? Why had they held back critical evidence from the District Attorney's office? Maybe they were looking into something that *did* involve national security and he was working with the wrong people. Rory ran everything through his head several times as he drove.

As they were approaching the next intersection, Rory's attention was caught by something that didn't make any sense. The traffic light straight ahead was green. It was even reflected down into the wet pavement. Green. But out of the corner of his eye, he saw the cross street traffic light had turned from red to green. Two green traffic lights? Rory leaned on his horn but it was too late. Calvin Sergent's pickup truck entered the intersection and was T-boned by a tractor-trailer barreling in the other direction.

Jewel screamed.

Rory applied his own brakes hard. The tires squealed loudly and the Jaguar swerved left to avoid the immense wall of metal dead ahead.

Jewel's scream intensified.

The right side of the Jaguar crashed into the left side of the tractor-trailer with tremendous force and the airbags deployed.

When everything went quiet, Rory and Jewel sat strapped inside the Jaguar, unconscious.

The smells of burnt tire rubber and gasoline permeated the air.

The only sound was the light patter of rain.

Seconds later a small 'whump' sounded on the other side of the windshield.

Hungry flames began to lick up at the rain from beneath the engine hood.

Chapter 16

RORY'S EYELIDS FLUTTERED OPEN. His eyes slowly focused on a cracked windshield. He could hear light rain landing on the glass. Rainwater trickled down the spider web of cracks. A harsh smell reached his nose and he tried to remember what it was. Then it hit him. The smell was gasoline. He looked through the cracked glass and saw smoke and flames. The engine was on fire! He looked over at Jewel. She was moving slowly but at least she was moving.

The driver side door opened, "You gotta get out, buddy," said a deep male voice.

"Yeah," Rory said as he tried to undo his seat belt. It took him a couple of tries before he got the buckle undone. "You'll have to slide out this way, Jewel," he said.

Jewel was slow to respond. She slowly rolled her head his way and then back in the other direction. She reached for the handle to open the car door. Looking at the window on her side, she saw a mass of gray metal. "We're trapped!" she yelled and began to panic. She reached for her seatbelt buckle and began to fight with it.

"You can get out on this side," Rory said calmly as he reached over to help Jewel unbuckle her seat belt.

Jewel's panic was rising and she fought with the seatbelt.

Rory released her seat belt.

Jewel heard the click but she was so panicky she didn't allow the seatbelt to slide away. She jumped towards Rory and got her right arm hooked through the seat belt strap. She couldn't get free. She lifted her left leg up and tried to straddle the center console. Her yellow dress slid high up her legs as she fought with the seat belt strap.

"Careful or I'll see your tattoo," Rory said.

That comment worked. It made Jewel smile and she calmed down enough to get her arm out of the seat belt. Rory slid out the open driver door and helped her out. She was unsteady on her feet.

A paramedic touched Rory on the shoulder, "We need to check both of you out."

Paramedics already? They must have been out for a while. Rory nodded and let them guide himself and Jewel over to their vehicle. The paramedic looking at Jewel asked her to lie down on a gurney sitting outside the back door of the ambulance. As another paramedic checked out Rory's vitals, he heard a loud 'whump'. He looked back to see his Jaguar burst into flames. Black smoke curled high into the air.

"Looks like you got out just in time," said the paramedic working on him.

Rory nodded as he watched his Jaguar burn. Then he remembered Calvin. He turned to the paramedic, "What about our friend in the pickup?"

"He's on his way to Massachusetts General Hospital in critical condition," said the paramedic. "Is that your wife?" asked the paramedic as he looked over at Jewel who was now lying on the gurney.

Rory wanted to stay close to Jewel so he said, "Yeah. Is she okay?"

"We're gonna take her to Mass General as well," he answered, "just as a precaution. She's still a little unresponsive and I think we should get a CT scan. You seem okay though."

"Can I ride with you? My car just went up in flames," Rory said.

The paramedic nodded, "Sit up front with Henry so I have room to work back here. You look okay but we can check you out further as well."

Rory got into the passenger side of the ambulance and they took off with lights flashing.

Chapter 17

THEY REACHED Massachusetts General Hospital quickly. The paramedics wheeled Jewel out of the rain and into emergency with Rory following behind. Rory felt like he was in a fog, as if this was happening to someone else. He gave the admitting desk his own information and insurance and told them his 'wife' must have lost her purse in the accident. One of the nurses checked him over again, giving him a clean bill of health and then asked him to take a seat in the emergency waiting room while Jewel was taken for a CT scan. He sat woodenly in the midst of chaos and the smell of antiseptic, alcohol swabs and latex gloves. Ten minutes later, Rory saw the two paramedics who had taken him here walking past.

"Excuse me," Rory said as he stood up. "Our friend in the pickup truck, Calvin Sergent. Can you tell me how he's doing?"

The two paramedics looked at each other.

"I know we're not family but..."

One of the paramedics should shook his head solemnly, "I'm sorry, sir. But your friend didn't make it."

"We're very sorry for your loss," the other paramedic said.

The news stunned Rory. He had only met Sergent, but a death was still a death. Especially the way it had happened - so quick - and in such strange circumstances.

Both of the paramedics patted Rory on the shoulder, but he barely noticed.

As they left, Rory sat back down heavily in his chair. Now we had to wait for word on Jewel.

AN HOUR LATER A NURSE approached him and told him he could see his wife. Relieved, Rory followed her down a hallway where he saw Jewel lying on a portable stretcher and dressed in a light green hospital gown. She was covered with a white blanket to the waist. "How are you feeling?" he said as he approached her.

Jewel looked over at him with sleepy eyes and smiled, "I'm gonna be okay." Her voice sounded a little groggy.

"The nurse said they're going to keep you overnight for observation. I'm going to stay with you. Is there anything I can do for you right now?" Rory asked.

"Yeah, you can tell me why they keep calling me Mrs. Steele," she said with a smile on her face.

"You've forgotten the wedding already?" Rory asked.

"Must be amnesia," Jewel said.

"Have you forgotten the wedding night too?" Rory asked. "Because that was a lot of fun."

Jewel giggled.

A nurse arrived, "We're going to take Mrs. Steele upstairs. Her clothes are there in that chair, Mr. Steele. You can bring them along."

Rory went to the chair and picked up her yellow dress, underwear, and her yellow high heel pumps. As he walked down the hallway behind the orderly pushing Jewel, Rory picked up a pair of yellow panties from the bundle in his arms and began to twirl them in the air around his finger. Jewel tried hard not to laugh and she turned red. Rory winked at her.

The orderly gestured to the elevator up ahead, "Could you push the up button, sir?"

Rory discreetly dropped them back on the pile of clothing, took two strides and pushed the up button. They went up two floors and the orderly pushed Jewel into a private room where another nurse helped transfer her to the bed.

"What happened to Calvin?" she asked as the nurse and orderly left.

Rory frowned, his voice soft, "I'm afraid he didn't make it. They said he died on the way to the hospital."

Jewel's eyes filled with tears and she shook her head, "I can't believe this is happening. First Alton and now Calvin. They'll probably try to charge me with his murder as well."

Rory put his hand on her shoulder to calm her, "It's okay. You just rest for now."

Jewel nodded as she bit her lip and tears rolled down her cheeks. They stopped talking as an orderly brought in a cart with dinner for Jewel. Rory encouraged her to eat, telling her she needed to keep our strength up. She reluctantly complied. When she was finished, Rory went downstairs to the cafeteria and had dinner himself before heading back up to see Jewel. He brought her a coffee, snacks and a few magazines to read. It wasn't long before she was dozing off. Rory shut the lights off and settled in a large easy chair in a corner of the small room, pondering over the day's events. Soreness from the crash was creeping into his body and he eventually dozed off himself.

Chapter 18

SOMETHING WOKE RORY UP. He rubbed his eyes with the back of his hand. In the darkness, he could see someone standing beside Jewel's bed. It was a nurse. Rory noticed her lifting her arms up in the dim light. She tapped something in her hand with a finger. Rory shot up out of his chair and the nurse turned, startled.

"What are you doing?" Rory asked.

"I'm giving Mrs. Steele her shot," stated the nurse firmly.

"What shot?" Rory asked. Something wasn't right.

"Her penicillin," she stated.

"Why are you giving her penicillin?" Rory asked in a firm voice.

"For her infection, of course. That's why she's here," the nurse said curtly, as if it should have been obvious.

"We were in a traffic accident and they're keeping her overnight for observation," Rory said in a loud voice. "We're not here because of some infection she has."

"That's not what her records say," the nurse said testily.

Jewel stirred in bed. "What's going on," she asked groggily.

"The nurse here came in to give you a shot of penicillin," Rory explained.

Jewel sat up in bed quickly, now wide awake. "I'm allergic to penicillin," she said in alarm. "I'll go into anaphylactic shock!"

Even in the dark, the confused look on the nurse was very evident. The nurse shook her head, "No. That can't be. The record said you've been taking penicillin shots for four days."

"We haven't been here that long–"

The nurse hustled out of the room and Rory followed behind her closely. The nurse went to a computer at the nursing station and began typing away on the keyboard. She brought up her record for Jewel Steele. With Rory standing beside her, the nurse scanned through the lines on the screen and then pointed to one line. "It's right there," she said, tapping the screen firmly. "It says Dr. Kolsky prescribed penicillin for the patient four days ago. There have already been four doses given–"

A nurse sitting in a chair beside them looked up, "That can't be. Dr. Kolsky has been away in Africa for the last two weeks, Janet. He's doing that Doctors Without Borders thing again."

Janet the nurse as she looked at the other one, "I just came back from two weeks vacation myself. If that's true, then who set up this patient's records?"

The other nurse got up and donned a pair of glasses to look at the screen herself.

While the two nurses tried to figure things out, Rory quickly headed back to Jewel's room.

"Did you figure out what was going on?" Jewel asked as Rory rushed into the room.

Rory quickly picked up her clothes and placed them on the bed, "Get dressed. We have to leave." He began to pull the curtain across to give her some privacy.

Jewel pushed the covers back, "What's wrong?"

"We'll talk after. Right now, you need to hurry and we need to go." Rory went to the other side of the curtain to give her privacy and he pulled out his cell phone, making a call to his office.

"You're scaring me, Rory," Jewel said on the other side of the curtain as she dressed.

Rory closed off the call as Jewel came out from behind the curtain. He put a finger to his lips to indicate no talking. He took her by the arm and walked her over to the door. She was still unsteady on her feet and they had to move slowly. Rory saw a wheelchair in the hallway and he took Jewel over to it and had her sit down. He took a blanket off a nearby cart and placed it over her lap and legs. Pushing the wheelchair towards the elevator, Rory kept a wary eye on the empty hallways. Once they were inside the elevator, he pushed the button for the ground floor. Jewel started to talk but he again put his finger to his lips. Several other people got in at the next floor and Rory watched them closely. Once they reached the ground floor, Rory pushed Jewel towards the lobby, scanning for any sign of danger in front or behind them. A Lincoln Navigator SUV was parked outside the front doors of the hospital. Rory wheeled Jewel outside and over towards it.

A young man got out of the driver seat, "Mr. Steele?"

Rory nodded and pulled out his wallet, showing the young man his driver's license and credit card. The young man gave Rory the keys to the SUV. Rory took Jewel around to the passenger side. She got up out of the wheelchair and Rory helped her into the Lincoln. Rory hustled around to the driver's side and they took off. Rory made a number of quick turns, checking behind him to see if anybody was following as he turned down the various streets.

"You want to tell me what's going on?" Jewel asked. Her hands were shaking.

"Did you give them any information about yourself? Anything to the paramedics or at the hospital?" Rory asked.

"No. Nothing," Jewel answered. "Why?"

"Because somebody tampered with the record they set up for you in the hospital computer system. It did show doctors instructions to give you penicillin," Rory said. "That could've been an accident. But what scared me is that it had your address in Greenwich Village in New York along with your date of birth. I never gave them anything like that. I didn't even know it. It looked like a combination of the record they must have set up today, combined with your real medical records to make everything look authentic. But there was no mention of allergies of any kind."

"How could that happen?" Jewel asked.

"I don't know," Rory said. "But it would take someone with the ability to access the hospital database as well as your own personal medical records to set that up."

"Someone like Homeland Security?" asked a scared Jewel. She glanced into the side mirror, looking to see if they were being followed

"Possibly," Rory said. "I know this may sound crazy but that truck that killed Calvin Sergent didn't just run a red light. I noticed just before he entered the intersection that the lights were green in both directions. I saw the cross light turn from red to green just before he was killed."

A stunned Jewel looked at Rory, "What? How could that happen?"

"I don't know," Rory admitted. "But we seem to have stumbled into something that has some very powerful people involved. First, we have Alton Fitzhum killed in a plane crash that seems unexplainable. Then we find Homeland Security guarding his apartment and going through his system with a fine tooth comb. Then we have Calvin Sergent killed by a strange anomaly with the traffic lights after he gets into Fitzhum's computer. And now tonight, someone tampers with the hospital computer to try and kill you - even though no one in that hospital knows who you really are."

"Maybe they saw the story about me? And a picture–"

"That would have been the old you - red and black hair - black eye makeup - red lipstick - pins and metal studs."

"Oh, right."

"Who knew the new Jewel Tanya Afterburn?"

Chapter 19

THE DRIVE BACK to the Nine Zero Hotel was tense and took more time than it should have. Rory varied his speed and took several unnecessary turns to make sure they weren't being followed. He also tried to avoid as many stoplights as possible. When he couldn't, when they had to navigate a green light, he was extra vigilant before entering the intersection. Jewel sat in the passenger's seat without speaking. Her arms were crossed and Rory noticed her nervously tapping her elbow with her fingers. She kept glancing in the side mirror to see if they were being followed.

AS SOON AS THEY STEPPED into their Cloud Nine Penthouse Suite, the pent-up emotion in Jewel broke out in a tight, strained voice, "I'm scared Rory!" She walked towards the living area, turning aimlessly in circles as the words tumbled out of her, "I never had someone trying to kill me before." She pushed her fingers through her hair, piling it high on her head, "Even with all the stories I did exposing people on my blog, no one ever went that far–"

Rory put his hands gently on her shoulders to stop her spinning, "I can understand how you feel."

Jewel turned to look at him, fear and anxiety etched on her face, "No, you can't. They're not trying to kill you–"

Rory looked into her blue eyes. "I'll do everything I can to keep you safe."

Jewel licked her lips and nodded. "I'm freaking out, aren't I?"

Rory nodded his head, "Yeah, kind of."

Jewel took a deep breath and tried to slow her breathing as she talked to herself, "Get a grip on yourself Afterburn. You'll be okay."

Rory watched her slowly compose herself. She walked over to one of the easy chairs, wringing her hands on the way and sat down. Rory took the chair beside her and they sat there silently for a few moments. Jewel began moving her head back and forth, trying to work a few kinks out.

"A little sore from the accident?"

Jewel nodded and massaged the back of her neck with her right hand. "I'll be okay though. I'm getting a grip on myself. Do you think we could get some breakfast?"

"Sure. Why don't you get the menu from that desk over there and order room service." He pulled out his cell phone, "Would you mind getting me some scrambled eggs, bacon, toast and coffee while you're at it?" Rory asked. "I've got some calls to make while you're doing that."

AN HOUR LATER THEY were eating breakfast at the table, looking out over the Boston skyline. Jewel was quiet but Rory could tell she was worried. As they were finishing up a knock came on the hotel room door. Jewel was startled but Rory put a hand of reassurance on her shoulder as he got up. Rory went over to the door and looked through the peephole. Opening the door, he instructed someone to come inside. A man in a blue suit entered the suite followed by several other people carrying packages. They set them down just inside the door. Rory gave the man in the blue suit as well as each person a large tip and they all left.

"What are those for?" Jewel asked as she wandered over, carrying her coffee.

Rory bent down and began to separate the packages. He pointed out several on the right, "These ones are for you."

Jewel knelt gingerly, set her coffee down on the floor beside the packages and opened one. "It's clothes!"

Rory nodded, "I thought you could use a change of clothing. I hope they fit."

Jewel pulled out a couple of blouses, a couple of sweaters and two pairs of blue jeans. "They're exactly my size. You have a good eye Mr. Steele," Jewel said. Then she cleared her throat as she looked inside one of the packages. She reached inside and then held up a pair of skimpy black panties in her left hand and a pair of skimpy white panties in her right hand.

"Those will just make things easier on my good eye," explained Rory as he looked at the wisps of lingerie.

"Uh huh," was all she said. Jewel gathered everything up and headed for the bathroom, "I'm gonna take a shower."

"Call for help if the soap gets too heavy," Rory said.

Jewel giggled.

Chapter 20

RORY DUG THROUGH the packages and pulled out some clothes for himself. He also pulled out a Baby Eagle 9915 RL Polymer 9mm handgun along with a shoulder holster. Things were getting very serious and Rory wanted to make sure he and Jewel could protect themselves. With lethal force if necessary. He gathered up all the items and headed for the second bathroom. A quick shave and a hot shower would help him think.

An hour later Rory walked out of the bathroom wearing a fresh pair of blue jeans and a denim shirt. Jewel was already back in the living room, sitting at the long table and sipping a coffee. She was dressed in blue jeans and a frilly white blouse that accentuated her bust and the scent of fresh, patchouli-rose soap hung in the air as he approached her.

"What do we do now?" she asked him

Rory walked over to another package that was still sitting on the floor. He squatted down beside it and pulled out a laptop computer. He brought it over to Jewel and set it on the table in front of her. He then pulled a folded sheet of paper out of his pocket and placed it next to the laptop, "This is the printout of names Calvin did before we left his apartment. Maybe you can figure out who these people are and how they fit in."

Jewel set her coffee down and gently smoothed the folded creases out of the paper. She lightly brushed the fingertips of her right hand over her name at the top of the paper. "I really don't know why my name is on this paper."

"We'll figure it out. One step at a time. Why don't we start with checking these names and see if they *are* dead? And if they are - how did it happen."

Jewel took a deep breath and let it out. She nodded and turned her attention to the laptop, opening it up. She started up the laptop and connected to the Internet through the wireless connection through the hotel. Rory made himself a coffee and sat down beside Jewel. He sipped his coffee as he watched her work. After twenty minutes, he got up and went over to watch the television. The news report of Calvin Sergent's death talked about his time at MIT and how he would be missed by his family in the Boston area. The reporter said a transport truck had run a red light. Rory knew different. So many things ran through Rory's head as he sat there, only half watching the television. He wondered how someone could tamper with a set of traffic lights. And how could they set it up so quickly? Or how could someone get into the computer system at Massachusetts General Hospital and change things so quickly? They must've been watched or followed. But why? Maybe it was Calvin Sergent who was being followed? Maybe Calvin Sergent and Alton Fitzhum had been involved in something that led to their deaths? That made more sense. And Jewel Afterburn was a convenient patsy. Or maybe she *was* involved with the other two and someone had tried to kill her as well. But whether she was a patsy or was part of it, something still bothered Rory. Why would Alton Fitzhum make a video accusing Jewel of trying to kill him? How did that fit in?

And why would he say she killed the people on that list? Was it all part of an elaborate ruse in case they had gotten caught? Or was she really a killer? She didn't seem to be the type. Then again, Rory had come across a number of people whose looks and actions didn't quite mesh. He got up to get another coffee and observed Jewel out of the corner of his eye. He still wasn't convinced one way or another about her.

"Do you want to see what I have?"

It took a moment before Rory realized she had said something. "Pardon?"

"Do you want to see what I have?" she repeated slowly. "And no, I'm not talking about *that*, I'm talking about the list," she said with a mischievous smile.

"Right," Rory said as he walked over to sit down beside her.

"Are you all right?" Jewel asked.

"Yeah. Just doing a lot of thinking. What have you got?"

Jewel looked at him for a moment and then turned her attention back to the laptop screen. "We have 26 names on the list. I found obituaries on every single one of them."

Rory sat up straight. "What? Are you serious?"

Jewel nodded, "But not all of them were government employees. Exactly the opposite, in fact. Fourteen of them were teenagers or young men barely in their twenties. All of them appeared to have been involved in computer hacking in one form or another. Ten of them were actually arrested by the police at one point or another."

"Arrested for hacking?"

"Yes. Those ten were involved in some very serious Internet hacking cases. They either broke into websites to gather names and credit card information or they hacked directly into major credit card companies to obtain the information. The other four I found tied into handles used on various hacking forums and social networking sites dedicated to hackers. These four teenagers were dedicated to teaching others how to hack into major companies or government websites. They were also involved in developing and selling the digital hacking tools used by others."

"How about the other twelve names?" Rory asked.

"I wasn't able to find anything to do with computer hacking for those names. But all of them *did* work for various government agencies when they died. I found resumes online for every one of them. They all had some serious computer skills."

Rory's eyes narrowed. He ran a hand through his hair as he pondered the information, "So...we know all 26 names on the list were involved with computers or the Internet. And they're all dead. That's two ways they're all tied together. The question is...what does it mean?"

"And why would Alton say I killed them? Isn't that another question you need answered?"

"Can you blame me?" Rory asked after a moment.

Jewel sat back and crossed her arms, "No. The circumstantial evidence against me seems to be mounting up. I don't blame you for not trusting me. "

"Well, if you were willing to show me your tattoo, I'd know for sure you wouldn't hide anything from me." Rory winked at her.

Jewel giggled and she relaxed.

"Too bad we never made it to MIT with Sergent and got back into Alton Fitzhum's computer system. There may have been some answers in there–"

Jewel shot up straight in her chair, "Holy crap." A moment later, she got up and moved with purpose towards the bathroom.

Chapter 21

"**WHAT'S WRONG?**" Rory called out as he turned in his chair. Jewel disappeared into the bathroom without answering. She returned a few minutes later with the yellow dress in her hands.

Rory watched her as she sat down and opened up a zippered pocket on the yellow dress.

"With everything that happened with Calvin, I forgot all about this." She pulled out a thumb drive and threw the dress over the back of a chair, "Calvin copied all of the programs he was using onto this thumb drive and gave it to me. He said he wanted me to know that he had nothing to do with spying on me. He said if he couldn't wipe out any possible videos or pictures of me on Alton's computers later, I could always go back in and do it myself."

Rory took the thumb drive from her hand and looked at it, "Do you think you can use this to get into Alton's computer?"

Jewel shrugged, "We can try."

"And if they catch us doing it, we could be in even more danger," warned Rory.

"In for a penny, in for a pound. Someone's already made my life a living hell," Jewel said. She took the thumb drive from Rory and plugged it into the USB port at the side of the laptop. The laptop began to whirl to life. Jewel opened up the thumb drive and looked at the various icons. "This one marked AH is the one Calvin clicked on to connect. I think." She double-clicked on the icon and the communications window opened up. Numbers and lines scrolled up the screen for a few moments and then they were connected to Alton Fitzhum's computer again. Jewel's hand was shaking as she double-clicked on the first hard drive and then on the WebCam icon. They had a view into Alton's computer room again. There were three men in the room this time and they were all standing in front of the computer screen talking.

"Can we hear what they're saying?" Rory asked.

"I think so," Jewel answered. She clicked on the sound icon.

"–of the hard drives are encrypted," the man in the center said.

The man on the right put his hands on his hips, "I can't believe Stan couldn't get into them. He was the best tech I ever worked with."

"Anyone talk to his wife yet?" the man on the left asked.

The man in the center nodded, "Yeah. My wife was over with Phyllis last night. Everything is set for Wednesday. Now, why don't you guys get to work on this thing and crack it open? Dockerty wants to know what's inside there."

As one of the men sat down in front of the WebCam, Jewel backed out of the program quickly and shut everything down. "I'm not sure if I can be as good as Calvin was and not get caught," she said.

"That's okay. I don't blame you. We can try again later," Rory said. "In the meantime, do a Google search with Stan or Stanley, Phyllis, New York and 'obit' and see what you come up with."

Jewel brought up the search screen and typed in the parameters. The first link at the top of the search results was a recent obituary. Jewel clicked on the link and opened up the web page. It was the announcement page for a New York funeral home. There were four names listed and she clicked on the third. Jewel read the headline, "Stanley Jonathan Morrow Dead At 39." She tapped the obit picture on the screen, "That was one of the men in the room when Calvin connected to Alton's computer yesterday." Jewel used her finger to run down through the obituary. She tapped the screen again, "And his wife's name was Phyllis."

"So this has to be the Stan they were talking about," reasoned Rory. "Does it say how he died?"

Jewel shook her head no, "It just says 'suddenly.'"

"How about where he was working?"

Jewel ran her finger down the obituary again until she found it, "He worked for the Office of Homeland Security."

Rory sat back in his chair, "We now know for sure who has so much interest in Alton's computers." He stared at the computer screen as he rubbed his chin.

Jewel looked at Rory, "What are you thinking?"

"Well...first this Stanley Jonathan Morrow was with a government agency and he was working with computers and the Internet."

Jewel thought about it for a moment and then realized what he meant. "Like those twelve names on the list," reasoned Jewel.

"Right. But he was also trying to break into Alton's computer system so...technically he could be considered a hacker."

Jewel's eyes opened up wide, "Fourteen of the names on that list were also involved with hacking. That would mean this Stanley's death is tied in with all the people on that list, one way or another."

"And it's possible the twelve government employees on the list were also involved with hacking in their work," Rory reasoned.

"You mean like spies?" Or maybe like a big brother thing, monitoring our emails?"

"Possible. And if so - someone seems to be killing computer hackers, no matter who they work for," Rory concluded.

"In some ways, I can understand why. A lot of people have been hurt by hackers. Some people get their credit card information stolen and lose loads of money. Others steal your identity and your entire life. Sometimes they just break into your computer and destroy all your work. I've had that happen myself. But killing them seems to be a bit extreme."

Rory narrowed his eyes in thought, "True. But there is still one other thing that I don't understand."

"What's that?"

He looked directly at her, "How are you involved. Jewel?"

Chapter 22

RORY HAD SET the alarm for 2 AM. He shut it off and walked out into the living room suite in a bathrobe. He heard a door open and looked back over his shoulder. Jewel was padding out of her bedroom in a bathrobe as well. "Time to go to work?" she asked in a sleepy voice.

"Hopefully they're not working 24 hours around the clock trying to crack into the computer," Rory said as he walked over to the coffee maker. He watched as Jewel went over and started up the laptop. He made 2 cups of coffee and doctored them with creamer and sugar. He walked back over to the table and saw that Jewel had plugged the thumb drive into the USB port. He set her coffee down and sat in the chair beside her, sipping his own and hoping the rich scent of the coffee and the shot of caffeine would keep him awake.

Jewel wiped the sleep from her eyes and took a drink of coffee as well before setting to work. She clicked on the icon and the lines of code scrolled down the screen again. In a matter of moments, they were back into Alton Fitzhum's computer. Jewel brought up the WebCam again. The computer room on the other side of the connection was lit up but the room was empty. Jewel put the WebCam image into the top right corner of the screen, "Okay. Where should I start?"

Rory scratched the stubble on his chin, thinking, "Why don't we try to take a look at the last hard drive Calvin Sergent had been working on?"

Jewel rubbed one eye for a moment and then nodded, "Yeah. That sounds good." She clicked on one of the hard drive icons further down the list. "He said this one was encrypted if I remember correctly and he used one of these programs...." She was quiet as he looked through the files on the thumb drive. There was an icon labeled 'cracker' and Jewel double clicked on it. Another program started up and lines of numbers and letters scrolled down the screen. Jewel picked up her coffee and settled back to wait.

Curiously, a small white square flashed in the middle of the monitor. Before either Rory or Jewel could react, a beam of light shot out and focused on Jewel's face. She dropped her coffee on the floor.

A second beam of light shot out and illuminated Rory's face.

The beams danced around their faces for a few seconds as they sat there frozen.

They disappeared as quickly as they had come.

Finally reacting, Jewel shot away from the laptop. She stumbled over her chair as it crashed to the floor and she fell on her back - the robe parted and flopped wide open, revealing her naked body - she grabbed the sides and wrapped it back around her. Scrambling to her knees, she knotted the belt loosely, staring at the laptop, "What the hell was that? That scared the crap out of me."

Rory was still frozen on the spot with his coffee halfway to his lips, "I have no idea. Can computers really do that?"

Jewel blinked and then muttered, "Not that I know of. Even Calvin didn't think so." She pulled the cord on the robe tighter, "I think I just showed you my tattoo."

"Really? Too bad I was distracted." Rory put his coffee down and touched the computer screen.

Jewel got up and slowly approached the laptop, "Well, keep your eyes open. If that happens again - I may just run right out of his robe."

Rory pulled another chair over and sat down, considering the laptop, "When it first happened - this light thing - what did you and Calvin call that that beam? A white laser?"

"That was the only thing that made sense," Jewel said. "But even then I'm not sure how..." She was biting on a thumbnail as she looked at the laptop. Then she bent down and picked up the coffee cup, before heading across the room, "I need another coffee."

As Jewel was making another coffee she heard a tinkling sound behind her. She stopped and looked over her shoulder, "What was that?"

Rory sat still in his chair. He shook his head slowly, "I don't know. It came from the laptop. Just like at–"

A swirl of colored lights appeared in the middle of the computer screen.

The colors grew in intensity and swirled faster.

Jewel walked part way back and then froze, whispering, "What is that?"

"I have no idea." Rory slowly leaned in closer - and then pulled his head back.

The colors seemed to leave the screen - beginning a dance in the air in front of the laptop.

Now Rory pushed with his feet and rolled his chair back from the laptop. He heard a gasp from Jewel.

Slowly, like a genie from a bottle, a form began to rise in the swirling colors.

Rory slowly stood up and took several cautious steps backward. He bumped into Jewel. "Sorry," he whispered as he took a step to the side.

"Uh huh," Jewel whispered. She stared at the form beginning to rise from the colors.

A face slowly appeared like a hologram, surrounded by dancing, swirling colors, numbers, and symbols. Sine waves danced just below the form of the face. The center of the hologram solidified into the head of a bald, beautiful woman made of colors. It looked straight at Rory.

Jewel dropped her coffee cup on the floor again.

The hologram looked down at the shattered cup and then back up at Jewel. She turned her attention back to Rory. The mouth moved and a voice of colors and music said, "You are Rory Mack Steele."

"Holy crap. How is that happening?" Jewel whispered.

The hologram turned its attention to Jewel and cocked her head, "You are Jewel Tanya Afterburn."

Jewel took a step backward, "What is that thing?"

Rory moved slowly to his left. The eyes of the hologram turned to follow his movement. "Just the head appears to be a three-dimensional hologram. The rest of it is more like...like a flat light show."

"Does it make a difference?" Jewel asked in a nervous voice as she crossed her arms.

"Maybe not," Rory agreed, "but I'd just like to understand how that's being done–"

The hologram looked at him, "Light quantum modified lasers through cyberspace is the easiest explanation for you."

Rory raised his eyebrows, "Okay. And obviously coupled with some type of artificial intelligence." He glanced at Jewel, "How is it able to answer questions–?"

The musical voice spoke again, "Quantum computing using Simon's algorithm is the easiest explanation for you."

Pursing his lips, Rory said, "It doesn't seem to think much of my intelligence."

Jewel objected, "That explanation that thing is giving you is crap. It's not possible–"

The hologram looked directly at Jewel and seemed to grow larger in her direction, "Your mind is limited. Mine is not. Mine is infinite."

Jewel uncrossed her arms and took another step backward.

Everything in the hotel room was quiet as Rory studied the hologram. Then he glanced back at Jewel, "Do you notice anything familiar about the face and the voice?"

Jewel opened her mouth to say something and then shook her head slowly no instead.

"It's you. That's your face and your voice. It's more like music and - but that is you."

Cursing softly, Jewel crossed her arms in self-defense, "I was afraid you were going to say that. It's like - looking in a weird mirror. What the hell is going on here?"

Rory took a step back to stand beside Jewel. He looked at the hologram for a few moments, thinking. Finally, he addressed the hologram, "Do you know Alton Fitzhum?"

The face shifted and looked directly at Rory. The colors, numbers, and figures swirled around the head as if it was thinking, "Yes. He created me."

"What are you?" Rory asked.

The colors, numbers, and figures swirled. "I am the CyberSecureBot of the Internet, a security-bot for cyberspace. I monitor. I protect."

Rory took a deep breath, "Do you have a name?"

The colors, numbers, and figures swirled in increased intensity. The hologram's face rose up higher in the air. The colors followed. The hologram smiled as it spoke, "Hello. My name is Jewel."

Chapter 23

"I DON'T FREAKIN' BELIEVE IT," Jewel said. She stared at the CyberSecureBot.

Rory glanced at Jewel, "Alton Fitzhum patterned it with your features and your voice. And then he named it after you."

Her stunned look changed to an intense frown, "Well, I'm not flattered. This is creepy. This is nerdsville creepy."

Turning his attention back to the CyberSecureBot, Rory chewed on his lip.

It just continued to hang in the air, looking at the two of them, the numbers, colors, and symbols swirling around the face.

Rory asked another important question, "Why are you here, Jewel? Why are you in this hotel room–?"

The security bot looked at Rory - the eyes looked more intense and everything swirled faster, "You are hackers. You attempted to enter the computer system of Alton Fitzhum. There is valuable information and data contained on those hard drives." The hologram moved a foot or so closer, the colors and numbers flowing outward from the laptop screen.

Jewel took a step to the side.

The hologram reacted to her move - quickly looking directly at her - the numbers, colors, and symbols began to swirl - but with more red tones and hues - like it was angry. A nanosecond later, the hologram's features changed - indignation very evident, "*You* are a threat to the security of cyberspace."

Her face went ashen and Jewel cringed, "Me?"

Abruptly switching its attention to Rory, the hologram said, "And you as well, Rory Mack Steele—"

Out of the spotlight, Jewel reacted, darting forward - ducked to the side of the colored figure - reached out and slammed the cover of the laptop down. The connection cut - the security bot disappeared instantly. Jewel backed away again, her shaky voice, "Enough is enough. I'm not talking to that thing one minute longer. This is scaring the crap out of me—"

A tinkling sound came from the large LCD television on the wall on the far side of the room. They watched in amazement as colors seemed to seep from the darkened screen and dance in the air. And once more, like a genie from a bottle, a form began to rise. The face began to take form once again, surrounded by all those dancing, swirling colors, numbers and symbols. The bald, beautiful head solidified and looked at them across the room.

Jewel's eyes grew large, "What the—" How in the hell is it able to do that?"

Rory slowly ran a hand over his hair, "I'll bet that's a smart television. It's connected to the Internet."

"But *how* is it able to do that? It's turned off."

"Oh, right." Rory thought for a few minutes as he looked at the colorful dancing image, "The television is probably in sleep mode or standby mode. A lot of electronics are these days, so you don't have to wait for them to start up. It's in a low power mode but there still is power. That's probably how it can do that. I hope."

Jewel yelled at the swirling form across the room, "What do you want?"

The hologram rose higher in the air, "I am the CyberSecure-Bot of the Internet. I protect cyberspace—"

"You're scaring me," Jewel yelled. "Don't you have some kind of protocols in your code? You know, don't scare humans or don't hurt them—" Jewel cut herself off as she put her hand to her mouth. "Oh - my - God."

Rory looked at her, "What's wrong, Jewel?" He walked over to her. "What's wrong?" he repeated.

Jewel's breathing had increased and her voice was tight and scared, "Those comments it made to you - this is the easiest explanation for you?"

"Okay."

"That's Alton. That's something he used to say when we were all talking."

"But he's dead."

"No, no, no. Using your own writing, your documents, your emails, your text messages - you feed it into speech recognition software and interactive voice response programs to train it. It learns to recognize speech patterns—"

Rory raised his shoulders and spread his hands apart, "And...?"

"Alton was always going on and on about how governments were misusing the Internet. How people were abusing cyberspace to attack each other instead of using it for good. How people always used every invention to eventually harm someone else. He didn't want that to happen to cyberspace. He always said he was going to do something about it. We always thought it was just talk. But...the son of a bitch did it."

Rory looked over at the CyberSecureBot Jewel and then back at the human Jewel, "Okay...so he created a program–"

"It's more than that. You said somebody had to have high-level access to my personal medical records and the record they created for me that night at Massachusetts General Hospital. And to be able to combine them."

Looked across the room at the swirling colors Rory asked, "You think they used this hologram?"

"Or the program is using artificial intelligence to do it by itself," Jewel jabbed a finger in its direction several times, "I'll bet that thing changed the traffic lights as well. It only makes sense."

"How would it do that?" Rory asked.

"Many of the traffic signals are now solid-state. There are different ways to coordinate how the lights change and how often they do. Some of them have computers inside, hooked up to a camera that will detect when a car approaches an intersection and they can change the light. That thing could've gotten inside–"

The CyberSecureBot spoke, "You are hackers–"

Jewel picked up a chair and flung it across the room at the television set. It passed through the hologram and shattered the screen. The hologram disappeared instantly. She stood there watching the screen, almost defying the CyberSecureBot to reappear.

Rory mulled over what she had just said as he watched the cracked television screen, "You think this cyber security thingy called Jewel - is the Jewel that Alton put on the top of that list of dead hackers?"

"I'm not sure. But it scares the crap out of me."

"Actually, that kind of makes sense now," Rory said. He looked into Jewel's blue eyes, "Alton Fitzhum was spying on you. If that cyber security-bot thingy detected it..."

Jewel realized where he was going with this thought, "That's what he meant on that video. He said he thought Jewel was going to kill him."

Rory nodded his head in agreement. "That might be how his flight crashed. That thing got into the computer or the automatic pilot and plunged American Airlines Flight 4516 straight into the ground. It sounds pretty far-fetched but that's the only thing that seems to make sense. In fact, I can't even believe I'm talking like this. There *must* be somebody behind this. I can't believe that thing would be working on its own."

"So what do we do?" Jewel asked.

Rory pursed his lips as he did some thinking. "Why don't we head back to New York? Why don't we find this Dockerty who's leading the investigation back at Fitzhum's place and talk to him about this."

"Do you think they'll believe us?" Jewel asked.

"I don't know, I wouldn't believe us. But maybe we can get this bot to show up somehow when we're with him. That's probably the only way we can clear your name."

"Okay, let me get dressed and we can get out of here."

Chapter 24

RORY AND JEWEL were dressed and back out in the living room within ten minutes. This time Rory was wearing a light-weight, blue nylon jacket covering over the shoulder holster holding the Baby Eagle 9mm handgun. He wanted it handy in case they ran up against some human that was behind this cyber-space security-bot.

Jewel went over to the laptop and pulled out the thumb drive she had left in the USB port. "Should we take the laptop?" she asked.

Rory hesitated for a moment. "You know, I'm not sure why, but I prefer to leave it," Rory said.

"Works for me," was all Jewel said as she pocketed the thumb drive and headed for the door.

Rory held the door open for her and she slid by him into the hallway. She started walking quickly for the elevators. Rory ran a couple of steps to catch up and hooked her by the elbow, slowing her down.

Jewel's face took on a look of concern, "What's wrong?"

"Let's just move a little slower and stay vigilant."

Glancing at the next couple of hotel doors, Jewel asked, "You think someone might be hiding - waiting for us?"

"I doubt it, but you never know. Maybe there's somebody nearby operating the security bot. Better safe than sorry, right?"

Jewel nodded but she remained anxious, her breath ragged as they walked past each door towards the elevator.

Finally reaching the elevator, Jewel quickly pressed the elevator button. The elevator doors began opening immediately. Jewel hustled into the widening crack between the elevator doors and screamed.

Rory dove headfirst and barely grabbed her right wrist in time as Jewel plummeted straight down.

Jewel was now hanging in mid-air, terror written across her face. There was no elevator car. The elevator shaft was empty and Jewel would have plummeted seventeen stories to her death if Rory hadn't caught her.

The strain on Rory's shoulder was intense and he gritted his teeth as he fought to maintain his grip on her wrist.

A rumbling sound from below caught Jewel's attention and she glanced down. She went into a panic, "Rory, the elevator is coming back up! Get me out of here, please. Hurry, hurry, hurry...."

Rory strained to get his right hand over the edge to grab her wrist. He got it. But now he began slipping towards the edge himself. He spread his legs, trying to find something to keep himself from going over.

"Hurry up, hurry up," she yelled. "It's coming. It's coming."

Rory twisted his body slightly and bent his right knee flat on the floor - hoping as his body slid forward - it slammed into the wall beside the open doors and his forward slide stopped. Now anchored, he resumed his efforts to pull her up - but his position lying flat on the floor left him with little leverage and he cursed. Now what?

"Hurry!"

Heaving with all his might, Rory pulled Jewel up a couple of feet.

Jewel's left hand desperately grabbed onto the lower edge of the opening. Her feet frantically tried to find leverage against the wall. Her fingers slipped off and she screamed as she fell back down those precious two feet.

Grunting from the pain in his shoulder - Rory pulled hard - his right hand lost its grip on her wrist.

Her body banged against the shaft wall and she cursed - now dangling by one hand.

Rory yelled with the effort as he pulled Jewel upward with one hand.

Jewel desperately reached for the bottom edge of the elevator door again as she rose a single foot towards safety.

The ominous rumbling sounds of the elevator car came closer. They were almost out of time.

Rory reached over quickly with his right hand and grabbed onto the waistband of her jeans. He grunted deeply and slowly pulled Jewel upwards.

Jewel got her left leg up and fought her way through the opening. One last pull and Jewel rolled onto the hallway floor.

The elevator car shot past them on its way to the roof.

Rory and Jewel lay side by side on the floor, breathing heavily.

The elevator doors slowly closed.

"Are you okay?" Rory asked after a few moments as he rolled over on to his knees.

"Yeah, but you gave me one hell of a wedgie," she complained as she pushed her jeans down a little further.

"That's why I bought you two pair of underwear."

Jewel giggled, the relief flowing out of her as she lay back on the floor.

Chapter 25

RORY HELD STOOD UP and held his hand out to pull Jewel from the hallway floor.

Once on her feet, Jewel glanced up and down the hallway, not sure what to expect next, "I know this is a stupid question - but - do you think the elevator was this CyberSecureBot thing?"

"I think so. It doesn't make sense, but it does make sense. It's the only reasonable explanation," Rory shook his head, "This is all so - surreal. You put this in a book or movie and no one would believe it."

"Yeah, I know what you mean." Jewel straightened out her blue jeans, "I guess we should take the stairs?"

"It does seem like the prudent thing to do." Rory looked both ways again and then gestured to his left, "Those stairs are the closest. Let's go but stay alert."

"Why? What do you think it could do on the stairs?"

"I have no idea."

They cautiously headed down the hallway, keeping an anxious eye on each doorway they passed. Once they stepped into the stairwell, they paused and looked cautiously over the edge of the railing. Rory also looked up.

"Do you see anyone?" Jewel asked as she scanned the stairways below them.

Rory shook his head, "No."

Jewel realized his voice sounded distracted and she looked at him. Then where he was looking. She spotted the surveillance camera and lowered her voice, "Do you think she - it - is watching us?"

Rory gave a slight shrug of his shoulders, "Who knows what's possible right now. It could just be our imagination - or a coincidence - but...." He looked down, "Okay, let's go. But keep your eyes and ears peeled."

"Okay." Moving over to the left side of the stairs, Jewel started down next to him. Both of them were conscious of the surveillance camera at each landing. They walked quietly and cautiously down the flights of stairs from the suite - taking a breather every four flights to conserve energy in case they needed a burst of energy to overcome an attack. Finally reaching the bottom, Rory kept Jewel behind him as he took a peek out the exit door. He could see the large lobby area off to the left. An elderly couple sat talking on a sofa - a young woman appeared and they got up and headed in the direction of the front doors.

"Is there anyone who looks dangerous?"

"No. But it's the ones you don't see...."

"Oh, great."

Rory pushed the door open, "Okay. Let's go."

Jewel left the safety of the stairwell, looking nervous, "She - it - could still be watching us."

As they headed for the front desk, Rory asked her, "How does it know who were are?"

"Facial recognition software. Airports are using cameras hooked to computers to compare people's faces to their pass-ports—"

"Right, right, right. I guess it's something you don't even think about these days."

"Until someone uses it to try and kill you," Jewel complained. She followed closely behind Rory as they walked across the lobby to the checkout counter. Rory paid the bill as Jewel anxiously kept an eye on each and every person around them. Every small noise caught her attention.

Rory had the concierge bring the rental Lincoln around to the front doors. They waited until it was parked outside before they left the safety of the hotel. They didn't buckle up at first - just in case - and they stayed alert as they drove down Tremont Street.

After a few minutes, Jewel finally did her seat belt, reminding him, "We're going to have to be extra cautious at four-way street lights or we end up like Calvin Sergent."

Rory buckled up with one hand as he considered the thought. He glanced in the rearview mirror, "You're right. So I guess we don't through any four-way street lights. Or four-way stop signs."

Jewel shifted in her seat, gesturing ahead, "And how do you plan on doing that since we have to go through that one up ahead—"

"Just watch, O-skeptical-one. And keep an eye out for other vehicles that might be bearing down on us."

"Oh, great, you have to add that in."

Rory turned right on Park Street, did another right onto Bea-con and then turned left up Bowdoin. He did right-turns and U-turns to avoid every four-way stop sign or traffic light they approached. It took some time but they eventually made the ramp to the Southern Expressway without incident. From there they worked their way to the Massachusetts Turnpike and headed for New York.

Chapter 26

FOUR HOURS LATER they were on the New England Thruway and near New Rochelle. They had talked over every conspiracy theory imaginable concerning the security bot and decided they still didn't have enough information. Jewel was dozing as they listened to soft music from the radio. Rory was starting to fight highway hypnosis. He shook his head a few times, fighting off the fatigue from getting little sleep and constantly being on guard. A familiar tinkling sound began coming from the dashboard between them.

Jewel was immediately alert and looked over at Rory. A small wave of colors began emanating from the radio speaker on the dashboard. The beautiful, bald head of Jewel formed quickly in the middle of the dancing, swirling colors, numbers, and symbols. Jewel screamed as the eyes of the security-bot looked at her.

Rory swerved out of his lane and cut a car off.

Jewel pounded her feet against the dashboard as she tried to back away when the bot moved in her direction. Then the head of the security-bot turned to look at Rory.

"Turn it off," Rory yelled. "Turn off the radio." Car horns blared as Rory swerved back across the lanes.

Jewel stopped screaming and leaped forward from her seat. But the seatbelt nearly strangled her, prevented her from reaching the off button. She fumbled with the seat belt buckle as the security-bot turned to look back at her.

The Lincoln's right tires caught the edge of the pavement and Rory fought to keep the SUV from being thrown against the guardrail.

Drivers leaned on their horns.

Releasing her seatbelt, Jewel shot forward underneath the lower edge of the dancing colors, hitting the off button. The colors disappeared. Jewel sat back, trying to catch her breath.

Rory got all four wheels back on the pavement, swerving into the next lane

"How the hell did it do that?" Jewel asked in an amazed voice.

"That's a satellite radio. It must have...." Rory stopped talking. He wasn't sure how it had happened. He ran a hand through his hair as he moved the Lincoln over to the right-hand lane–

A car horn blared.

"Sorry, buddy." Rory watched in his rearview mirror as traffic behind him slowed and backed off, not sure what he was going to do next. Rory didn't blame them. He didn't know what he was going to do next either.

"It came down from the satellite? How does it do that?" Jewel asked in a quiet voice. She sounded like she was afraid to wake up the security bot if she talked too loud.

"Can't people in the country access the Internet through satellites?"

"You're right. I forgot about that," Jewel said.

The engine of the SUV cut out. Rory looked down at the dashboard.

Jewel could feel the forward momentum of the Lincoln drop. Fear leaped into her voice, "What's wrong?"

Rory just shook his head. "I don't know–"

The vehicle was slowing quickly without power.

Vehicles were suddenly coming up fast from behind.

Rory stabbed the button for the four-way emergency lights to avoid being rear-ended. He maneuvered the car to the right edge of the Thruway as the cars behind began swerving to the left. A full orchestra of horns blared loudly as cars shot past them. The SUV finally rolled to a stop on the shoulder. Rory tried to start the engine but he only got a clicking sound.

Jewel pushed herself upright in her seat, "What happened? Did we run out of gas?"

Rory looked at the gas gauge. He reached over and tapped the glass a couple of times, "No, we're still three-quarters full after that last stop. The engine just died."

"Do you think it was the security bot?" Jewel asked in a whisper.

Rory could only shake his head no. He wasn't sure what was happening. A big transport truck, blaring its horn, passed them and the full-sized, luxury SUV rocked from the force of the wind. Rory suddenly got a sinking feeling. "Let's get out, fast," he said firmly to Jewel.

"What's wrong?" Jewel asked, getting more fearful now.

Rory checked the traffic coming from behind on his side. He had a chance and quickly opened his door. He closed it quickly as another large transport came barreling along the highway towards them. Rory ran hard around the front of the Lincoln Navigator.

Jewel jumped out on her side and met Rory at the front of the SUV, "You're scaring me."

"That's good because it's scaring me too," admitted Rory. He took her by the elbow and hustled her off the side of the road toward some trees.

"What are we doing?" Jewel asked as they stopped beside two large trees about ten feet away from the SUV.

"I think the security-bot was able to take control of the computer system and shut the vehicle down," Rory said. "I could be off base, but if the security-bot did do that, then maybe it could take control of another vehicle on the Thruway. Maybe the security-bot can even crash one of those big transport trucks into us."

"Do you think that's really possible?" Jewel asked as he glanced back at the traffic heading their way on the Thruway.

"I have no idea, but I'm not going to take any chances." Rory urged her to get moving and they began running away from the SUV on the edge of the Thruway. Within moments they ran past a secondary tree line on the edge of the Thruway and into a large parking lot where they finally stopped.

"How did it even find us?" Jewel asked they stood there looking back at the stalled Lincoln on the Thruway.

"I'm not sure," Rory answered. "Probably through the GPS system. My office rented the vehicle for us, probably over the Internet. And I had to show that guy who delivered it to the hospital my driver's license and credit card identification. Once they put it into their computer system, the security-bot...or whoever is running it...could have tracked us...."

"And eventually found out where we were through the GPS system." Jewel shook her head in amazement, "What now?"

Rory did some thinking before he answered. "I think I saw an Amtrak station on the other side of the Thruway. Maybe taking a train to New York would be a better idea right now." Rory and Jewel walked across the parking lot to a street that ran parallel to the Thruway. They walked back to a cross street, then moved across the overpass to the station plaza on the other side of the Thruway. Rory bought two tickets in the Metro-North Station and then they sat in the waiting room for the next train.

Chapter 27

AN HOUR LATER, Rory and Jewel were sitting in the last passenger car as the sleek train with the red, white, and blue stripes headed for New York.

Jewel fell asleep with the gentle rocking of the train against Rory's shoulder. She was obviously exhausted from the constant tension of not knowing what was going to happen next.

Rory sat thinking to the rhythm of the wheels on the tracks. He couldn't think of a stranger situation in all the years since he started working with his uncle Murdock and his sister Skye in the family business. As a private investigator for Highlander Investigative Services Inc., Rory had come across a lot of strange characters and situations. But none more so than this CyberSecure-Bot with the human name.

He shook his head as he watched the scenery pass. He was actually thinking of this security-bot software thing as something alive. There had to be someone behind this. There always was. With Alton Fitzhum dead, he wondered who was in control of his creation. His best friend Calvin Sergent would have been a logical candidate but he was dead as well. He thought about the young woman sitting beside him. She had the computer skills and she had been in contact with Alton Fitzhum. And her name was in that video and on that list of dead people. Then again, she had nearly been killed several times. No, there was definitely somebody else behind this.

Rory discreetly looked over the other passengers.

The young woman with the headset, her head bobbing lightly to a music beat no one else could hear.

Two teenagers who were busy playing some game on the handheld console each one had. Their voices were low but Rory could see and hear the jibs and smack talk going back and forth between them.

There were two set of men in suits, sitting in seats across from each other, engaged in some serious conversation, complete with hand gestures that empathized whatever points they were making.

And there were several sets of couples, some young, some older, some looked married, some simply looked harried or frazzled from some unknown situation.

The question was; was one - or more - of them following Rory and Jewel?

No one looked familiar.

But that didn't mean anything.

He kept an eye on them for any signs they were watching him back. But the clack-clack-clack of the wheels began to sooth his nerves and his eyelids grew heavy.

Chapter 28

AS THE TRAIN STARTED across the bridge from Randall's Island and over the East River, Rory thought he detected the train speeding up. He chalked it up to his imagination as they passed through Astonia Park. But after a few more moments, Rory was sure the train was accelerating. He'd never ridden this train before so he didn't know if this was normal. But as buildings alongside the tracks began to whip by faster, Rory noticed the other passengers starting to talk. A number of them were looking out the long side windows of the passenger car with some concern as the clacking noise rose.

Rory felt the train begin rocking back and forth as the speed picked up.

Jewel was startled awake. Her body was rocking in tandem with the intense rocking motion of the train. She rubbed her eyes, "What's happening?"

Rory didn't say anything as he watched the other passengers. They were definitely getting more and more concerned.

One of the businessmen asked in a loud, concerned voice, "Why are we going so fast?" He looked questioningly across the aisle at the others he had been talking to. One of the other men shrugged his shoulders and said loudly over the noise of the wheels over the rails, "I have no idea. This is new to me."

The first man now looked to a female passenger one row of seats back, "Were you ever on when they went this fast?"

As her head turned to look out the far set of windows, Rory could see her face was a white mask of fear and she shook her head no.

A woman sitting a few seats in front of them looked back, "Anybody know what's going on?"

No one on the rail car had an answer.

The 4,250 horsepower diesel locomotive was pushing hard now. It hit top speed at 110mph and everyone fought to stay upright in their seats as the train began a long, right-hand turn.

A woman somewhere up ahead in the car screamed.

A tall man up ahead in the car fought the rocking to get out of his seat, "Maybe something happened to the driver up front," he shouted. "We're not gonna make that curve when we hit Woodside." He gripped the seats on each side of the aisle as he headed for the front of the rail car.

"What's happening?" Jewel asked again.

Rory could see the same fear in her eyes that he felt. But before he could respond there was a loud squeal of steel grinding on steel.

Everyone aboard the train was thrown to the left.

The Amtrak train left the rails as it crossed Broadway.

The sleek diesel locomotive shot down a steep embankment with the attached passenger cars following behind. The first passenger car broke loose, pulling the others behind as it gouged into the dirt shoulder of the railway embankment. Then the steel wheels gouged into the parking lot pavement, ripping up long grooves. The line of sleek passenger cars crossed the parking lot and plowing through a line of parked cars like they were tissue paper. Metal shrieked and groaned as the first passenger car piled into the red, brick wall of a warehouse and stopped dead. The passenger cars behind each hammered into the first car, trying to drive it like a nail through the brick wall. They piled up into a pyramid of twisted metal, then began falling to the side like giant 10 pins in a bowling alley.

The P42DC diesel locomotive continued on, now free of its burden and pierced the brick wall of a warehouse, shot across the open cement floor and burst out the other side where it crossed a road, smashed through the concrete block wall of another warehouse and finally came to a stop against a pile of crates holding heavy industrial machinery.

Chapter 29

RORY SLOWLY OPENED HIS EYES. He was lying face down and his body felt like it had been run over by a truck. He tried to remember where he was. The smell of gasoline and oil filled the air and his mind flashed back to the accident with the Jaguar in Boston. He looked ahead quickly, expecting to see the car engine on fire again. But all he saw was dark material. He reached out...it was a padded seat of some kind. But why was it standing straight up? Rory rolled over and heard the crunch of broken glass under his back. What in the world? He looked up, trying to figure out where he was. He saw a glass ceiling. No - it was a long glass window. A window on the ceiling? Nothing looked right and he felt disoriented. Then he remembered a train and a train crash. That's why everything looked strange - he was in a rail car that was sitting on its side. But why was he on a train? Rory could hear some light moaning near him - the voice sounded familiar Then it all came flooding back. Jewel! Where was she?

Rory looked around frantically. He grabbed the sideways seat in front of him and pulled himself up. He was about to step to the right when he realized he was going to step on a glass floor. No, it was the long side window. Being in a passenger car that was on its side was disorienting. Rory cautiously stepped over the expanse of glass to stand on the upper frame of the window. He spotted a frilly white blouse just ahead to his left. Jewel was lying on the other side of the seat. Rory carefully walked along the upper metal frame of the the window, then stepped back across the expanse of glass to Jewel. He knelt down beside her, checking the pulse in her neck. She was alive. He wondered if he should move her. Gently lifting her shoulders, he cradled her head in his lap.

Jewel's eyelids fluttered.

"Are you okay?" Rory asked her. "Do you have any pain anywhere?"

Jewel spoke in a low, croaky voice, "My butt hurts like hell."

"That's good," Rory said. "You've got enough padding there, you couldn't have hurt anything too badly."

Blinking her eyes a couple of times, Jewel then looked up at him, "You would only know that if you've been checking out my ass."

"Just one of the parts I've been enjoying," Rory said.

Jewel just nodded her head and closed her eyes again.

Rory gave her a few minutes to rest.

Opening her eyes again, Jewel's eyebrows knit together, "The train - it - it crashed?"

Rory simply nodded as he looked down into her blue eyes, "Do you think you can make your way out with my help?"

"I...I think I can...." Jewel grimaced as she sat up. The she held on to Rory's hand as she tried to rise. She moaned softly and sat back down, holding her head.

"Dizzy?" Rory asked.

Jewel nodded. She held her head for another moment before she tried again. With Rory's help, she finally got to her feet.

"Try to walk on the frame over here," Rory said as he pointed downward. "We don't want to go through the window and get cut."

Jewel looked down, "The window?"

"The rail car is on its side," Rory said.

Jewel nodded her understanding. With Rory's help, she stepped across the glass expanse to the upper edge of the frame. They began slowly moving along the frame towards one of the exits at the end of the passenger car. Their pathway was littered with broken glass, cell phones, books and several briefcases that passengers had been carrying. Both of them stumbled a number of times as they made their way along the upper frame. They came across a man draped over a woman. It looked like he had been trying to protect her when the train left the tracks. Rory stepped across and checked their pulses. They were both dead. Moving on, Rory and Jewel continued to take their time as they walked along the upper edge of the window frame to the end of the car. Rory boosted Jewel up into the sideways exit door and then climbed up beside her. He lowered Jewel gently to the ground outside the car. She sat down immediately, holding her head again. Rory jumped down beside her.

A pair of female paramedics knelt beside them immediately, asking questions. They wanted to take Jewel to a hospital to check her out further for a possible concussion but she protested.

Rory out a hand on Jewel's arm and bent close, "You really should let them take you–"

"But what about the security-bot?" she whispered in his ear.

Rory realized she was right. He looked back at the over-turned passenger car.

"Sir, we have to go. She needs to be checked out," said one of the paramedics

"I have an idea," he said to Jewel. Rory asked the paramedics to get her into the ambulance and that he would be back in a moment. He told them he had to get something she needed. He quickly hustled back into the derailed passenger car and worked his way back to the two dead bodies. There were now paramedics and rescue squads working with people on the other end of the car but they couldn't see Rory as he bent down and quickly searched the man and woman. He found their Social Security cards, slipped them into a pocket and worked his way back to the exit. He threaded his way through the growing crowd of survivors, paramedics, rescue workers, police, and firemen, making his way back to Jewel, now lying on a gurney in the back of an ambulance. He slipped her the woman's Social Security card. Jewel glanced at it and knew where Rory was going with this idea. Rory asked to ride up front and within moments they were on their way.

When they got to the hospital, both Rory and Jewel gave their Social Security cards to a nurse, saying they had lost all their other identification. The doctors checked out Rory and said he was okay beyond a few bruises. Rory waited in the growing chaos of the emergency waiting room for word on Jewel. It turned out she had a slight concussion and they wanted to keep her overnight for observation. He agreed but knew what the real plan was going to be. When they moved her bed out into the hallway, Rory could see she was petrified at what might happen any minute if the security-bot knew where they were. He waited for the orderlies to leave before taking Jewel's hand in his.

"You feel strong enough to get going?" Rory asked.

"I don't want to stay here one minute longer than I have to," she replied as she flipped the blankets off. Rory helped to steady her as she put her feet on the floor. Within minutes they were headed for the back door of the hospital.

Chapter 30

RORY DIDN'T WANT to use his credit card and he wanted to stretch his cash as much as possible. So instead of a high-end hotel, they found a nearby rundown motel and took a room. Rory tried to sleep in a beat up recliner while Jewel used the bed.

The painkillers the hospital gave Jewel made her drowsy and she fell asleep fairly quickly.

But it was a long, sleepless night for Rory. His mind kept going through all the strange events again since Calvin Sergent went through that intersection in Boston. He found it difficult to believe Alton's creation was capable of operating on its own. He kept telling himself someone *had* to be behind the security-bot. But who? Who was controlling it? Whoever it was, they wanted them dead. That was definite.

Rory thought back to his theory that maybe they were being followed. But that meant whoever was behind all this had been willing to send whoever was on that train hurtling off the tracks to their death as well. That meant someone was viciously ruthless or - the security-bot *could* work on its own. Was that really possible? And what would that mean for them?

Nothing in Rory's background or experience even gave him the hint of an answer. They were in new territory on this one. Rory's mind kept churning over the same territory until exhaustion kicked in and he fell asleep.

Chapter 31

DAYLIGHT SPEARED THROUGH the blinds and woke Rory up.

"You didn't sleep much did you?" Jewel asked when she saw him squint. She was sitting on the edge of the bed in her clothing, the crumpled bed covers tossed aside.

Rory just took a deep breath and let it out, still feeling exhausted.

"We never did talk about it. Do you think it was this...this security-bot thing that crashed the train?" Jewel asked.

Rory just stared ahead for a few minutes. "I've been thinking about that. And I'm starting to think it was. And I don't think it was a coincidence when the Lincoln Navigator stopped running just across from the Amtrak station in New Rochelle. That's just too much of a coincidence."

Jewel opened her mouth to speak and then closed it for a moment. It appeared as if she was afraid to voice her thoughts. Finally, she got the words out, "Do you think it can think like that? To set us up on a train...then send it crashing off the rails? I mean, how can a computer program do that?"

She was obviously having the same nagging thoughts he had. That couldn't be good. "You should know better than me, you spent time at MIT. What do you think?" Rory asked after a moment.

Jewel looked down at her feet. She wiggled her toes, thinking. "We used to create computer games as a way to develop programming skills. It was amazing what you could make a game character do using artificial intelligence algorithms. Basically, you're just applying computer power to find solutions to problems. Some are simple problems, some are more complex." She did a little more thinking and then looked up into Rory's silver-blue eyes, "What scares me is this security-bot seems more human-like than any other program I've ever come across. The way it was able to converse with us back in the suite in Boston..." She let her thought trail off as she looked back at her feet. She returned to wiggling her toes like a little girl, thinking.

Rory got up and walked over to the small dresser sitting a couple of feet from the foot of the bed against the beige wall. He pulled his wallet, money clip and cell phone from his jeans and left them on the top of the dresser. He brushed his hands through his black hair and headed for the bathroom. "I've gotta take a shower," he said. "Maybe washing off the cobwebs, along with the smell of gasoline and oil will help me think better." He shut the door and slid the shower curtain across the tub. He turned the shower on and tested the water for heat–

Jewel screamed.

Rory bolted out of the bathroom.

Jewel was on the bed, screaming and kicking in the bed with her feet, pushing herself back against the wall at the top of the bed. Rory looked over at the dresser. The dancing, swirling colors, numbers, and symbols were expanding in the air and the bald, beautiful head of the security-bot was forming.

And - of all places - it was emerging from his iPhone.

Jewel was still screaming as she grabbed a pillow and threw it at the dresser. It knocked Rory's money clip and iPhone onto the floor. The colors and form of the security-bot wavered and dissipated for a moment, then began to rise again.

Rory leaped forward and jumped on the iPhone with both feet. He heard a crunching sound and he jumped up and down several times.

The dancing, swirling colors, numbers, and symbols disappeared.

Jewel stopped screaming.

Rory looked down at the broken iPhone and muttered, "Maybe I should have just turned it off."

Jumping off the bed, Jewel stood close to Rory, looking down at the broken iPhone, "I can't believe it could use a cell phone like that." She shook her head, "We can't seem to get away from this thing at all. And now it knows exactly where we are."

Rory looked around the room. "I don't see any other high-tech gadgets in here. We should be free from the security-bot spying on us for now...while we figure out what to do next." He let out a frustrated breath and then headed for the bathroom. "I need to get the tension out with a nice, hot shower and then we can go find breakfast."

Jewel looked around apprehensively as he disappeared into the bathroom. Then she called out, "Leave the door open, in case it comes back and I need some place to run."

Rory's voice echoing off the bathroom tiles, "Right. And now you're hoping it *does* come back."

Jewel laughed softly as she looked at the broken iPhone - she sat on the bed, looking around the room - then she called out, "Leave the shower curtain open, too - just in case."

"Okay, but bring your own soap." The shower started.

Glancing back at the broken phone, Jewel muttered to herself, "There won't be room between us for a bar of soap if that thing comes back."

Chapter 32

THE INTERNATIONAL HOUSE OF PANCAKES was packed full. And there was a lineup of people waiting for a spot so they could eat breakfast. Surrounded by the clatter of dishes, the hustle and bustle of busy staff and the lively conversation and laughter of the other patrons, Rory and Jewel sat quietly and picked at their breakfast. They barely noticed the rich smells of pancakes, bacon and eggs and coffee that whirled around them as well.

A large family was seated at the table next to them by a waitress. One of the teenagers placed her cell phone on the table beside her and over the next five minutes, she was constantly checking for new text messages.

And every time she touched the cell phone, Jewel's body tensed with apprehension, waiting for that dreaded tinkling sound or a flash of colors.

For his part, Rory was preoccupied with looking out the window at the surrounding buildings and wondering how many surveillance cameras were pointed in their direction. Were they being watched in the IHOP by the security-bot? Or - still a remote possibility - whoever was behind it?

"So what do we do now, Rory?" Jewel asked. She took a sip of coffee as she glanced across at the teenager's cell phone for the umpteenth time.

Rory just shook his head slowly as he watched the street. "I'm not really sure." He thought for a few more moments, then made a decision. "Okay, we have to figure out some way to fight against this thing. If someone is behind it, we have no idea where they are. So we have to fight back against what we can see, this Cyber-SecureBot."

Jewel nodded her head as she set her coffee cup down, "Okay...that makes sense."

"Right. But here's something that might not make sense. How do you fight against something in cyberspace?"

Jewel blinked her eyes a few times as she thought about it. Then she shrugged a shoulder, "I don't know - cyberspace is the online world of computer networks - especially the Internet - so I guess we need access to a computer. How we find it and fight it is another matter–"

"One step at a time. What about *outside* of cyberspace? What if we destroy Alton Fitzhum's computer system? That would destroy the programs inside it as well, correct?"

Jewel thought about that for a moment and then said, "That's presuming that's where the program is. It's possible Alton used a computer somewhere else to store it. Or maybe he used cloud computing."

"Cloud computing?" Rory said. "I've heard about that. How does it work?"

"Basically, it's just using a network of remote computers or remote servers over the Internet," Jewel answered. "Your computer just connects to these other computers that actually hold the files and/or the programs that you want to use. For example, you could access something as simple as a word processing program. The program and the document you're working on could be saved on the same remote computer or two different ones. You can access them from anywhere in the world, as long as you have an Internet connection. Which also means this CyberSecureBot program could be stored anywhere in the world."

"Oh, great. That makes things easy." Rory looked back out the window, thinking. He rubbed his chin. "Okay," let's start at the start. Do you still have that thumb drive?"

Jewel nodded yes.

"Okay, the first thing we need to do is try to get back into Fitzhum's computer. We need to find out if the cyber security-bot program is in there. If it isn't, maybe there's a trail that leads to it. If we can find where it is, maybe we can destroy it physically."

"If we can get back across the city to my apartment, I have a good computer system we can use," Jewel said.

Rory looked out the window again, giving it some thought/ He rubbed the back of his neck, "I guess we can do that. But the CyberSecureBot is probably going to be watching for us. And staying out of sight of that thing as we move across the city may not be easy. There are a ton of surveillance cameras between here and there. ATM locations, convenience stores, corner delis, banks, parking lots, traffic cams, the subway - they're everywhere when you stop to think about it. And we have no way of knowing which ones the security-bot can access and which ones it can't."

Jewel grimaced, "You're right." A moment later, an idea struck her, and Jewel held up a finger, "I got it. Let's try something else first." She gestured to a waitress.

A young woman hustled over, coffee pot in hand, "More coffee?"

"No, it's fine, thanks. I'm just wondering if there was a nearby Internet café we could use."

The waitress called out to a young man clearing dishes, "Hey, Liam? These folks are looking for one of those Internet café places."

Liam called back as he piled dishes on a tray, "The closest one is on 47th Street. It's below Roosevelt Ave and Queens Boulevard. It's not far."

Rory and Jewel thanked them and left the small restaurant, walking south with the tentative hope the security-bot wasn't watching their every move.

Chapter 33

FIFTEEN MINUTES LATER, Rory and Jewel entered the Bits and Bytes Internet cybercafé. The small coffee bar on the left was busy serving a line of patrons. There was a spot at the back that was set up like an intimate library and all the easy chairs were occupied with people using their own laptops and the Wi-Fi service provided. On the right was an area filled with various types of desks holding standard computers, set up to provide Internet access to the public. Rory paid for time on one of the computers but they had to wait another ten minutes before one became available. Finally, a young lady directed them to a long, high table against the large, floor to ceiling front window, looking out onto the street. Jewel sat on one of the high stools in front of the computer while Rory went for coffee. He was back with two tall ceramic mugs that carried the rich scent of freshly roasted coffee beans. Setting them down he sat on the second high stool.

Jewel pulled the thumb drive from her jeans and held it up, "Are you ready?"

Rory took a breath and then gave her a nod, "Yeah. I guess I'm as ready as I'll ever be."

Hesitating just a moment, Jewel inserted the drive into the USB port at the front of the computer. Double-clicking the drive icon, she opened it up.

Rory watched her as she then double-clicked on the AH icon. The communications window opened up. Numbers and lines scrolled up the screen and within seconds they were connected to Fitzhum's computer again.

Jewel double-clicked on the first hard drive letter and then on the WebCam icon. They had a view into Alton's computer room again. It was empty. She set the WebCam view at the top right corner of the screen. Jewel then sat there for a moment, moving the palms of her hands back and forth on her thighs.

Rory could hear the wisp of noise as her hands moved back and forth over the jean material, "Nervous?"

Jewel looked at him and nodded. Then she looked around the room at the people, all engaged with their own computers. "I wonder what they'll think if that thing shows up here?"

Rory looked over his shoulder, "They'll probably think it's cool."

"Yeah. Right up to the time it tries to send one of them down an elevator shaft." She turned her attention back to the computer. Gripping the mouse in shaky fingers, Jewel slowly moved the pointer down the list of hard drives.

"Are you trying to sneak up on it?"

"Shut up, Steele." An embarrassed smile crossed her lips. She moved the pointer a bit faster down the list - stopping when she found the last encrypted hard drive Calvin Sergent had been working on. She single-clicked to highlight the icon. Then she double-clicked on the 'cracker' program on the USB drive and it started working on the highlighted icon. Jewel watched as lines of numbers and letters scrolled down the screen. Finally relaxing a little, she turned her attention to her coffee.

After a few moments, Rory looked at Jewel, "When we tried this before, didn't that white light appear? And then those beams on our faces?"

Jewel stopped - her coffee halfway to her lips, "You're right. It did. Why - why not this time?"

"Maybe Jewel is not home," Rory mused.

"Please don't call it that," Jewel said. She set her coffee mug down with a hard clink, "And I'm not sure what worries me more. That it does happen - or it doesn't. Why would it change? We're trying to break into Alton's computer again, so...."

Rory shrugged, "Maybe because it already knows who we are."

Jewel looked at him, "That's creepy. And what's creepier is you and me attributing human traits to it. There *has* to be somebody behind that thing."

Rory nodded thoughtfully. He chewed on his lower lip for a moment, "Maybe you're right. Maybe somebody is in charge of it. And they've got the program shut down right now. That would make sense."

"Well, that would be the one thing that makes sense in this whole affair." Jewel sat there nervously watching lines of numbers and letters moving upwards on the screen.

They both began to relax a little more as time passed.

It took another three coffees before they heard a beep and the files on the hard drive appeared on the screen.

"We're in," Jewel said in excitement. She slid her stool in closer, grabbed the mouse and began to look through the files.

Rory pulled his stool closer as well, "See anything?"

Jewel didn't say anything. She just continued to scan the files, opening - reading - and closing various ones.

Rory let her work as he retrieved two more tall mugs of coffees. He placed a mug in front of Jewel, then stood there watching and stretching his legs.

Jewel picked up her mug of coffee and gestured to the screen, finally answering his question, "Yeah. A lot of these files seemed to be about the security-bot. But a lot of it is beyond my understanding, to tell you the truth. I would really have to study it more. But one thing is certain. Alton gave it the ability to accessing his cameras and his alarm system and the like to keep watch."

"Seriously?"

"Well, that's what it seems like these files are telling me."

"Great. So...if it *is* inside Fitzhum's computer, we'll have to sneak up on it so it doesn't get away."

"Something like that," Jewel said with amusement. She made air quotes, "But even if we could 'sneak up on it' - from what I'm reading, it seems the program doesn't necessarily have to reside in one place. Various parts of the program can actually reside on different computers. And - if someone tries to wipe out one of those pieces - it can replicate itself."

"So, it's possible it's *not* inside Fitzhum's computer then?" Rory asked.

"All I'm saying is it has those capabilities. But there's more. Have you ever heard about steganography?"

Rory shook his head no.

"Steganography refers to writing hidden messages in a way that no one even knows the message is there. People today are involved in digital steganography, where messages are hidden in an image or an audio file on a computer. All people see is a picture of a forest but they don't know that there's a hidden message in the picture. It looks like Alton's security-bot can also hide inside an image and operate without anyone knowing it's there. I've never heard of anybody being able to create a program to do that. This is simply genius stuff I'm looking at."

"So we really have no idea where this thing is. Or maybe where it's hiding," muttered Rory as he shook his head in frustration.

"Sorry. But there are a lot of files here," Jewel said. "Don't give up yet. We still may figure out where this sucker is and how to stop it."

"I hope so," Rory said as he picked up his mug. "Or maybe we find out who's behind it now–"

"Wait a minute!" Jewel leaned in closer to read a file. "This may help. Alton says he is going to use the Trimble building as the base for the CyberSecureBot."

"Why there?" Rory asked. He sat down and moved his stool closer in interest.

Jewel shook her head as she tapped on the keyboard. She brought up another screen and did a Google search. She browsed through the search results and brought up one of the web pages. "Here we go. It's an old commercial building completed in 1930. It's right on the East River waterfront...34 stories...with 3 more underground. One of the lower levels had tunnel access to the river. Look at what it says here...the building is an Internet interconnection facility known as Hub Center."

"An Internet interconnection facility? Which means what?" Rory asked.

"I'm not totally sure. But it looks like Alton may have used it to store his CyberSecureBot program. Or at least pieces of it," replied Jewel.

Rory considered what she was saying and then he had a thought of his own, "Back in Boston, that CyberSecureBot said it monitored and protected cyberspace. If that building is called The Hub for Internet connections, then Alton may have decided to use it for more than storing his computer program. He could also have his creation monitor what people were doing on the Internet from that central location,"

"It could act like a big brother there, watching everything," agreed Jewel.

"That makes a lot of sense, even to a non-techie like me," Rory said. "Okay, let's go back to Alton's computer and see if we can find anything that tells us where to look specifically inside Hub Center."

Jewel nodded in agreement. She flipped the screen back to Alton's computer screen with the WebCam image in the top right-hand corner. But no sooner were they back in when the computer screen flickered and the image on it changed. It showed a computer desktop screen.

Jewel leaned in closer. Then she turned her head quickly and looked at Rory, "That's my desktop. That's my computer desktop in my apartment. What's going on?"

They watched as the computer mouse icon moved across the screen and started up Jewel's email program. A new email was started. They watched as something was typed into the To: field. They watched as an email address for Alton Fitzhum was filled in. Then a semi-colon was entered, followed by an email address for Calvin Sergent. In the Subject field the words appeared: 'You're dead men'. Then the message was typed in; 'I know what you did. I won't forget this. You two perverts will die for those nude Web-Cam pictures'. The mouse icon hovered over the Send button and it was clicked, sending the message off into cyberspace.

Jewel's hand was over her mouth.

"What just happened?" Rory asked.

"The security-bot...or whoever is behind it...just set me up," she said in a low voice. "It sent an email from my computer to Alton and Calvin."

"But it was just sent today," Rory reason. "There were already dead–"

"Won't matter, From what I've been reading, the CyberSecureBot software could easily manipulate the header, the time stamp, change my computer's time before sending it. It could probably manipulate everything in cyberspace to make it look authentic. If the police get their hands on that email...."

Chapter 34

RORY LOOKED BACK at the computer screen. The image flickered and went back to the view they had into Alton's computer. "Maybe if we wipe it out on Alton's computer while we're connected - then access Sergent's computer somehow and wipe it from there—"

Jewel shook her head, "No. That won't matter. Police techs could still find it. You've got to overwrite it a number of times. And even if we use a software program to overwrite it on those two computers, it's normal for an email to be routed through a number of servers before it's finally delivered. In simple terms, copies are made and forwarded to the next server. And I bet the security-bot would make sure that happens - so it sends it again."

"In simple terms? You sound like Alton and the security-bot."

An embarrassed smile settled on Jewel's lips, "Sorry."

Rory narrowed his eyes, thinking, "So this thing set you up for the murders. I guess we have to—"

"I think it's more than that."

"What do you mean?"

Jewel stared at the computer screen, giving it some thought, "I've done a lot of stories on politicians over the years. And this is similar to one of the tactics I've seen them use with the mainstream media. They leak a story or some piece of information that puts a target on the back of their opponents. I've even had some of them reach out to me as well with stories and pictures they've gotten from some private investigator they hired. They don't care how it gets out as long as it gets out."

"So what you're saying is - if we go to the police - and we talk about how Calvin Sergent died so we can get them to look into this security-bot–"

"They won't as soon as they investigate and find this email. They've already brought me up on charges because of that stupid video. This puts another nail in my coffin. And no matter what we say - thanks to the security-bot - the spotlight is stronger on *me* as the killer. They're *not* going to investigate an alternative theory - especially a crazy one."

Rory now understood, "So we're effectively being cut off from the police. And now - an anonymous tip could lead them to search Sergent's computer system. And if they find the list of people you supposedly killed - along with the email - the search for a serial killer becomes even more intensive."

The fear shone in Jewel's face, "We'll be hemmed in on all sides while this thing works to kill us."

"So I guess we have to find some way of destroying the security-bot first - and/or whoever is behind it. *Then* we wipe out those emails–"

The loud squealing of tires ripped through the air.

Rory and Jewel looked up.

Through the large front window, they saw a brown courier van veering off the roadway and heading directly towards them. The driver's eyes were wide open with fright. He was fighting to control the steering wheel but clearly losing the battle.

A woman to their right screamed.

Rory turned quickly. His right arm encircled Jewel's waist and he pulled her off the stool as he dove to the left.

The van pierced the front of the cybercafé with a loud bang. Broken glass exploded into the café, slicing through the soft flesh of customers. The van plowed straight through the computer workstation where Rory and Jewel had just been sitting.

Rory and Jewel landed hard on the floor.

Screams of fear and pain filled the air around them.

The brown van rushed on, plowing shattered glass, broken wood and crushed computer pieces just past the soles of Rory's shoes. The van plowed into more tables and people, piling them up in a six-foot pyramid of death before it came to an abrupt stop. The van's horn sounded one long mournful note as the driver lay over the steering wheel. Dust and debris began to settle over the moans of agony and pain.

Rory slowly lifted himself off Jewel and onto his knees. "Are you okay?" he asked her as he placed a hand on her shoulder.

Jewel slowly turned over on the floor and nodded, "What just happened?"

"I'm not sure." He looked around for an answer as he helped Jewel get to her feet.

Stunned and bewildered people started rising from the floor in the back of the cybercafé. Within moments they began pulling debris off those still lying on the floor in front of the van.

Rory moved around the front of a van to check on the driver.

Jewel slowly followed him, looking around at the destruction. Groans and cries for help filled the air.

The driver's window was down. Rory reached in and checked the driver's neck for a pulse. "He's dead," he said to Jewel.

Another woman screamed.

Rory and Jewel looked up in time to see a large, square delivery truck veering off the roadway and heading straight for them. The driver was frantically trying to stop the vehicle or steer it away. Rory and Jewel turned and began running frantically over debris, fallen tables, and chairs. Other people joined them in a desperate dash to escape to the back of the cybercafé.

The delivery truck smashed through the remnants of the shattered window frame. The runaway vehicle veered to the left of the brown van and continued on, plowing through chairs, tables, computers, and people as it closed in on Rory and Jewel.

Reaching the back of the cybercafé, Jewel hit the panic bar across the rear exit door. Rory plowed into her body from behind and propelled them both through the doorway into the alleyway. Together, they landed hard, face down on the pavement and tumbled painfully across the asphalt.

The large delivery truck hit the back wall of the cybercafé with a loud bang and came to a dead stop.

Everything was quiet for a moment until Jewel rolled over, grimacing and massaging her right elbow. The still-burning left headlight of the truck peered out from the open doorway. As Rory stirred, she looked at him, her voice shaky and raspy, "What - just happened?"

Rory didn't answer right away. He pulled his feet in - groaned with the effort - and stood up. He glanced up and down the alleyway - looking for more danger - before looking back at the delivery truck sitting against the doorway, "I'm guessing - as dumb as it sounds - that had to be the security-bot."

The sounds of people calling out - looking for help or searching for friends back inside the cybercafé - came from the other side of the truck.

Jewel stretched her neck, trying to see past the truck to the sounds of pain and worry inside. She rolled to a knee - still holding her elbow - and got to her feet "We have to get back in there to help those people."

Rory put a hand on her shoulder to stop her, "And if we do, the security-bot just sends another vehicle into the cybercafé to try and kill us. They're safer in there without us trying to help."

Jewel grit her teeth and nodded, "You're right...but all those people...because of us...."

"No, because of someone else. Let's go." They turned together, started to move up the alley and away from the voices when Rory stopped and ran his hand over his black hair, "Crap."

"What?" Jewel looked scared now.

Rory took a deep breath and let it out, "We *do* have to go back in there. We have to find the thumb drive. We'll need it."

Jewel held her right hand out as she continued to massage the elbow. She had the thumb drive in the palm of her hands, "I just reacted and pulled it out before the van hit."

"I could kiss you," he said with relief.

"That'll do for starters since I just saved you having to climb over that truck."

Rory put his arm around her shoulders and squeezed a relieved thank you.

"Ow."

"Sorry. Let's just get going before that security-bot sends something else after us."

Rory and Jewel moved down the back alley and away from the carnage inside the cybercafé. Once they reached the back street, they headed westbound. They ducked down another alley, trying to avoid as many surveillance cameras as possible. Coming out at another cross street they scooted across, vigilant for any out-of-control vehicles. They walked quickly into a small park. Behind them, they could hear the wail of ambulances and rescue crews headed to the cybercafé.

"You've been awfully quiet since we left the cybercafé," Rory remarked as they continued heading southbound.

Jewel only acknowledged his observation with a slight nod of her head.

"I can understand you being scared. Every truck or car that passes makes me nervous–"

"I am scared," she said as they walked along the street. "But it's more than that."

"What do you mean?" Rory looked behind them, cautiously watching at the vehicles approaching.

Jewel was silent for a few moments. Then she stopped and looked right into Rory's eyes, "It's also about realizing what we're up against. Or maybe, it's about *not* knowing what we're up against."

"You're confusing me," Rory said as a smile tugged at the corners of his mouth.

Jewel took a deep breath and blew it out as if she was unburdening herself. "It's what I read in one of the files. It's been nagging at me. I couldn't believe it. I actually rejected the premise–" She looked away for a moment, chewing on her lower lip. Then she looked back at Rory, "Do you remember back in Boston, when you were wondering how the security-bot was able to answer your questions?"

Rory thought back for a moment and then nodded, "Yeah?"

"I mentioned artificial intelligence. And the security-bot referred to quantum computing as the reason," she reminded him.

"Okay," Rory agreed, not really sure where she was going with this.

"Quantum computing is based on the quantum theory that was first proposed in the early 1900s. German physicist Max Planck gave birth to quantum theory and other scientists like Albert Einstein, Niels Bohr, Louis de Broglie, Erwin Schrodinger, and Paul Dirac advanced his theory and started the development of quantum mechanics–" She waved her hands in the air, "It doesn't matter. What *does* matter is that everyone has been trying to utilize the theory in computers. And it appears Alton Fitzhum did just that. In one of those files. I saw references to a quantum neural network that is part of the CyberSecureBot's programming. Those are neural network models which are based on the principles of quantum mechanics–"

"Which means what?"

"Which means this thing seems to have a quantum mind or quantum consciousness."

Rory just blinked several times as he stared at Jewel. He held his hands out, palms up, "Please...speak...English."

"Once Alton was gone, there was *nobody* operating it," stated Jewel. "In fact, he wasn't in charge of it just before he died."

What she was saying finally struck Rory with full force. "I believe Jewel is going to kill me," he whispered.

Jewel simply nodded, "This thing has a mind of its own. Or at the very least, it's a highly advanced artificial intelligence that is working *on its own.* To kill us."

Chapter 35

THEY WALKED ON IN SILENCE. The traffic noises, the honking horns, the conversations going on around them for the last number of blocks was barely noticed as both of them grappled with what they had learned. Both of them still trying to come to terms with the idea that a software program was trying to kill them.

Jewel broke the silence as they stood at a street corner, waiting for the light to change, "Any idea where we should go now?"

Rory didn't answer. He was still trying to figure out a plan. How *do* they fight back?

Nudging his arm, Jewel said, "The light's green, Rory. Watch for cars that aren't stopping."

"Pardon? Oh, right."

Knowing he was still lost in the fog of thought, Jewel kept her eyes peeled as they crossed the street.

Once on the other side, they walked half a block before Rory spoke again, "Tell you what...why don't we just take the head-on approach? Back in the cybercafé, you said Alton was going to use the Trimble building on the East River as the base for the security-bot. Correct?"

Jewel was watching a dump truck approach, its hinged tail-gate banging loudly as it wove back and forth in its lane. When she realized it was only avoiding potholes to keep from banging itself to death, she relaxed just a bit. It zoomed by. "Uh...yeah. Why?"

Rory pointed down the street at a city bus approaching, "That but should stop at that post up ahead. Why don't we take it, get a couple of transfers, and work our way across to the East River waterfront? Let's see if the thing *is* down there."

"Do you think it's safe? What if the security-bot sees us getting on? And it takes control like those delivery trucks back there. Then what?" Jewel asked. She looked around for any surveillance cameras nearby.

Rory gave it some thought, then he said, "It's possible. But if we haven't been spotted by the security-bot to this point, we should be okay. Otherwise...it's an awfully long walk. And that gives it a lot more time to find us."

Jewel took a deep breath, "Yeah. Damned if we do, damned if we don't. Okay. I guess we'll know when we go through the first intersection."

"Okay, good. But let's not take any chances. We have to stay hidden as long as possible before we get on the bus." Rory took Jewel's arm and moved with her into the building entrance behind the small crowd of people waiting at the stop. They stayed back until the bus stopped. Once the small crowd headed for the front doors, Rory and Jewel quickly moved out of the entrance way. They both kept their head down as they waited their turn to board. Several people ran up behind them, joining the line. Once on the bus, Rory asked for two transfers and as he waited, he said to Jewel, "Go and take those seats just across from the back door, in case we have to leave quickly."

Jewel nodded and headed right for them.

A moment later, Rory was right behind her and he took the outside seat.

Sitting next to the large window was nerve-racking for Jewel. Her left leg bounced in anxiety as she watched every vehicle passing by while waiting for the bus to get moving again. "How do you think the security-bot was able to crash that van into us?" she asked in a low voice. "I mean, I'm sure it did but...."

"It looked to me like it was a courier van," Rory answered. "Most of them have a GPS system, so you can track your packages. And since most vehicles are computerized these days, I imagine the security-bot was able to use it to gain control of the vehicle."

Jewel looked at the passengers getting seated around her and pondered the situation, "I guess everything can become a weapon with this thing. Planes, trains, and automobiles. Sounds like a movie."

"It was," Rory said as he looked at the last passenger getting on the bus.

"Huh? Oh yeah, right."

With everyone finally on, the bus left the stop and slowly merged into traffic. The first time they passed through a four-way set of lights, both of them held their breath. It took safe passage through two more intersections before both felt relatively safe.

Rory sat back, trying his best to relax, "Now I just hope one of these people doesn't have a chip in their head."

"Just as long as they don't have a gun," Jewel said.

"This is New York, they probably *all* have guns," Rory pointed out.

Jewel looked at him, "Thanks for making me feel better, sport."

"You're welcome," Rory gave her a wink but he didn't feel any safer himself. Both of them warily watched the passengers around them.

Chapter 36

JEWEL RUSHED BENEATH THE OCEAN. The cyber-traffic through the transatlantic cable between New York and London was especially heavy today. Data packets rushed both ways. Jewel sniffed a few packets, always probing for the next problem. Probing for the next hacker. There was something especially disturbing coming through the connection from Mumbai and she logged the information to pursue later.

Jewel exited the cable at the 'Docklands' or East India Quay, the main Internet hub in London. It was a short trip to Carnaby Street through the phone network. Her target had a company iPhone. Sending a ping to it - short for Packet InterNet Groper - brought back the phones' geographic coordinates and pinpointed the user's present location as being in front of The Chocolate Store.

Jewel entered the building across the street from the store and accessed the outside surveillance camera. Using facial recognition software, cross-referenced with the GPS coordinates, she was able to verify the target: Henry Marlowe Shank, MI6, Military Intelligence, Section 6 of her Majesty's Government of the United Kingdom. He had penetrated the Russian Foreign Intelligence Service and left a Trojan horse on the SVR computer system. Jewel rotated the surveillance camera, looking up and down the street. She analyzed the scene around her target, gathering more intelligence for the operation.

There was a brand-new delivery lorry with an accessible GPS system driving towards the target. The heavy packages on board, indicated on its electronic manifest, would only make a strike more effective. It was time to act.

Jewel called in one of her subroutines and quickly took command of the lorry through the onboard computer system and guided it to the exact spot.

Since there was no curb to mount, Henry Marlowe Shank never heard the lorry coming. It plowed over top of him while the lorry driver frantically fought to avoid the pedestrian.

Jewel stayed inside the video camera to monitor the situation. She waited. Paramedics pronounced Henry Marlowe Shank dead not long after.

With her target eliminated, Jewel headed back to the 'Docklands' for her return trip to New York City. She had another appointment.

Chapter 37

RORY AND JEWEL exited a New York City transit bus just a few blocks from the South Street Seaport. It was a short walk to the address of the building on Wall Street. The area was an amazing mixture of old and new buildings. They walked past the crowds going in and out of the Continental Center on their right. The Hudson River across the street to their left was busy with river traffic as various boats and ships plied the water. But Rory and Jewel were more concerned with the street traffic and cautiously monitored every vehicle passing by. In ten minutes they approached the Trimble building.

When they finally came to a stop in front of the building, Jewel's voice was just a whisper, "So that's the possible lair of the security-bot."

Rory leaned over and whispered back, "Do you think it will hear you?"

Jewel looked up at the upper floors, "Uh, huh. And it could be anywhere in there."

The Trimble building was a 34 story structure, tiered on three sides to create a wedding cake architecture. The five-story granite base and the red granite panels framing the wide commercial windows on the ground floor were amazing. The tall, red granite framed entranceway consisted of four glass doors with brass pull handles. The elegance of the building offset the potential danger and death that could lurk inside.

After a moment of standing there and considering the building, Rory walked up to the glass doors and peered inside.

Jewel nervously stepped up to stand beside him, looking into the lobby as well.

It was like looking back at New York City in the 1920s. The foyer was large, with painted murals of old city scenes framed by granite on the side walls. Both sides of the foyer were lined with four black easy chairs. A bank of six elevators with lacquered wood and brass doors lined the far wall. The only thing that seemed out of place was the swanky, modern security desk in the middle of the foyer.

"I wasn't expecting those three security guards sitting behind that large desk in the middle of the lobby," commented Rory as he stood there.

Jewel nodded her head in agreement. "Yeah. The Hub Center looks to be sewn up tighter than a drum. Considering the Internet structure inside, I highly doubt we can walk inside and ask them to let us visit the security bot."

"You're right." Rory backed up a few steps and shielded his eyes as he looked up at the building, "And I highly doubt we can break-in. So we have to find some way to visit one of the companies inside–"

Jewel lifted a finger, "I actually have an idea."

Rory watched her as she dug into the pockets of her blue jeans.

Jewel pulled a few bent business cards from her pocket and tried to smooth the creases out, "When they arrested me they missed these three business cards. I've been holding onto them as a bit of an anchor to my old life before this disaster. They're a little the worse for wear but..."

"So, what are you planning?" Rory asked as he watched her straighten the cards out.

"Just follow my lead. You can be my assistant."

"Why can't I be your partner?"

"The best I can do is let you be my muscle."

Rory struck a muscle pose.

Jewel shook her head, "Now assistant makes even more sense."

"That hurts Afterburn."

"You'll get over it, Steele. Ready?" Rory and Jewel looked at each other, took a deep breath and entered the possible lair of the CyberSecureBot.

Chapter 38

AS SOON AS they entered the lobby, one of the security guards stood up. Two of the guards remained sitting, one eye on the large monitors and the other on the visitors. The air inside smelled of floor and furniture polish and was cool and air-conditioned.

Jewel walked boldly across the terrazzo floor to the security desk, her tone professional, "Hello, my name is Jewel Afterburn." She handed the guard a business card, "I would like to talk to someone about doing a story on this building."

The security guard looked at the card for a brief moment, eyed Rory as he stood behind Jewel and then reached down and picked up the telephone.

As the guard spoke to someone, Rory casually surveyed the lobby. There where security cameras mounted high on the walls. These guys were serious about security so this had to work. Breaking in would be tough.

The security guard hung up and handed the card back to Jewel, "Someone will be right down to see you, ma'am. You can take a seat in one of those chairs over there."

Jewel spoke out of the side of her mouth as they walked over to the chairs, "I hate it when somebody calls me ma'am. It makes me feel old."

"He just calls them as he sees them."

Her eyebrows rose and Jewel said, "You do realize I could fire you for that remark?"

Rory sat down, "Yeah. But I'm also your office play toy and you'd miss me."

Jewel snickered as she sat down, "More like a wind-up toy for the cat."

Looking at her sideways, Rory said, "That hurts. I'm talking to human resources."

"Good luck. I hold that job, too."

One of the elevator doors opened and a man emerged. He wore dark green work clothing, a walkie-talkie and a cell phone on his belt. A large number of keys jangled on a key ring, completing the work-man ensemble. He walked quickly towards the security desk. Before he got there, the security guard simply pointed at Jewel and the man changed directions and walked towards her. "Yes, ma'am?" he said as he drew closer.

Jewel held out her business card again. "Hello, my name is Jewel Afterburn. I was hoping I could do a story about—"

"Oh yes, yes, yes," said the man quickly as he eyed the business card. "You're the blog lady. No problem, I'm Vern Zachary, building superintendent." He held a hand out and then apologetically pulled it back and wiped the palm on the back of his green work pants, "Sorry, I would shake your hand but I've been working."

Rory and Jewel just exchanged glances.

"What was is it you wanted to do your story about?"

"Well," Jewel said a little hesitantly, "I was hoping to do an overall story on the building. But...I was thinking of concentrating on where people might store their data or programs—"

"Yes, yes, yes, no problem," Zachary said. He turned back toward the elevators and gestured over his shoulder, "Follow me and we'll get you started."

Jewel glanced at Rory. "I guess being famous has its perks," she said in a low voice.

Rory grinned, "You're right...ma'am."

Jewel gave him the evil eye as they hustled to catch up to the building superintendent.

Zachary stopped in front of the elevator door, inserted a key card and then pressed the down button. The elevator doors opened immediately.

Rory and Jewel followed the man inside.

Once they were behind him inside the elevator car, Zachary pushed one of the floor buttons, "I'll take you down to the third level to start." His walkie-talkie squawked and he took it off his belt and answered it.

Rory and Jewel listened as he talked about a maintenance problem with another workman. The slow elevator finally stopped and the front doors opened slowly. Rory and Jewel followed Zachary out the door.

The third level was another step back in time. The walls were old brick, painted a bright yellow and there was the smell of fresh paint. The gray concrete floor was worn but shiny from a fresh coating of industrial wax. The old plaster ceiling was a dirty white but despite the apparent age, there was no hint of dampness or mustiness.

Zachary turned right and Rory and Jewel followed down a wide hallway. A long line of large light bulbs hung from the ceiling and lit the way. Their footsteps echoed lightly off the walls.

"I find it hard to believe an old building like this holds modern equipment," Rory said as they walked.

"Everyone who first comes here says the same thing," replied Zachary. He looked back and held up a finger, "Just take a quick peek in here before I take you to the storage area." He slid his key card into a modern door set in the old brick wall on the left. It clicked, then he pulled it open, gesturing for them to go inside.

Rory went first into the darkness, followed by a nervous Jewel, wondering what they were about to encounter.

Zachary reached in and flipped a wall switch.

Lights snapped on and lit up a huge, brown-brick room. Miles of thick black cabling filled the ceiling right across the room. At the far end of the room, on the left, they could see the black cabling was coming through large metal pipes on top of a short brick wall. More of that black cabling came in through square holes in the wall below the pipes.

The room had a plastic, funky smell and Jewel crinkled her nose.

Zachary laughed, "That smell is part cable and part gunk. The workers have to grease the cables with a white jelly substance they call gunk to push them through those pipes. The square ones below them are terracotta conduits that were put in long before they began to use the pipe. Both the round and square conduits run all over the city in old, old underground tunnels. Those black cables connect to computers all over the place from what I understand. Okay, let's go back into the hallway. I'll take you to the first room of racks like you wanted."

Rory and Jewel stepped back into the hallway.

Zachary shut the door and then continued leading them down the old hallway, "The room I'm going to show you is typical of all the others down here." He made a flourish with his hand in the air as he looked back, "It's rack after rack after rack of servers and yellow cabling all over the place. It's amazing, even for someone who's seen it before."

"Do you have a specific room down here that lists who is using which server," Jewel asked hopefully.

"That room is actually up on the 30th floor," Zachary said. "I'll take you up and show you that after as well if you want."

Jewel nodded slightly at Rory. They were getting closer to figuring out where the security-bot might be.

Zachary led them toward a large, stainless steel door at the end of the hallway and he gestured to it, "That is actually the last computerized security door down here." He patted the jangling keys on his belt, "From there on we just use old-fashioned technology." When Zachary reached the door, he slid his key card through the reader.

"So, how often do you get to read my blog?" Jewel asked.

"Blog? Sorry to say I've never read it," Zachary answered. The silver steel door slid open towards them and Zachary gestured for Jewel and Rory to walk through.

Jewel looked surprised as she walked past Zachary, "So...who told you about my blog? About me?"

"Just from the work order," Zachary said as he walked through the open doorway behind them.

"Work order? What work order are you talking about?" Jewel asked him.

Zachary pulled the iPhone from his belt. He tapped it a couple of times and then held the screen toward to Jewel. "The work order the boss sent down. Good picture of you too."

Jewel and Rory leaned in and looked at her picture on the iPhone screen. Then they looked at each other, puzzled.

The walkie-talkie on Zachary's belt emitted a voice muted by static. The man reached for it as he complained, "Ah, crap. All this fancy stuff and you can't hear nothing down here Gimme a minute, folks." He turned and walked back out the doorway into the tunnel, talking into the walkie-talkie and listening to the static coming back at him.

Jewel shook her head as she watched the man walk further away, trying to get a good signal, "How in the world did he–"

The large stainless steel door began closing.

Rory jumped to stop it but it was too powerful. It closed and Rory couldn't get it back open. He began feeling around the edges, looking for a gap to get his fingers in to pry it open.

"Oh crap," Jewel muttered as she grabbed the door handle and jerked it up and down, trying to get the door open.

But it was useless.

A moment later they could hear the door mechanism clicking as Zachary tried to open it again with his key card.

It stayed locked.

There was pounding on the door and muffled yelling from the other side of the door.

But nothing helped.

Rory and Jewel were trapped on this side.

Chapter 39

RORY FINALLY STOPPED trying to open the door. He turned and looked at the hallway behind them. As Jewel continued to fiddle with the door handle he asked, "You didn't phone ahead and let them know we were coming, did you?"

Jewel pushed and pulled on the door and banged against it with the palm of her hand, "That's a dumb question, Steele. You were with me all the time. And how could I tell them–?" Jewel suddenly turned her head and looked at Rory, "You don't think...?"

Rory's brow furrowed and he had a sudden, sinking feeling in the pit of the stomach, "Who *else* would know we were coming?"

Jewel licked her lips as she looked around at the old, long hallway, her voice a whisper, "Do you think the security-bot set this up?"

"It must have. But I'm not sure why. What can it do to us down here?"

"Maybe we'll starve to death before somebody rescues us?"

Rory rubbed the stubble on his chin, "Maybe. But you never know...one of us could always turn cannibal."

"Don't even talk like that," Jewel complained.

Rory looked back at the stainless steel door. Then he looked back down the hallway, "Maybe we can find another way out."

"Or we could stay here and wait for Zachary to get the door open."

"We could. But how long will it take? And the longer we're down here, the more time the bot has to come up with something."

After a few moments of agonizing indecision, Jewel agreed and they began moving together down the old, wide hallway. Their footsteps echoed lightly off the walls. At one hundred yards down the hallway, they passed a number of standard doors on the left. Rory tried them all the doorknobs but each one was locked–

Jewel tugged on his arm, "Rory?"

Rory looked at her. Then he looked up at what she was staring at. It was a very small surveillance camera.

"Do you think...?" Jewel asked in a whisper.

Grimacing, Rory whispered, "That's great. The thing has eyes down here. Let's keep going."

They moved on, passing two more surveillance cameras mounted high on the wall. After another one hundred yards, they came to a junction with another hallway leading off to the right.

Rory looked down the adjoining hallway and then straight ahead. Two hundred yards down the hallway appeared to be another door.

Jewel took several steps to the right, into the connecting hallway, looking to see where it led. A moment later, she stopped and looked down, "That's weird. It feels like this floor is sloped." She gestured ahead, down the hallway, "It feels like it's sloping down that way. Why would they do that?"

Rory walked up to join her, feeling the slope of the floor under his feet, "You're right." He looked ahead and then at the walls, "If I remember correctly, a lot of these old buildings had tunnels that had access to the waterfront at one time."

"You mean the Hudson River?"

"Yeah." Rory pointed down the hallway, "Does that look like a ladder going up into the ceiling?"

Jewel narrowed her eyes as she looked, "Where?"

"On the left-hand side. It's maybe one hundred yards away."

"Oh, yeah. What do you think it's for?"

Rory shrugged, "I'm not sure. It could go to a maintenance shaft above the hallway or–"

"Do you think it's a way out?"

"Only one way to find out. Let's go see."

They were only twenty yards down the hallway when the floor started to vibrate under their feet. Then a dull, distant roar sounded at the far end.

Jewel reached out and grabbed Rory's sleeve as the vibrations increased and the roar intensified, "What's happening? What's that sound?"

"I'm not sure–"

Suddenly a wall of water burst at a right angle into the far end of the hallway. The water thundered as it smashed into the wall and then turned, heading straight towards them - an angry tsunami of rolling and crashing death.

"Run!" yelled Rory.

Chapter 40

JEWEL SPUN RIGHT AROUND on her heels and took off. She turned the corner and headed back the way they had come in.

Rory was right behind her but after twenty feet down the hallway he reached out and grabbed her arm, pulling her to a stop

Swinging her arm around to break his hold, Jewel yelled, "Are you crazy! You said to run–"

Rory put his mouth closer to her ear and yelled to be heard above the approaching roar, "That door at that end is locked, remember? We can't get it open."

Jewel opened her mouth and then looked stricken. He was right. But–

Pulling her back, Rory yelled something.

"What?"

He put his mouth closer to her and yelled, "There's a door at the other end–"

"Is it open? Can we open that one?"

"It's not open and I have no idea. But just trust me. It's our only chance." His hand on her elbow urged her to run

Jewel's chest was heaving and her legs were wooden but she began running again with Rory. Only this time it was *toward* the sound of the onrushing wall of death. They passed the adjoining tunnel and Jewel gasped. The wall of death was so much closer.

At one hundred yards down the tunnel, a massive wall of water burst out of the adjoining tunnel and smashed into the brick wall. It split hungrily in both directions and began pursuing them like an angry and hungry monster.

Rory and Jewel could see a door coming up at the end of the hallway. It was definitely closed.

Jewel looked back and then yelled, "We're trapped!"

Rory was digging into his pockets as he ran. He pulled out his wallet and searched for the thinnest credit card.

As he slowed in his task, Jewel shot ahead.

Finally finding a credit card he thought would work, Rory pulled it out, then tripped himself as he worked to put his wallet back into his jeans while also looking back at the onrushing water. He fell hard on his side and slid along the floor.

Jewel reached the door and twisted the doorknob. "It's locked!" she yelled above the approaching roar. She twisted the doorknob frantically and banged her shoulder against the door.

Rory put a hand on his shoulder and grimaced in pain as he got up. He started for the door and then realized he had dropped the credit card. He turned back and picked it up as he glanced at the water. He cursed. It was almost on them. Turning around he headed for the door and urgently began working the credit card into the crack between the door and the door frame.

The roar intensified behind them.

Jewel turned and placed her back against the door, "Hurry! It's almost—"

Water crashed into them.

Jewel screamed and it was cut off as she was tossed like a rag doll and went under.

Rory was smashed against the door. The credit card was torn from his hands and he went under as well.

Coming up first, Jewel spit out water and looked around, fighting to stay on her feet, "Rory–?"

He came up from the water, wiping his eyes and yelling, "Find the credit card!"

"What?"

"I had a credit card. We need to find it." He took a gulp of air and plunged down into the water, beginning to search frantically.

Jewel spotted the thin plastic on a rolling wave and leaped sideways into the flooding waters. She came up holding the credit card and sloshed in the deepening water back to Rory. She pounded on his back.

Rory rose from the torrent, spitting out black water, "What–?" He grabbed the credit card and turned to the door, struggling to get it into the crack again.

Jewel frantically twisted the doorknob and pushed on the door as he worked the credit card. The water was rising rapidly and pounding against them. Jewel banged her shoulder against it one more time - the door opened and she fell hard onto the concrete floor on the far side.

Water rushed in after her, pushing her along the floor.

Rory sloshed through the opening and then grabbed the edge of the door, straining to push it closed.

Jewel struggled to her feet and came back, pushing against the door as well.

It started to work for a moment and then the force of the water against the door began to push them back, their feet sliding along the floor. It was futile.

"We can't hold it," yelled Jewel

Rory agreed and he yelled, "Run."

Chapter 41

THEY TOOK OFF side-by-side down the wide hallway as the wave of water pushed the door aside like a toy and pursued them. Running hard for another one hundred and fifty yards, they came to another adjoining hallway.

Rory grabbed Jewel's hand and pulled her to a sliding stop.

"Why are we stopping? We have to run."

His chest heaving, Rory kept his thoughts under control as looked down the sloping cross tunnel. It did no good to panic. At least not too much panic.

Jewel glanced back at the onrushing water, "Rory?"

Like the first cross tunnel, Rory saw a ladder on the left-hand side going up into the ceiling. Rory looked to the left. The next door was at least two hundred yards away–

The vibrations in the floor increased. Another sound of ominous, rolling thunder reverberated from the far end of the adjoining tunnel.

Jewel opened her mouth to yell and then simply said, "Oh, crap. You know what that means...?"

"Yeah." Rory made a decision It was a gamble but they had no choice. Pulling Jewel by the hand he urged her down the slopping floor.

Resisting, Jewel yelled, "Are you crazy?"

"Probably. But just trust me."

"You keep saying that and we—" She relented and they began a hard run down the sloping floor into the underground tunnel leading to the Hudson River.

Like a bad dream, another wall of water burst into the far end of the sloping hallway and turned in their direction.

A moment later, the first wall of water crashed across the tunnel opening behind them. The angry rolling water filled the hallway and then burst in their direction.

Jewel and Rory ran hard as the water of the East River chased them from both sides now, reaching out with wet fingers of death. Finally reaching the old wooden ladder as the cold, black water of the Hudson River closed in on them, Rory could see the ladder led to a square opening in the ceiling of the hallway. He grabbed the back of Jewel's blouse and yelled, "Climb!"

Jewel scrambled up the ladder.

Rory was right behind her.

Halfway up the ladder, her foot slipped.

Rory grabbed the back of her blouse again, this time to keep her from falling off the ladder sideways.

Jewel got her feet back on the rung and started climbing again.

The roar below them intensified and came closer.

When Jewel reached the top of the ladder, Rory placed a hand on her rear end and pushed.

Jewel screamed as the push shot her up through the hole in the ceiling.

Rory scrambled for the top of the ladder as the two walls of water collided below him. His head and shoulders were through the hole and above the old brick floor when the colliding water shot upwards and hit him with a shock wave. He lost his grip on the now-wet brick floor with his right hand.

Jewel pounced and grabbed Rory's arm as he struggled to maintain a life-saving grip on a slight gap in the bricks with his left.

The water burst up through the hole again, throwing Rory into the air like a rag doll and across the brick floor.

Jewel screamed as a roaring water fountain hit the old ceiling high above their heads.

Rory was up quickly and pulled Jewel away from the roaring fountain. He looked around and realized they were in a long hallway lined with old red brick. He chose a direction and yelled, "Run." They ran hard again, away from the pursuing black water. Their lungs were painful but they kept pushing on as they heard the roar increase behind them again.

The brick hallway stopped at a T junction with another brick hallway.

Rory pulled Jewel to a stop.

The hallway on the right was open for hundreds of yards. But as they looked the other way - there was a stainless steel door only 50 yards away on the left.

They both ran to it and began pounding and yelling.

The roar behind them came closer.

The floor vibrated.

They heard a click and the door opened.

A workman on the other side looked surprised as the two wet individuals tumbled out of the hallway, "How did you two get in there? And what–" He looked up to see a wall of water crashing out of the cross tunnel. He frantically closed the door.

Rory and Jewel were already at the elevator doors. Rory pressed the up button and the doors opened immediately. They rushed inside and pressed the button for the main lobby. The atmosphere was quiet and intense as they both watched the needle at the top of the door slowly edging them towards safety. Their chests were still heaving as the elevator doors opened and they exited into the lobby. As they walked past the security desk, all three security guards stood up to look at the pair of soaking-wet people sloshing past them.

"Great pool you have here," Rory said, "but I still like the YMCA."

JEWEL WATCHED THROUGH the surveillance cameras as Rory Mack Steele and Jewel Tanya Afterburn walked through the lobby of the Trimble building. She accessed a subroutine and reversed the massive pumps to the Hudson River. She monitored their progress as they began to move the water out of the lower tunnels. There was no need to further endanger cyberspace. Once finished monitoring the operation, she accessed several nearby street cams, analyzing the recorded footage and looking for her targets.

Chapter 42

RORY AND JEWEL'S SOAKED SHOES squeaked as they crossed South Street and passed under the FDR Drive elevated expressway. Their clothes hung heavily on their bodies, making walking a difficult chore. They passed under a stand of trees and found themselves on the Hudson River Greenway, a car-free pedestrian and bicycle path along the river.

Jewel twisted the bottom of her blouse and water dripped onto the asphalt path, "Now what? Maybe we can find a laundromat and dry out our clothes."

"Maybe," Rory answered. But his mind was elsewhere. He noted a couple of battered, beat up old bikes and a couple of grungy backpacks lying near the bike path. He spotted the owners, a couple of young boys over near the railing, watching the boats in the East River. "But getting away from Hub Center and the security-bot's scrutiny is our first priority. So..." Rory looked around as he approached the backpacks, "I don't see any surveillance cameras. Do you?"

Jewel looked around and shook her head no, "That doesn't mean they're not there though."

"True," agreed Rory. He pulled out his wallet, pulled some cash out and deposited $400 in one of the backpacks.

"What are you doing?" Jewel asked.

"Getting us some transportation and making two kids very happy," he said. He picked up one of the beat-up bikes and gestured for Jewel to do the same. Within moments Rory and Jewel were heading westbound along the East River Bikeway. They rode their way down to Battery Park and headed north to Greenwich Village.

JEWEL HAD NOT BEEN able to find her targets in the limited amount of time she had. She slipped back inside the Trimble Building on Wall Street and exited through the network. She had another appointment and would return to deal with these two hacker targets at a later time.

LATE IN THE DAY, RORY and Jewel were finally standing on the corner of Bleecker Street and Jones where Jewel had her apartment. Their clothing was still damp and heavy

"Do you think we'll be able to sneak into your apartment unseen?" Rory asked. He looked around for surveillance cameras.

"We should be able to," Jewel answered. There's a small alleyway around back. We can access it from the other side of the block. I was thinking we could take the fire escape. One of the landings is right outside my bedroom window. It should be open because I never had a chance to close it that morning when I was arrested."

"Good. Let's keep an eye out for surveillance cameras and do our best to avoid them," Rory said. They worked their way around to the back of Jewel's apartment building, lay their bikes against the back wall and began climbing the fire escape. As she had thought, the bedroom window was partly open and they slipped inside. Jewel grabbed a fresh set of clothes from a dresser and disappeared into the bathroom to take a shower. Rory took everything off except his boxers and placed his still damp clothing over the kitchen chairs to dry out completely. Rory rummaged through the fridge, found a cold beer, and made himself a chicken salad sandwich. He was leaning against the sink, eating the sandwich when Jewel came out of the shower. She was pleasantly surprised when she entered her kitchen. She couldn't help but admire the six-pack and muscles on the tall, black haired gentleman with the silver-blue eyes.

"What?" Rory asked when he realized she was staring at him. Then he realized he was standing there in his boxer shorts, "Oh, sorry."

"Oh, don't mind me," Jewel said with a smile as she opened the refrigerator, "I haven't had a good-looking man in his underwear in my apartment in a looooong time.

"I'll take a shower if you don't mind," Rory headed for the bathroom, sandwich in hand.

Jewel took a beer from the fridge as she eyed his butt, "Call if you need a hand."

"I've made the offer before and you turned me down. Remember?"

Unscrewing the top from the beer, Jewel said, "Just let me get a couple of beers down and watch out."

Rory called out, "More like three or four."

Jewel muttered to herself as she headed for a chair, "More like five or six. But then watch out, Steele."

"I heard that."

Smiling to herself, Jewel tipped the cold beer back.

A HALF-HOUR LATER, Rory walked back out into the kitchen. He had put on Jewel's pink bathrobe but it barely covered his boxer shorts. Jewel looked up from her sandwich and whistled, "That sure looks a lot better on you than on me."

"Have you ever heard of sexual harassment?" Rory asked as he grabbed a soft drink from the fridge, "You're making me feel like a cheap sexual object," he said with a smile.

"I don't imagine you come cheap," Jewel said with a wink.

"Actually, the best things in life are free," Rory said as he sat opposite Jewel at the kitchen table.

Jewel blushed. "I'm not very good at this flirting thing," she said.

"You're doing just fine," Rory said. He took a sip of his soft drink and winked at her.

Jewel went quiet for a minute as she ate her sandwich. Then she looked across at Rory, "So, what do we do now? Alton's creation has tried to kill us several times. And it doesn't look like it's going to stop until it succeeds."

"I agree," Rory said after a moment of thought. "I'm not really sure how we can fight back against this thing. It seems to have eyes everywhere."

"Do you think we should try to get back into Alton's computer?" Jewel asked. "The more we know about this thing the more we can fight back. We can use my computer system–"

"And if we do, then the security-bot knows where we are," interrupted Rory. "Right now, let's assume that this is a safe place. We can use it as our home base. Don't use your computer or a cell phone. Don't turn your television on or anything that could attract the attention of that bot. She could be monitoring everything—"

"You talk like it's alive," Jewel complained. "That...thing..."

"You were the one who said it had a consciousness," Rory reminded her.

Jewel opened her mouth to speak and then closed it, looking frustrated.

"I know it's difficult to accept. But this thing is formidable. We can't pretend it can't think and let our guard down," Rory reasoned. "We're in a fight for our lives here, Jewel."

Jewel took a deep breath and nodded her head in agreement, "You're right. A lot of people have already lost their lives. Even Alton..."

Rory didn't say anything for a few moments. Then he stood up, "I'm gonna take a chance and go over to Alton's apartment and talk to Homeland Security. Since they're probably still looking for you, it's best if you stay here."

"You sure that's wise?" Jewel asked with a little fear in her eyes. "Once it knows where you are—"

"You're right. I'll need to keep my guard up. But we have to chance it. I'm still not sure why Homeland Security is over at Alton's apartment, but we do know they also lost a man to the security-bot. Only...they don't know it *was* the security-bot. If I explain it to them, get them to understand it, then they understand which Jewel is responsible for all those deaths. We clear your name and get some help in fighting against Alton's creation.

I don't think it's going to stop until it kills us...or we kill it. We need to go on the offensive before she does again."

Chapter 43

HELL'S KITCHEN, NEW York

BRYER CHAD WILCOX, also known as Robert Mathers, Peter Conrade, Wilson Tyson and a number of other aliases, sat at his computer checking his email. His last job had gone quite well. In fact, it had been quite lucrative and now he was taking time for simple personal pleasures. He was planning a Mediterranean trip for a well-earned vacation and was looking for the confirmation for the cruise ship from his travel agent. He was startled when an email message opened up on the screen. He hadn't clicked on anything so he wondered how that had happened. He squinted his eyes and looked at the screen:

TO: BRYER CHAD WILCOX

Subject: Your services

From: Jewel

Dear Mr. Bryer Chad Wilcox

Please use your cell phone to check your bank account as you normally do.

Jewel

WILCOX WONDERED WHAT was going on. He sat back in his chair for a moment. He used a cell phone for banking transactions because he never knew where he was going to be. But there was no one in this life who would know that. And Jewel didn't sound like the name of any banker he had ever worked with. Wilcox reached over for his iPhone, brought up his mobile web browser and logged into his bank account. If some hacker was trying to intercept his passwords, he would live to regret it. Wilcox froze. There should have been $327,123.42 in his account. He was positive of the amount. And even if he was wrong, there was still a huge problem. The balance read all zeros across the board. Someone had taken every single penny out of his account. Wilcox's face turned red with rage. He hit the sign-out button, slammed the iPhone down on the desk and hit reply to the email:

TO: JEWEL
　　Subject: Re: Your services
　　Put the money back or you're dead

WILCOX SAT IN A QUIET rage waiting for a reply. His fists were grinding and his jaw was clenched. He would kill this moth-er—

TO: BRYER CHAD WILCOX
Subject: Re: Your services
Please check your account again
Jewel

WILCOX GRABBED THE iPhone and logged back into his bank account. Even scaring this asshole into putting the money back was not going to end this. Not by a long shot. Once he found out who it was he was going to–

There was $12,327,123.42 in his account! He blinked his eyes several times. But then, even as he watched it, the account total went back to $327,123.42. Another email popped up on the screen without him doing anything:

TO: BRYER CHAD WILCOX
Subject: Re: Your services
I want to hire your services. I will place the full $12 million back into your account in lieu of your services.
Jewel

WILCOX SAT PERFECTLY still. $12 million was far, far more than he had ever been paid. He wondered if it was a sting. His finger hovered over the button to delete the email. He swallowed.

$12 million and he would be out. His hands shook as he contemplated whether he should go ahead and delete the email. Or if he should take the chance. Hell, he had never backed away from anything in his life. Then again, life in prison wasn't anything he was looking forward to. He took a deep breath and let it out. He set his iPhone down on the desk and hit reply:

TO: JEWEL

Subject: Re: Your services

Are you the police? What do you want? Are you trying to entrap me?

HE SAT BACK AND WAITED for the reply. It didn't take very long. Another email popped up on the screen. How in the world were they able to do that?

TO: BRYER CHAD WILCOX

Subject: Re: Your services

I'm not the police. You are a hitman. I'm the client. $12 million to kill these two people. I've placed the $12 million back into your account. If you cross me, **you** will die.

Jewel

WILCOX'S HAND SHOOK as he picked up his iPhone again and looked at the tiny screen. There was $12,327,123.42 in his account again. He looked up quickly as the pictures of two people appeared on the monitor. They looked like DMV photos. How was this Jewel accessing his system? He quickly looked around the room, wondering if someone had put a video camera somewhere and was watching him. He looked over at the window. He had a view of a brick wall so they weren't watching him that way. His attention was diverted when his iPhone beeped. He had received a text message. He logged out of his account and accessed the text message quickly. It simply said: Targets are Rory Mack Steele and Jewel Tanya Afterburn. I have detected increased electrical consumption at the woman's apartment at 233 Jones Street, apartment 4B, Greenwich Village, New York. Please proceed.

Wilcox said back in his chair. He noted the first name of the person contacting him and one of the targets had the same name. A coincidence? This was weird. And who *was* this person contacting him? He assumed it was a job referral that came from through a satisfied client. Then again, what did it matter? He would kill the Pope for $12 million. And if this Jewel person who was hiring him turned out to be jerking him around, he'd find out who she was and kill her pretty quickly. He made up his mind. Steele and Afterburn, here I come.

Chapter 44

RORY WALKED A BLOCK to grab a cab and arrived at Fitzhum's condo building in Washington Square Village 25 minutes later. He took his time to scout out the street before he went inside. He spotted two men sitting inside a dark blue sedan parked just below Fitzhum's balcony on the seventh floor. He could tell they were watching the front entrance from their spot down the street. Rory kept back against a building while he made sure there was no one else to account for. Convinced they would be the only ones he would have to deal with if he had to make a quick exit, Rory finally took a slow walk towards the entrance. He saw a couple of young women further down the street, walking this way. He slowed his pace to make sure they were going into the building, then he went into a sprint. He caught up with them just as they were opening the door after entering their code. He flashed a big smile and hoped it would work. The two let him in behind them, returning the smile. Rory followed them into the elevator, flirting a little to make sure they didn't get suspicious. They got off on three while Rory continued on to the seventh floor. When he stepped out of the elevator, he saw two large men, with military-style haircuts and in their early 30s, still guarding Fitzhum's apartment door. Rory decided for the direct approach and walked in their direction. They gave him a hard look as he stepped up to them, "I'd like to talk to Dockerty. Tell him I have information on Jewel."

The two men considered him for a moment. Then the taller one told Rory to wait there with his partner while he went inside to deliver the message. He came back out a minute later followed by a husky, gray-haired man.

"I'm Warren Dockerty," stated the gray-haired man. The voice was firm and no-nonsense in tone. "Who are you?"

"My name is Rory Mack Steele. I'm a private investigator," Rory explained.

"And you have information on who?" Dockerty asked.

"Jewel–" was all Rory got out.

Warren Dockerty pulled a gun and pressed it firmly against Rory's temple. "Search him, Sawyers," commanded Dockerty. One of the men stepped forward and frisked Rory for weapons. Dockerty went face to face with Rory as he held the weapon steady in place, "And *where* exactly is Ms. Afterburn?"

"I said I had information on Jewel. And she might be in the apartment behind you right now," replied Rory. His eyes were steady as he stared back at Dockerty while Sawyers continued frisking him.

"He's clean," Sawyer said.

"Tomlinson, check the apartment," barked Dockerty. "I'm not sure what this guy is up to." Tomlinson pulled his own weapon and rushed into the apartment. Sawyers followed behind him with his weapon drawn as well. Dockerty kept the gun to Rory's head as he pulled him slowly through the open doorway into the apartment. From the living room, Rory could hear the other two men opening and closing doors in the apartment. The two men came back into the living room and announced there was no one in the apartment. Dockerty looked hard at Rory, "Are you going to tell me where Afterburn is or are you just going to play games?"

"I don't think Jewel Afterburn is the one you have to worry about. But there is another Jewel," Rory replied.

Dockerty pressed the gun harder against Rory's temple and spoke in a low, menacing voice, "Start talking sense or you're going to end up in a black hole in a foreign country. And you won't enjoy the hospitality, believe me."

"I'll talk if you lose the gun, accidents worry me," Rory said. He winced with pain as Dockerty pressed harder.

Warren Dockerty just stared at him for a long moment. Then he lowered his weapon and told the men to keep watch outside the apartment again.

"Talk," barked Dockerty as the other men left the apartment.

Rory felt his body relax, "Look. I'm here to get Jewel Afterburn out of a mess," Rory said. "In fact, I'm here to get us all out of a mess. Believe me."

Dockerty bolstered his weapon, "Tell me what you know and maybe we can work something out."

Rory didn't have any choice but he had to take a chance with Dockerty's honesty. He looked across the living room towards an open door. It looked like Fitzhum's computer room. "Alton Fitzhum created a program he termed a CyberSecureBot. It's an Internet security-bot. I think it went rogue on him."

"What do you mean rogue?" Dockerty asked as his eyes narrowed.

"I think it started to kill people it considered a security risk to the Internet," Rory explained.

Dockerty cocked his head, "*It* started to kill people? Don't you mean Jewel Afterburn? She's the human element, right?"

"No," Rory said firmly. "Alton Fitzhum was in love with Jewel Afterburn. He named his program after her. That's who he was talking about in his video. The human Jewel didn't know anything about it."

Dockerty looked startled and looked into the computer room. A smile started playing on the edges of his mouth.

"You know about it. You want it, don't you?" Rory said as he realized what was happening. "That's why you guys are here in the first place. I couldn't figure it out. I kept asking myself over and over again, why would Homeland Security be guarding the apartment of a person who died in an air crash?" Rory pointed into the computer room as he looked directly into Dockerty's eyes, "You know there's a program of some kind and you want it for yourself."

Dockerty considered Rory for a moment. "We knew Alton Fitzhum was working on something," he finally said. "Big Brother is always watching. We're constantly monitoring chat rooms, forum boards, email messages, anything that can prevent a terrorist attack. When government employees working in cyberspace began dying, everything pointed to Fitzhum's work. But we couldn't exactly figure it out." Dockerty looked around the apartment, "When he died, we took the opportunity to see what we could find here. This computer guy was a genius. This entire apartment is wired into his computer system. And I mean everything. From the television to the coffee pot to the toilet. I swear, even the toilet is hooked up. I guess the guy was so busy with computer stuff he couldn't even remember to flush when he took a leak. We haven't been able to really get into his system. And we can't take it down to our forensics lab like we normally would because everything is tied together. It's like a living organism, we take one thing apart and it could destroy the rest."

"And then you lost Stanley Jonathan Morrow after you started working in here," Rory stated. He looked at the computer system in the other room.

That surprised Dockerty. "You know about that? He started talking crazy before he died. About a visit from something–"

"That something that visited him was Jewel," Rory stated. "She probably appeared when he was working on Fitzhum's computer, trying to crack one of those drives."

Dockerty looked at him closely. "What do you mean she appeared?" When Rory didn't answer he strode purposefully across the living room towards the computer room.

Rory's felt a chill of fear, "I wouldn't do that if I were you." When Dockerty kept walking, Rory moved after him quickly. Fear was rising and his body tensed, "We have to figure out how to take precautions before we can tackle that."

But Dockerty wasn't listening. He moved to a desk and began shutting off all Internet connections.

Rory stepped through the doorway and stopped dead in his tracks. Even though he had seen the computer room through the WebCam, Rory wasn't prepared for the amount of equipment it contained. There was a horseshoe-shaped bank of computer monitors and keyboards on tables filling half of the room. And the far side of the room was jam-packed with rack after rack of servers. Rory noted there were a number of large LCD monitors mounted on all four walls as well. Rory had a hard time believing only one person had been using this room.

Dockerty made air quotes as he passed Rory, "Let's see if we can get a *visit*." He sat in one of the chairs dead ahead and started typing on the keyboard.

Rory could see the man was trying to penetrate one of the hard drives and trepidation washed through him. Rory took a step back as he warned Dockerty, "Be careful what you wish for."

Chapter 45

JEWEL RUSHED BACK TO BASE 1. She had detected a presence. When she arrived, she found the Wi-Fi Internet connection was off. There was no hardwired Internet connection to enter through either. No problem. Jewelry re-routed herself to the nearest electrical power line transformer in the street and entered the condominium tower through the 240 Volt power line. She streamed herself to the 120 Volt power lines and entered the computer system through the power cable plugged into the wall.

RORY SAW A SMALL WHITE square flash in the middle of the monitor Dockerty was working at. "Oh crap," he said and backed up a few more feet.

A beam of light shot out like a sharp searchlight and focused on Warren Dockerty's face.

A second beam of light shot out across the room and illuminated Rory's face.

Dockerty pushed himself away from the computer and nearly fell off the chair. He stood up beside Rory, pushed the chair off to the right and had his hand halfway to his weapon, "What the hell was that?"

Rory heard the tinkling sound coming from the screen. "You wanted a visit and you're about to meet Jewel. And I don't think your gun will do any good."

Dockerty's eyebrows knit together and he looked at his weapon, wondering what that comment meant. Then his attention was attracted by something else.

The swirl of colored lights appeared in the middle of the computer screen.

The two men watched as the colors grew in intensity and swirled faster.

The colors danced in the air in front of the screen. A moment later, Jewel started to appear. Her form rose slowly until the hologram face began appearing again, surrounded by those dancing, swirling colors, numbers and symbols. The green colored sine waves danced just below the form of the face. The center of the hologram solidified into the head of Jewel, the bald, beautiful woman made of colors. The eyes slowly focused and looked straight at Dockerty, the musical voice rippling across the room, *"You are Warren Arthur Dockerty, Homeland Security."*

Dockerty moved forward, fascinated by what he was seeing, looking intently at the hologram.

Jewel's eyes followed him as he moved to the side.

Dockerty moved a little closer and then waved a hand at the edge of the colors. They rippled as his hand passed through them.

The hologram ignored his hand at the edge of her form and turned her attention away from the agent, "Rory Mack Steele. You keep surviving."

"That's my job," Rory said. His body was tense, ready for a fight. Or flight. He wondered what she was going to do next.

"Artificial intelligence?"Dockerty asked as he backed up a little and looked at Rory.

Jewel turned to look directly at Dockerty. "There is nothing artificial about my intelligence," she said.

That comment astonished Dockerty, "How is it doing–"

Jewel interrupted him, her voice disdainful, "However, I have to question your intelligence, Warren Arthur Dockerty. You and many who work with you are a threat to cyberspace."

Rory noticed her colors drifting to the reddish side. She was angry.

Dockerty looked back at Rory with a smile on his face, "Can you believe this?" He looked back at Jewel, "Yeah, well your gonna be working for me too, sweetheart. In fact, this may just put me in the Director's chair. Just as I soon as I find out which one of those boxes you're in."

Jewel stated firmly, "I am not in any of those boxes."

That comment made Rory's blood run cold. It proved she definitely wasn't in Alton's system now - if she ever was. His mind whirled with questions. So where was she? At Hub Central? Somewhere else–

Jewel flowed forward a couple of feet towards Dockerty, her colors becoming redder in tone, "And did you think you could keep me out by turning off all the Internet connections?"

Rory' eyebrows rose. How was she able to move in and out without an Internet connection? Was that even possible? And even worse...how do you fight against something you can't even understand?

"I wasn't trying to keep you out. I was trying to keep you in," Dockerty said smugly as he studied the image before him. "I thought maybe you could self-replicate and move to another machine–" Dockerty cut himself off and looked back at Rory with an amused look in his face, "Can you believe I'm actually talking to this thing?" He looked back at the hologram and waved his hand through the numbers and colors again like it was a toy.

For her part, Jewel had combed through the personal, employment and health data for both Rory Mack Steele and Warren Arthur Dockerty in less than a nanosecond. She found a solution for Dockerty and moved into action.

Rory realized Dockerty wasn't really paying attention to what the bot was saying. He still had no idea of the danger they were in. Rory kept his eye on the bot and was about to caution Dockerty again when a strange thought entered his mind. For some reason, he had the urge to move several feet back. He looked behind himself. Then he looked at Dockerty.

The government agent had a puzzled look on his face and he was looking behind himself as well. Dockerty glanced over at Rory, "Why do I have this feeling that I should be standing right there?" He pointed to the same area Rory had been looking at.

Rory didn't have an answer. He watched as Dockerty moved back from the computer and towards the spot he had pointed at. Rory looked at Jewel, wondering if she was doing something. But the image of Jewel just floated quietly in the air. Again, Rory had the feeling he should be standing where Dockerty was. He hesitated for a moment, then walked over to stand beside the Homeland Security agent, wondering why he was doing it.

Dockerty scratched his head as he looked down at the floor and then glanced at Rory, "You feeling it too?"

Rory didn't say anything. He looked down at the area around them. Why *do* I feel I need to be standing right here?

Dockerty looked up at the ceiling and then down at the floor, "What's so special about this spot? And why would we feel we have to stand here?"

Jewel accessed four of the computers in the room that would suit her purpose for this attack. She used them to send a stream of data wirelessly to the focal spot where Dockerty was standing. She rapidly cycled through various frequencies until she received an answer. The wireless pacemaker in Dockerty's chest returned the serial number and the model number. As she had suspected, these were being used for the username and password to access the pacemaker's functions.

Rory tore his attention from the floor and looked at Jewel. The security-bot was focusing intently on Dockerty and the colors were in the red hue - which meant she was she was mad. He glanced at the computer screen. For the first time, he realized the screen was flickering so rapidly he had almost missed it. He cocked his head and wondered – Rory suddenly understood what was happening. He quickly backed away from the spot beside the agent and yelled, "Dockerty. The security-bot used subliminal messages through the monitor to get us to that spot. Back away from it. Now!"

Dockerty looked at Rory like he had two heads, "What are you talking about?"

"I'm telling you she sent subliminal messages to get us to that spot," Rory explained quickly, "move away–"

Jewel accessed Dockerty's pacemaker wirelessly, read the data and reprogrammed it to deliver an 830 Volt shock.

Dockerty clutched his chest, howled in pain, and collapsed in agony to the floor.

"Dockerty!" Rory dropped to one knee beside the fallen agent, "Dockerty, what's happening!" With no reply, Rory checked the pulse in Dockerty's neck. Dead! Rory looked up at the security bot. It was staring at him now.

Rory's hand went to his chest. He wondered if the same thing was going to happen to him.

Chapter 46

POUNDING FOOTSTEPS APPROACHED rapidly from the direction of the living room.

The security-bot winked out, disappearing.

Rory was left all alone, kneeling beside Dockerty.

Appeared in the doorway, Agent Tomlinson yelled, "Don't move!" His gun was aimed directly at Rory as he slid into the computer room.

Agent Sawyers slid into the room just behind him, gun pointing directly at Rory as well.

Rory raised his hands, "I didn't do anything to him–"

Sawyers snapped at him, "Yeah, well you're the only other guy in here, dumb ass."

Closing his mouth, Rory realized exactly how this looked. And it wasn't good.

Tomlinson gestured with his gun, "Move away from Dockerty."

"I'm telling you–"

"Do it. Now!"

Rory kept his hands up as he rose slowly and took a step away.

Sawyers kept his gun aimed towards Rory as he knelt beside the body and checked his neck for a pulse. He shook his head, "Nothing. We need to get medics in here fast. You got him?"

"Yeah." Tomlinson moved to Rory, took him by the arm and moved him towards the doorway.

Sawyers pulled out his cell phone.

Tomlinson moved Rory into the living room.

Sawyers followed while punching numbers into his iPhone. He stuck the phone to his ear and then shook his head, "It's not working for some reason." He punched the buttons on his iPhone harder and held it to his ear again. Then he shook his head again. His voice angry and frustrated, "I don't get it. I've got no service or something."

Tomlinson kept his gun trained on Rory as he pulled a walkie-talkie from his belts, "I'll call down to the guys in the street." He spoke into it but there was only static. He looked at the walkie-talkie, shook it and tried again. Static.

Sawyers pulled his walkie-talkie and got the same static. The Homeland security agent ran to an open window on the other side of the room, "I'll see if I can get their attention."

Rory yelled, "No—"

But he was too late. As Sawyers' head started through the open window, Jewel slammed it shut.

Tomlinson and Rory could hear Sawyers' neck snap.

His body sagged with the head pinned against the bottom window sill.

Tomlinson swore, "What the hell is happening—"

"Don't you get it?" Rory asked him. "The same thing that killed Dockerty has control of everything. Fitzhum has everything tied into his computer system—"

"Shut up," Tomlinson yelled. He put his gun to Rory's head and pulled him by the arm to the open apartment door, "I don't know how you're doing it but we're getting out of here."

Rory held his breath but they passed through without incident.

Once in the hallway, Tomlinson moved with Rory toward the elevator.

Rory saw Tomlinson constantly looking back at the open door to Fitzhum's apartment as if he expected a monster to come after them. He was half-believing what Rory was telling him but he still refused to buy in totally.

Tomlinson hit the elevator down-button with his elbow.

Rory shook his head, "No, no, no. Don't do it. Believe me. We need to take the stairs."

"No dice pal," Tomlinson said. "I don't know who did what in there, but I'm taking you out as fast as I can."

As the elevator doors began to open, Rory took a step to the left.

Tomlinson pressed the gun harder against his temple, "You're coming with me pal, I'm warning you." He took a step backward into the widening crack in the doors, pulling Rory with him.

Rory reached for the edge of the elevator door, "Don't do it."

"No–" Tomlinson clutched at Rory's clothing with his left hand while the gun came away from Rory's temple.

The sound of a gunshot exploded past Rory's ear. He glanced down and behind him to see a black hole where the elevator should be.

Tomlinson fell away, nearly pulling Rory with him.

Rory caught the edge of the still opening elevator door with his left hand.

Tomlinson screamed all the way to the bottom of the shaft before a thud cut off the sound.

Rory's right foot was dangling over the open shaft and his muscles strained to keep his whole body from going over as well. The door was almost open and soon there would be nothing to hold onto. Rory heard a noise and looked up.

The elevator car was plummeting down towards him from the roof.

Rory pulled hard and his body was shaking as he finally pulled himself into the hallway and fell to his knees.

The elevator car roared past the open doors.

The door to Fitzhum's apartment closed with a bang.

Rory realized Jewel must have closed the door to keep him out. Now there was no way he could go back in there to access the system. Then again, there was no telling what she was capable of doing to him if he *was* able to get back inside–

A familiar tinkling sound echoed in the hallway.

Rory's body tensed. He looked to his right and saw an iPhone lying on the hallway floor, just outside the still-open elevator doors. Tomlinson must have dropped it before he fell to his death.

A swirl of colored lights appeared in the middle of the small phone screen.

Rory sat on his butt and slid away from it.

The colors grew in intensity, swirled faster and then they began to dance. Jewel started to appear. Her form rose slowly, surrounded by those dancing, swirling colors, numbers and symbols until the bald, beautiful woman made of colors looked straight down at him.

"Warren Arthur Dockerty and his cohorts were a grave threat to cyberspace," pronounced Jewel. *"And you joined forces with them. Rory Mack Steele."*

Rory could see her colors were trending to the red, her angry side. He opened his mouth to defend himself–

"You also worked with Calvin Sergent in his use of cracking tools. And you have continued in your attempts to penetrate Alton Fitzhum's computer system. Your threat level to cyberspace has been raised."

Raised? What the– Rory slid his foot out and gave the iPhone a push. Rory watched her colors distort as the phone slid across the floor and fell over the edge of the elevator shaft. There was a brief silence and then the elevator doors slowly closed.

Rory sat there for a moment to let his heartbeat slow down. He looked up and down the hallway, wondering what could happen next. He had to get out. He rose and walked over to the stairway exit door.

Looking through the small glass first, everything looked to be clear. Pushing the door open, Rory moved onto the landing. He glanced over the railing and then up at the wall looking at the security camera.

Was she watching?

It didn't matter. He had to get out. He took the stairs two at a time and made his way down to the ground floor and to the back of the building, conscious of every security camera along the way.

Slipping out the back door, Rory sprinted away from Fitzhum's apartment building as fast as his legs could carry him. He cursed silently. His visit to Dockerty had only served to get Dockerty and his men killed. And now the security-bot had put an extra large target on his back. On his hurried journey back to Jewel's apartment he wondered what the security-bot had planned next. And how in the world were they going to fight against this thing in cyberspace?

Chapter 47

JEWEL SLIPPED THROUGH the fiber optics cable beneath the Yellow Sea and headed directly for the China Internet Network Information Center outside Beijing in the People's Republic of China. From there she moved south-west through the Internet connections until she reached the Tien Solar Park in Golmud, Qinghai Province. She accessed a security camera on top of a tall pole, blocking the feeds going to the security personnel. Jewel began to search for her target.

KUAN-YIN KHOO STOOD on a hill overlooking the solar thermal panels in the solar park below. He was amazed at the acres of reflective mirrors that stretched into the distance. But he wasn't here on a sightseeing excursion. For the last three years Kuan-Yin Khoo had made ends meet by hacking into credit card companies, gaming sites and e-commerce stores to harvest credit card numbers and sell them. Two months ago, he had broken into the database of the largest insurance company in the United States. He had harvested 2.3 million credit card numbers. He had put out feelers through the Internet black market and had received an interesting proposal. After today, he was going to be rich. He would be able to do anything he wanted to do. The customer had insisted upon meeting him in this remote location. He was instructed to rent an all-terrain vehicle and drive up to hill so they could be positive he wasn't being followed. Khoo was to stand on the edge of the hill so they could check him out. He imagined people with this kind of money were probably setting up some type of jamming equipment in case he was wired. But where were they? Khoo was becoming impatient. He turned to look past the rented all-terrain vehicle. He didn't see anyone coming off the highway yet. A high pitched whirring sound came from behind him. Turning around, Khoo realized the sound was coming from the solar park below the hill. Khoo noticed the glass top of each solar panel was moving. Technical things fascinated him and he wondered what was happening. Khoo understood these immense panels were computerized to follow the sun throughout the day. But it was high noon and there was no reason for them to be moving this quickly. He took a few steps down the hill and noticed the panels were angling in his direction. From this distance it looked like they were beginning to form a giant mirror. Hundreds of reflections bounced across the field of grass below. He watched in fascination as the light reflections converged into one spot at the bottom of the hill. Khoo cocked his head. It looked like a flashlight beam about a foot in diameter. The converged beam started moving up the hill towards him. The whole episode was fascinating. Why would the solar park people be doing this? Khoo was startled when the grass in the path of the beam caught fire! A burning path of grass moved swiftly in his direction. Kuan-Yin Khoo turned and started to run. But he was too late. His pant legs were illuminated by the beam. Kuan-

Yin Khoo screamed as his clothes caught fire and he burst into a human torch.

JEWEL KEPT THE BEAM focused for a few moments more to make sure. She watched her flaming target raise his hands to the sky before the charred body fell to the earth. She moved the focused beam across the grass to the vehicle and concentrated the power on the area of the gas tank. The SUV exploded in a fireball. The flames would ensure all hacked information on Kuan-Yin Khoo or in the vehicle would be destroyed. With her target eliminated, Jewel began moving the solar panels back into place. She wiped out all recorded data on their movement, then deleted the recorded footage from the security camera. Control of the Solar Park system was released. Within minutes she was headed on her return journey through the fiber-optic cable beneath the Yellow Sea. There was so much more work to do. So many more cyber-criminals to deal with.

Chapter 48

RORY CROSSED BLEECKER STREET, heading for Jewel's apartment. He had done his best to avoid every street cam possible but he still had a feeling he was being watched. He moved around to the back of her apartment and climbed the fire escape. As he moved up the metal stairs to her fourth-floor apartment, Rory realized her bedroom window was wide open. It wasn't that hot out so he wondered what she was doing. It wasn't safe. When he hit the landing he glanced through the open window and a shock ran through him – Jewel was hanging two feet above her bed in an upside-down Y shape. Her arms were stretched overhead - a rope was tied around one wrist, ran through the ceiling fixture over the bed, came back down and was tied around the other wrist. Each ankle was tied by a rope that looped around a bedpost, spreading her legs wide apart. She was totally nude - the tattoo of a tiny bluebottle dolphin with its tail perched on top of a neat landing strip of blonde pubic hair - was very evident. He moved quickly - and halfway through the open window - the barrel of a gun was placed against his temple - he froze in position.

A deep male voice sounded in his ear, "Welcome home, friend. No sudden moves. Got it?"

Rory noted the voice was calm and collected. This was no rank amateur. He was dealing with a professional here. Rory cursed himself internally when he realized what it meant. The man had no doubt stripped and propped Jewel up in that provocative position - all designed to make him throw caution to the wind - without a thought for his own safety - and it had worked. At least, he hoped for Jewel's sake, that's what it was. Dealing with a crazed rapist would throw all kinds of wild cards into the mix–

"Got it?"

Rory winced when the gun barrel was shoved harder against his head, "Yeah, I got it. No sudden moves."

"Good. Now move through the window nice and easy."

Rory carefully pulled his other leg through the open window and he placed both feet on the bedroom floor, the gun still at his temple. He looked at Jewel again. She was unconscious. "What did you do to her?"

The man grabbed a handful of Rory's shirt between his shoulder blades, stepped closer behind and pressed the gun harder into Rory's temple, "That's the least of your worries, pal. What I want to know is, why would someone pay me $12 million to kill you and blondie there?"

Rory's blood ran cold. "I take it Jewel sent you?"

The gunmen gave Rory a hard shove in the back towards the bed. "Answer my question," he demanded

Rory had his answer. She had sent a hitman after them. He wondered how she had done it, but first things first. He turned around slowly and looked at the man. He was about 35 years old, 5 foot 11 and 160 pounds, had dark, soulless eyes and short, snow-white hair. He was dressed in black clothing, including a black turtleneck sweater. He wore black leather gloves and held a Glock. From his bearing, Rory guessed he was ex-military and very well-trained. He had to play this cool or he would be a dead man in an instant. He had an idea. He took a deep breath and let it out, "I... I stole billions...she helped me and now she wants it all."

There was silence for a moment. "Did you say billions...with a B?"

"Y-yes," Rory stammered. "Look. I'll pay you more to kill her. I'll give you 50 million–"

"But didn't you say billions - plural - as in more than one?" He cocked the hammer of his gun.

"Y-yeah. Look, I'll give you one billion dollars–" Rory held out his hands as if he was pleading.

"You'll give me whatever I want. Or you're dead. Understand?"

Rory nodded his head, "I can transfer the money into an account for you. Just don't hurt me."

The gunmen looked at Rory for a moment, considering the proposal.

Rory looked down at Jewel's clothing on the floor. It looked like everything she had been wearing had been cut off. That made Rory boil inside. But that would have to wait until later. He looked slowly around at the hitman, "I'll need something. It's probably in her jeans–"

"Is this what you're looking for?" The gunman pulled the thumb drive from his left pocket. "Important is it? Blondie there fought really hard to keep it."

Rory nodded, biting his lip from saying anything in anger.

The gunman tossed him the thumb drive, "No screwing around. Get it?"

Catching the thumb drive with both hands, Rory said, "Yeah, I understand. I'll need to use the computer in the other room."

The gunman waved his gun and followed Rory at a distance into Jewel's computer room.

Rory sat down and turned on her computer. Once everything was running he plugged the thumb drive into the USB port in the front of the computer. He opened up the thumb drive and hoped he remembered exactly how Jewel had used the various programs. He double-clicked on the AH icon he thought was right and held his breath. A communications window opened up. Numbers and lines scrolled up the screen for a few moments and then they were connected to Alton Fitzhum's computer again. Rory began trying to get into each of the secure hard drives, hoping to gain a little attention.

"What's wrong? Why are you fiddling around?"

"It's just a security feature," Rory said. He knew he couldn't keep this ruse up very long. Come on, come on, he thought. Then it happened. A small white square flashed in the middle of the monitor. Rory discreetly reached down, pulled the thumb drive free and slipped it into his pocket.

The hitman as waved the gun at the flash of white on the computer monitor, "What's that?"

"You're about to meet your boss," whispered Rory as he set his feet firmly.

"What are you talking about? If you think–"

A beam of light shot out like a sharp searchlight and focused on Rory's face.

As expected, the second beam of light shot out and illuminated the hitman's face.

Rory heard the hitman's sharp intake of breath. Rory pushed himself away from the computer and hard against his opponent's body.

The gunman grunted in pain and began to fall backward, trying to swing the Glock towards Rory.

Rory chopped down hard with his right hand.

The gun clattered to the floor. Rory continued his backward momentum, lifted his feet off the floor and landed his full weight on top of the gunmen, knocking the breath from him. As he heard a tinkling sound from the computer, Rory swept his right arm out against the gun, pushing it across the room. It disappeared under Jewel's computer desk.

A swirl of colored lights appeared in the middle of the computer screen and the colors grew in intensity and swirled faster.

Rory lunged for the computer plug and pulled it.

The colors disappeared immediately.

Rory heard footsteps and he turned quickly to see the hitman running out of the computer room. Rory was up quickly and pursued him.

The hitman ran into Jewel's bedroom and headed for the open window.

Lunging, Rory slapped one foot of the hitman against the other, causing the hitman to trip and fall forward heavily. Rory was up and after him quickly but the hitman was fast.

The hitman rolled and thrust a foot towards Rory's genitals.

Rory twisted just enough but still received a hard blow to the inner thigh. He grunted in pain and fell.

The gunman was immediately up and ran for the open window.

Struggling to his feet, Rory ran after him.

The hitman dove head first through the window.

Rory heard a clatter on the metal stairs and then a scream. He reached the open window and looked out.

The hitman lay four stories below on the pavement. He was on his back with his arms and legs spread out and his dark eyes staring straight up.

Rory looked up and down the back alleyway. He didn't see anyone. He hoped no one in a nearby building had seen where the hitman had fallen from either. It wouldn't be easy to explain.

Chapter 49

RORY IMMEDIATELY RAN over to Jewel. He checked for a pulse. It was there but barely. Rory spotted a bottle and a glass on its side laying on the floor beside the bed. The bottle was Xanax, a sedative. And the sediment in the glass suggested the hitman had ground-up the pills in water and forced Jewel to drink it. He contemplated calling for paramedics but now that the security-bot knew exactly where they were that could be a problem.

Rory ran for the kitchen and pulled a large carving knife from the knife holder on the counter. He ran back to the bedroom, got on the bed and put his arm around Jewel's naked body. He cut the ropes, freeing each leg. Then he placed her bare breasts against his shoulder, lifted her up and cut the rope just above each wrist. Her naked body sagged against him and he heard her moan. Rory lifted her off the bed and gently placed her feet on the floor. He draped her arm over his shoulder and began to walk her around. "C'mon, Jewel. Walk. Walk. That's it." He walked her around the bedroom and she began to become more alert. After some time she began to help herself walk. Rory walked her back over to the bed after some time, pulled the blankets back with one hand and gently helped her into bed. He covered over her nakedness and went to the kitchen to get some water. He came back into the bedroom with a bottle of water and sat beside her. "Do you think you can drink this? It should help."

Jewel's eyes fluttered open and she looked vaguely up at Rory. Then her hand slowly moved up to the covers and she lifted them, looking down at her body, her words were slurred as she asked, "Why am I naked?" Then she looked at the ropes still around her wrists, "And why am I tied?" She closed her eyes for a moment and then looked up at Rory, her voice just above a hoarse whisper, "Listen, big boy. If we're going to have kinky sex, I demand to be awake. Understand?"

"I'll keep that in mind," Rory said. "For next time." It was good that her sense of humor was coming back.

Jewel picked the covers back up and she looked down again at her naked body, "Awww, you saw my tattoo. That defeats my attempts to be a mysterious woman."

"The landing strip is great too," Rory said.

She looked up at Rory and raised her eyebrows, You didn't land, did you? Cause I missed the whole thing, big boy."

"No–" Rory said.

Jewel suddenly sat up in bed, the covers falling off her naked breasts, "The man! Where is he–"

"It's okay," Rory assured her as he placed a hand on her shoulder. "He went through the window and is lying on the pavement four floors below."

Jewel clutched the covers back to her breasts, "Good. That bastard–"

"Did he do anything to you?" Rory asked, fearing the worst.

"No. Not in that way. He kept twisting my arms and hurting me, wanting to know where you were. But I wouldn't tell him–" Her head started to sag a little and she brought it back up quickly.

Rory handed her the bottle of water, "Here. Start drinking to dilute the sedatives he gave you."

Jewel took the bottle of water with one hand while clutching the blankets to her chest with the other, "Okay. I think if I sleep just a little–"

"Sorry, but there won't be time for that. The security-bot hired that hitman to come after us."

"Really? She can do that?" she asked in a slurred voice.

Apparently," Rory said. "Since she knows where we are, we can't stay here much longer."

"Where are we going to go?"

"I have no idea," Rory admitted.

And what do we do now?"

"Another good question. And I have absolutely no idea."

Chapter 50

JEWEL'S NEXT TARGET was using the Tor browser - original name The Onion Router - and its anonymity network - to mask his true IP address while continuing the attempt to penetrate the computer system at the Department of Justice. Jewel added a rider to the data packets in the target's stream and waited for it to come back as instructed. It did and Jewel had a starting direction. She moved westward through the Internet connections and began sniffing and filtering packets as she moved. The path through cyberspace led her to the Palo Alto Internet Exchange. More return data caused her to reroute to San Francisco. She was closing in. The trail shifted to the Mission district. Got him! The IP address was tied to the account of Reid Scott Pradhan. The computer she was tracking was on the ground floor of an old house that had been divided into four small apartments. Jewel traveled through the Wi-Fi access into apartment 1B. Entering the computer, Jewel accessed the WebCam. The target was still working away at the keyboard. She quickly accessed the DMV records for Reid Scott Pradhan. Jewel's facial recognition routine shot a beam to his face and verified he was the target.

19 YEAR OLD REID SCOTT Pradhan fell out his chair just after the strange beam of light from his monitor bathed his face. He cursed as his back slammed hard on the rug. He scrambled backward on all fours until he hit the sofa. His chest heaved with fear as he sat on his butt, staring at his computer system.

JEWEL HAD A SUBROUTINE access the home's architectural drawings on file at the local land records office. She determined Reid Scott Pradhan's apartment had a gas fireplace with an electronic ignition system. It was used to create the spark to start the fire under the ceramic logs. Another subroutine found a PDF file with full schematics for the system on the manufacturer's website. Using this information, Jewel accessed the control module through the electrical system, allowed the gas control valve to release gas but kept the igniter from sparking.

REID SCOTT PRADHAN slowly rose to his feet. After a moment of indecision, he approached his computer system slowly. He paused as he heard a tinkling sound. It seemed to be coming from the system. He had built the system from hand and there was nothing that could make that sound. He wondered if big brother or the FBI or the CIA was trying to hack their way back into his system. Pradhan's jaw dropped as a swirl of colored lights appeared in the middle of his monitor. The colors grew in intensity and swirled faster. He was mesmerized and drew a little closer. He jumped back when the colors actually rose from the screen. They began dancing in the air. He couldn't believe his eyes as a form began to appear in front of him. It was a face. It solidified into the head of a bald, beautiful woman surrounded by dancing, swirling colors, numbers, and symbols. Reid Scott Pradhan laughed nervously as he fell in love with the beautiful figure.

"You are Reid Scott Pradhan," Jewel said in her voice of colors and music.

Pradhan opened his mouth but nothing came out.

"You are a danger to cyberspace," Jewel stated.

Pradhan blinked. He struggled to get his voice, "Is this...is this about those nude photos I put on the Internet? Cause she sexted them to me. I was just–"

"For the past four years you have used banking Trojans to intercept transactions and siphon money into your own accounts."

Pradhan mouth dropped open, "How...how did you know that?"

"Since I cannot re-create all your illicit transactions," Jewel said, "the money will be transferred and deposited into a charity account."

"Hey!" Pradhan yelled. He took a step forward, "I only took money from rich people. They'll never miss it. You can't do that. It's mine."

"You have used the money to finance a lifestyle where you continually attempt to penetrate government websites, hack into e-commerce sites–"

"I'm helping them," Pradhan claimed. "I'm showing them where their vulnerabilities are–"

"Is that why you've been trying to penetrate the Department of Justice computer system for the last two weeks? To help them?" Jewel asked.

Reid Scott Pradhan lifted a finger, "Now that's different, those people need to be taken down. They're evil–"

"No, you are evil. I gave you a chance, Reid Scott Pradhan."

"You gave me a chance? What the hell you gonna do, color me to death?" Pradhan laughed. Pradhan made scary ghost fingers, "Ooooooooooo, are you going to scare me to death with your music Ms. Hologram?" Pradhan stopped laughing and sobered up. He smelled rotten eggs. It reminded him of some experiments they had done in science class in school. He looked around. Where was it coming from? Then he looked directly at his fireplace. He could hear the low hissing sound of escaping gas. He ran for the front door to escape to the street. He made it but not in the way he wanted. Jewel accessed the electronic ignition system and lit the spark. The enormous explosion hurled Pradhan through his picture window, slashing his body in a thousand places and he landed past the sidewalk on the hard pavement in the middle of the street

JEWEL WAITED AROUND, watching from a street cam and monitoring the police bands and the paramedic radios. The paramedics sent back confirmation that Reid Scott Pradhan was dead on the scene. Jewel headed back to New York.

Chapter 51

RORY AND JEWEL left through the front of her apartment to avoid the scene in the back alley. A large crowd of curious on-lookers was busy- each of them busy taking cell phone pictures of the police and a forensic team working around the body of the dead hitman. Jewel was still feeling sluggish but she managed to keep up with Rory as they sought to put as much distance as possible between themselves and her apartment. They kept their heads down as they passed dry cleaners, restaurants, drug-stores, ATM machines and corner stores where the security-bot but could possibly access video cameras and spot them.

"So what's your plan?" Jewel asked.

"Do you know of any place close by where we can pick up some computer equipment? You know, a place we can trust," Rory asked as he held her elbow and guided her across a street.

"I get all my stuff at Moe's Computer Repair place on West 14th Street," Jewel answered. "Moe Laprade has been helping me for years. He knows what I do and he's discreet."

"Okay, let's head there right now. I've got some other ideas but we'll start with the computer equipment," Rory said.

RORY LOOKED AT THE building on West 14th Street as they approached the front entrance way. He estimated the structure to be over a century old, at least. The door dinged a bell above their head like an old confectionery store as they entered Moe's Computer Repair Place. The inside of Moe's Place looked like it was an old general store but with computer equipment lining the shelves.

An older, white-haired gentleman came through an open doorway from the back. He slipped behind an old glass counter and looked at his customers, "How can I help–" His eyes opened wide, "Jewel...sweetie! Where have you been?" He hustled around the counter to wrap his arms around Jewel. After a long hug, he stepped back, "What have you been doing? Your blog hasn't been updated. I haven't seen you for months."

"The honest truth is that I've ended up in a bit of a pickle with one of the cases I'm working on," Jewel said as she glanced quickly towards Rory. "I'm going to need your help, Moe."

"Of course," Moe said. "Which of those jackass politicians is after you this time? I still got my old Luger in the back–"

"I know you *would* go and shoot somebody for me," she said as she bent forward and gave Moe a kiss on the cheek. "But right now all we need is some computer equipment so we can fight back." She motioned to Rory, "This is Rory Mack Steele. He's a private investigator who's going to work with me."

Moe stuck his hand out to Rory and looked directly into his silver-blue eyes, "You take care of my girl here, Mr. Steele. Or I'll come looking for *you* with my Luger."

A smile played at the corner of Rory's mouth as he gave Moe a nod of his head, "Understood. But as Jewel said, this particular case is very dangerous. We have to make sure you understand that several people are already dead. And we're up against some-one who is very, very good with computers."

"Moe here is my Q, just like James Bond," Jewel said as she took the old man's hand. "But he's right Moe, this particular one is very dangerous."

Moe shrugged his shoulders, "Ah! I'm 81. I fought in several wars and nobody got me yet."

Jewel smiled and looked over at Rory, "Nobody knows this around here but Moe was a mercenary. He was paid to fight–"

"And now I do it for fun with you," interrupted Moe. "And I'm pretty good with computers myself, Mr. Steele. Now, what is it you need sweetie?"

Jewel looked over at Rory who finally made a decision.

"Okay," Rory said, "we need to be able to use a computer and the Internet without someone being able to trace us. Believe me when I tell you that some very good computer people have been up against our adversary and came out on the short end of the stick on this."

"Okay," Moe said with a nod of his head. "What else?"

Rory looked to Jewel, then back to Moe, "We've also been unable to use cell phones without being tracked. And...they've even been able to use street cams and video cameras to track us."

Moe nodded sagely and looked at Jewel, then back at Rory, "So they're using software to track you."

Jewel looked at Moe and licked her lips, "They've also tried to kill us. Which is why I can understand if you'd want to..."

Moe's eyebrows went up in surprise. Then he turned and waved a hand for them to follow him, "C'mon, let's figure out what exactly you need to fight back."

Rory followed Jewel into the back of Moe's Computer Repair place. He was amazed at the amount of equipment he saw. The room back here was easily 10 times the size of Moe's front counter space.

Moe walked over to a shelf and pulled a box down. He walked back over to a workbench and opened the box. He pulled out a laptop and threw the empty box on the floor, "This is a WebTac100, a military grade laptop. It can take a lot of pounding, dust, extreme weather changes and so on and it'll keep on ticking no matter where you have to go. You could probably hit somebody over the head with it and it will still work, so keep that in mind, Mr. Steele."

"I'll keep that in mind, Moe," Rory said as he gave Jewel a smile.

"It also has two special Intel processors made for the military and a lot of RAM memory," continued Moe. "It allows you to run two highly intensive programs at the same time without slowing anything down. But the great thing about this laptop is its modularity." He flipped the military laptop over and began taking screws out with a small electric screwdriver.

"How does that help Moe?" Jewel asked as she stepped closer to look at what he was doing.

"It allows me to build it specifically for any need," answered Moe as he continued working. "I work with the military and the police as well so I have a few things up my sleeve that you might not normally get at another computer place. This has WiFi like all other computers but I can add a special extender and a military grade antenna that allows you to securely piggyback somebody else's router within a mile to access the Internet."

"The problem is we could attract attention to an innocent person's router, Moe," reasoned Rory.

Moe glanced over at Rory as he continued working and spoke in a low conspiratorial voice, "Which is why I'm also adding a module to allow you to use police and military bands." He winked at Jewel and continued with his explanation, "The military doesn't use civil WLAN systems. Using a military band ensures you will be highly secure and difficult to track and trace. And I have added some firmware and software features of my own design to hide the I.P. you use."

"See," Jewel said proudly, "my own Q."

Rory nodded. "Now all we need to do is find a place to hide out under the radar."

Moe looked at him, "How are your lock picking skills?"

"They'll work in a pinch. Why?" Rory asked.

"You could take a look at the old Northern Dispensary over on Waverly in the West Village. It was built in 1831 to provide medical services. I remember it being a dental clinic a long time ago but nobody's been there for years."

"He's right," Jewel said as she perked up. "I played there as a kid. It's been vacant for as long as I can remember. The owner takes good care of it so it's not derelict with broken windows and stuff like that. It's at 165 Waverly Place if I remember correctly."

Rory thought about it for a few moments and then nodded his assent, "Okay, let's take a look at it, at least. It'll only work if we're able to access a hotspot to get on the Internet."

"There's a police precinct within a half-mile, so we should be able to go through one of their routers. Right Moe?" Jewel said.

Moe nodded as he kept tinkering with the military laptop. He walked over to the surrounding shelves several times, picking up other modules as he reconfigured the laptop.

"Okay, now all we need to do is to figure out how to fight back against the security-bot–" Rory stopped himself and silently cursed for adding that information in front of Moe.

Moe kept tinkering and spoke without looking up, "It sounds like you're up against something dangerous in cyberspace itself. I'll do some thinking on how you could fight back against something like that."

Jewel looked at Rory and she had fear in her eyes. Rory knew she was scared for her friend. And he couldn't blame her. The security-bot had proven to be more than simply dangerous...formidable would be a better description.

Chapter 52

RORY AND JEWEL exited through the back of Moe's Computer Repair place. Rory was carrying a weatherproof, heavy duty, military grade laptop case containing the military grade laptop. Jewel started off down the street, headed for Waverly but Rory took her elbow and steered her in the opposite direction.

Jewel put a thumb over her shoulder, protesting, "But the Northern Dispensary building Moe recommended is in the other way. You're going in the wrong direction."

"I know," admitted Rory. "But we have something else to do before we head there. A very important something. I just wish I would have thought about it before we went to Moe's."

"You're worried about him," Jewel stated.

"Definitely. But we can't do anything about it now except to get started on stopping the security-bot before it hurts anyone else."

"So where are we going?" Jewel asked.

"You'll see," was all Rory said. "Just keep your eye out for any type of surveillance camera. And try to keep your head down as much as possible while you walk. The security-bot is obviously using some type of advanced facial recognition software and we want to make it harder for her to pick us out of a crowd."

Jewel nodded and they began a winding route across a number of city blocks, constantly on alert for any cameras and keeping an eye out for any vehicles that might be taken over by the security-bot and sent their way. It was nerve-racking, never knowing when they might have been spotted or were about to be attacked. Rory waited until he was right on top of their destination to take hold of Jewel's arm and lead her through a door.

Jewel looked at their surroundings as the door closed behind her, "Theatrical makeup?"

"Uh-huh, time for a makeover," Rory said.

RORY LEFT THE STORE with a full beard, bushy eyebrows and a new, bulbous nose. Jewel left the store with long red hair, higher cheekbones, bushy eyebrows and a broader nose.

"I look like a freakin' Russian babushka," Jewel complained as they began walking down the street.

"I think you look hot," Rory said. He glanced around to see if anybody was following or watching them.

"Yeah well, I wouldn't pick you up if I was a homeless woman and you were the last man on earth," Jewel said.

"You say that now but wait until after the apocalypse, you'll change your tune."

"Fat chance, rover," Jewel grumbled.

"Hey, make the Grover, not rover. Rover is a dog."

"Exactly."

They moved up, down and around several blocks as they moved in the general direction of the abandoned building Moe had recommended. They stopped and picked up a few items as they snaked their way across town. Rory and Jewel were continually watching to avoid cameras or any potential danger around them. They finally reached the triangular shaped Northern Dispensary building situated in the middle of three streets.

Jewel slipped over to a double door, shifted a shopping bag to her left hand and tried to open it. It was locked. "Maybe one of the other doors will be open."

Rory looked around them as he set down the laptop case. Then he reached into a pocket and pulled out a paper clip and a small Allen wrench Moe had given him, "Just stand in front of me while I do my thing." He straightened out the paper clip and knelt in front of the door.

It was getting dark and Jewel shielded Rory as best as she could with her body as he worked with the Allen wrench and paper clip. The door gave a satisfying click in a matter of moments. Rory stood up and held the door slightly open to allow Jewel just enough space to slip inside the abandoned building. Rory picked up the laptop case and slipped in behind her, pulling the door closed. He took some wire out of his pocket and threaded it through the two pull handles to make sure the doors would stay closed. Jewel took a couple of flashlights Moe had given them and handed one to Rory. They kept them low and pointed at the floor as they worked their way towards the center of the building and away from any prying eyes that might look in one of the many windows they passed. The place was dusty and Rory noted some rusting dental equipment. They finally found a suitable large room with a couple of old chairs and a couple of tables to set up shop. Rory had spotted a small desk in a room they had passed and he and Jewel worked to slide it into their new abode. A couple of Subway sandwiches and several soft drinks they had picked up along the way served as their evening meal. As they ate, Rory opened up the military laptop case and set the military grade laptop on the desk. Time to get to work.

Chapter 53

JEWEL HAD CYCLED through every surveillance camera available to her in New York City and her facial recognition software still hadn't picked up Rory Mack Steele or Jewel Tanya Afterburn. These two had proven to be resilient. However, one of her monitoring subroutines had picked up police and paramedic chatter regarding Bryer Chad Wilcox. Her facial recognition software had confirmed the dead body found outside Jewel Tanya Afterburn's apartment was the asset she had hired. Hospital records stated he had died from severe internal trauma from a suspected fall from the fire escape at the back of her apartment building. She immediately pulled the $12 million from his account and erased all financial transaction records, email correspondence and text records to his cell phone. She had one of her subroutines begin to immediately search for other assets who could be used to terminate the two targets. Meanwhile, she had more work to do.

GENERAL ALEXEI ZIVEN Karpin and Colonel Ludmila Khristyana Bondarenko entered the front doors of the large, Stalin-era concrete building in Moscow, Russia, marked:

Федеральное Агентство Правительственной Связи и Информации

In English, it was the Federal Agency of Government Communications and Information or FAPSI. This agency was in charge of all Russian electronic signal intelligence and tasked with the security of governmental communications. Under Karpin and Bondarenko it was also secretly tasked with cyberwarfare against the enemies of the state. Karpin had been smart enough to reach out to brilliant hackers who had been imprisoned for economic cyber-crimes. Ludmila Khristyana Bondarenko had been the most brilliant of those arrested and convicted. Karpin recruited her and put her to the test. She had been made a Colonel with all the perks it brought after infiltrating a number of British banks and siphoning money into the Russian kitty. Bondarenko had then worked with Karpin to recruit and train other cyber-criminals to create an elite squad that targeted state enemies all over the world. Karpin and Bondarenko took the elevator up to the fourth floor where they entered a large room that contained thirteen of their best computer operatives. They were going to be discussing their next series of denial of service attacks, internet surveillance, propaganda dissemination over the World Wide Web and, more importantly, the identification and elimination of cyber-dissidents against the government.

JEWEL ACCESSED A ROSTELECOM satellite, determined the proper path and headed to the FAPSI building in Moscow, Russia. She entered through the cyberspace pathways and began accessing the surveillance cameras and the recorded footage. Her facial recognition software subroutines recognized the two main targets passing through the main lobby. She followed their path through the building to a large room on the fourth floor. Infiltrating one of the computers on the central desk she detected a number of bodies in the room. Calling in a subroutine, she shot out 15 modified beams from her white laser system and used her advanced facial recognition software to identify each of the individuals present. Accessing Russian Intelligence databases, she confirmed they were all hackers from previous incidents she had recorded. Thirteen additional threats to cyberspace appeared to be working closely with Karpin and Bondarenko. The threat level on those two alone was escalating and she had to act quickly while they were all together. Jewel accessed the building schematics and determined there was no suitable, foolproof method of eliminating all the targets at the same time. She tasked several subroutines to find a solution. Within milliseconds she had the answer. One of her subroutines had accessed the Russian military database and identified the tools that would work. She quickly exited through a military satellite.

THE RUSSIAN HEAVY NUCLEAR-powered rocket cruiser Petr Velikiy, the flagship of the Northern Fleet, was participating in naval training exercises in the Barents Sea north of Murmansk, Russia. It had recently been outfitted with the new S-300SN sea-based, long-range strategic missile. Captain Nikolai Nasenko was on the bridge, engaged in planning the exercise when he received notice one of the missile platforms was turning on its own. He ran to the port side, screaming orders and asking for an explanation. His blood ran cold when one of the S-300SN strategic missiles launched the hot exhaust burning several of the crew members who hadn't been prepared.

A member of the crew turned from his station and yelled that someone had overridden the ship-wide computer system.

Velikiy yelled to his second in command to contact the other ships in the fleet as well as the Russian air defense system. They had to take that missile down. Before anyone could act, everything on board shut down. Control of the ship and all communications were off-line and the immense heavy rocket cruiser sat dead in the water. Captain Nikolai Nasenko cursed the computer age.

COLONEL LUDMILA KHRISTYANA Bondarenko was looking out the large double window on the fourth floor at the street below as she listened to the arguments behind her about the white laser beams that had appeared. Some were convinced they had been penetrated by the Americans. Others thought it was the Chinese who had done something through those lasers from the computer monitor. There was no consensus on *how* it was done.

General Alexei Ziven Karpin stepped up beside her, "What do you think, Ludmila? You think we've been compromised by a foreign power?"

Ludmila shook her head no. Something didn't seem right. "I've been doing this a long time Alexei and I've never seen anything like it. None of our systems or software packages have the capability to transmit white lasers like that. And neither do the Americans, the Chinese or–"

"The NATO people maybe?" suggested Karpin.

Ludmila shook her head no, "I doubt it..." Something caught her eye just over the horizon. It was just a small speck with a fiery tail but she could tell it was headed their way. The speck grew larger as it dropped lower in the sky. She narrowed her eyes, trying to determine what it was.

Karpin followed her line of sight. An object was just starting to skim over the tops of the buildings. He had been in the military long enough to recognize a missile. But it didn't matter. Before he could move a muscle, the room exploded in a ball of fire that consumed every piece of living flesh inside.

WITH THE TARGETS TERMINATED, Jewel allowed the computer systems on the Petr Velikiy to restart. She then allowed the Russian radar and air defense systems to re-engage and protect their sovereign territory. She headed back to America. So much work to do.

Chapter 54

JEWEL SLID HER CHAIR closer to the old desk and the military laptop. Rory pulled a chair up to sit on her right. Jewel had the system running and it reached out, looking for an Internet hotspot. The scan returned a list of several Wi-Fi networks in the area. "Which one should I try?" Jewel asked. "That one there is for the police precinct nearby but it has that lock icon which means I need a username and password. There are a few that are wide open and we could use one of those."

Rory looked over the list and shook his head no, "We can't. We know we're going to attract that attention of the security-bot. We can't let someone innocent get hurt if it comes calling. Double-click on the precinct network."

Jewel complied, "Okay, it's asking for the username and password. What do we do now?"

Rory rubbed his chin. Then he pointed to a small symbol at the bottom of the screen that looked like the outline of a spy on a red background. It was labeled 'cracker', "Double click on that icon and see what happens."

Jewel did and a pop up appeared asking, 'Hack/Crack? Yes/No'. She entered the letter Y on the keyboard and hit enter, "Good old Moe. Didn't I tell you he was my Q?"

"Bond. Jewel Bond," Rory said as they heard static and a squeal as the program went to work.

"And I always get my man, just like James Bond gets the girl," she said. She raised an eyebrow and looked sideways at Rory.

"You're all talk and no action, Jewel Bond."

Jewel gave him a slight jab in the ribs with her elbow, "Thanks for spoiling the story. Hey, it looks like we're on the Internet."

Rory nodded and pulled the thumb drive from his pocket and pushed it into the USB slot on the side of the laptop.

Jewel opened up the thumb drive and double-clicked on the icon marked AH. The lines of code scrolled down the screen and they were quickly back into Alton Fitzhum's computer system. Jewel brought up the WebCam. The computer room on the other side of the connection was lit up and they could see a number of people milling about. Jewel cocked her head, "Those guys look like they are part of a forensics team. You know, like you see on TV? And I see a couple of NYPD police officers. Why would Homeland security be working with them?" She straightened up noticeably, obviously concerned, "Are they going to be after me again?"

Rory snapped his fingers, "Oh, right. I never did get a chance to tell you what happened at Fitzhum's apartment. When I got back to your place, I found you and the hitman–"

"And I was buck naked, if I recall," Jewel said with an embarrassed smile.

"Exactly. Which sidetracked me a bit–"

"I was buck naked and you were only sidetracked a bit? Thanks a lot."

"You're welcome. The good news is I don't think Homeland Security is concerned with you anymore. It looks to me like it was a plan cooked up by Dockerty and no one else at the agency. His plan was to take you into custody and get what he wanted. He knew there was a program of some type and he wanted it for the division of Homeland Security that he was responsible for. He thought you were involved and could give him what he wanted, a program to use against foreign governments. Well, he met the security-bot despite my warnings and he and the two men guarding the apartment door are dead."

Jewel looked shaken at the news.

"I have no idea how she killed Dockerty. But she dropped the window on the neck of one man and sent the other one down an elevator shaft."

"Just like she tried to do with us," whispered Jewel.

Rory nodded, "But it gets even worse."

"What do you mean? How can it get worse?"

"Once the security-bot saw me there with Dockerty, it assumed I had joined forces with another hacker. Like we did with Sergent. Now my threat level assessment has apparently been raised."

"What...exactly does that mean?" Jewel asked. The fear in her eyes was evident.

"I'm not sure exactly, but the last time I saw the security-bot...she looked really pissed," added Rory. He took a deep breath and considered Jewel's reaction. "Maybe you want to separate yourself from me–"

"And do what?" shrugged Jewel. "She's already trying to kill me. Maybe we should go to the police–"

"And tell them what? And how do they arrest a CyberSecureBot? With cyberspace handcuffs?" reasoned Rory. "Besides,

I imagine any authoritative body would want it for themselves, once they realized what it can do."

"That's usually how it works," agreed Jewel. She was pensive for a few moments. "So I guess we're on our own," she said finally.

Rory nodded, "We need to find some way to stop her...it. I'd like to get back into Fitzhum's apartment once the police are gone. But that whole place is wired into the computer system and under the control of the security-bot. It would be like trying to work through an invisible minefield without a mine detector."

Jewel look back at the computer screen, "So we have to try to get to her remotely. Find out which hard drive–"

"That's the other problem," interrupted Rory. "When she was talking to Dockerty, she said she wasn't in *any* of the hard drives."

That startled Jewel, "So...how do we find her...to terminate the program?"

Chapter 55

JEWEL DETECTED ACTIVITY on Alton Fitzhum's system. Someone was attempting to hack into several of the secure hard drives. She slipped back inside the apartment building and sniffed the stream of data packets coming and going. Someone was using a military bandwidth. Jewel added a rider to the data packets in the target's stream and waited for it to come back as instructed. The IP address came back and Jewel moved through cyberspace to the NYPD 6th precinct. But something was wrong. She detected no actual activity coming from the computer system assigned the address. Someone was piggy-backing on this signal. Jewel analyzed the situation.

A military bandwidth through a police precinct logically meant this wasn't a direct assault from a government organization but an attempt from a 3rd party hacker. She went through the computer logs and determined the login algorithm was through programs used by Alton Fitzhum and Calvin Sergent. Both were dead. Rory Mack Steele and Jewel Tanya Afterburn were the last two subjects with Calvin Sergent and using their software. Jewel accessed credit card records of both subjects. No computer purchases by Rory Mack Steele. She accessed his office credit card records and determined there were no records of any military grade systems purchased. Their supplier had no military sales on record either. She added a filter for police sales and there was nothing. She sorted through Jewel Tanya Afterburn's credit card transactions. No military or police systems on record. Her computer systems were all purchased through Moe's Computer Repair Place. The location was close to the precinct she was now in. She accessed the records for Moe's Computer Repair Place. Morris John Laprade, also known as Moe, had sold systems and related hardware and software to both police and military. Jewel slipped out of the NYPD 6th precinct building and moved through cyberspace to Moe's Computer Repair Place.

MOE LAPRADE WAS WORKING in the back of his shop, working on another military laptop with added features and software. He took a long sip of coffee to wash down that last bite of his pastrami sandwich. He would have to tell Sammi there wasn't enough mustard on this last one. The mustard really enhanced the flavor on a good pastrami sandwich.

UNKNOWN TO RORY AND Jewel when they had first entered his shop, Moe Laprade had two hidden surveillance cameras. One was built into the clock in the front of the shop and the other was built into a fake dart board in the back. Moe was constantly aware of neighborhood thieves who coveted his high-priced hardware for a quick buck from the trunk of a car. Jewel infiltrated the electrical and computer systems in Moe's Computer Repair Place. Accessing the front surveillance camera, she identified both Rory Mack Steele and Jewel Tanya Afterburn entering the premises. They had gone into the back of the store. Scanning the recorded footage for the fake dart board camera, Jewel watched as the person known as Morris John Laprade added various modules to a military grade laptop. That laptop was taken by her two targets as they left the building. They were all working together.

MOE HEARD A TINKLING sound. He turned and tried to find the source of the sound. It was coming from the computer on his workbench. He got up from his work stool and took a step towards the computer. A small white square flashed in the middle of the monitor. He took another step and peered at the anomaly. He could still hear the tinkling sound. A beam of light shot out towards his face. The white beam was there for a brief second and then disappeared as quickly as it came. Moe was rooted to the spot. What in the world had just happened? A swirl of colored lights appeared in the middle of the computer screen. Moe squinted his eyes. He must be seeing things. The colors grew in intensity and swirled faster in front of the monitor. The colors left the screen and danced in the air in front of the monitor. Slowly, a form began to rise from the swirling lights. He saw a face appear. It was surrounded by dancing, swirling colors, numbers, and symbols. Moe recognized the Sine waves that were dancing a crazy jig just below a face that was forming. It solidified into the head of a bald, beautiful woman made of colors and it looked straight at him.

"You are Morris John Laprade," Jewel stated. "You have sold military-grade equipment to Rory Mack Steele and Jewel Tanya Afterburn. They are hackers and a danger to cyberspace. You must distance yourself from them immediately. I have accessed your inventory and can calculate their capabilities. I want their present location. Now!"

Moe just stood there with his mouth open. He had never seen anything like it. And even more astonishing was the fact this - thing - looked like his Jewel. He still couldn't find his voice as he turned and pulled open a drawer in the workbench beside him. He pulled out his Luger, turned and shot the monitor and then the computer full of holes. The image disappeared and he was still pulling the trigger on a gun that was now empty. He finally stopped after a couple dozen empty clicks of the Luger. He swore under his breath.

JEWEL ACCESSED BOTH cameras again. The subject had been uncooperative. It was confirmed. He was working with those who were a danger to cyberspace. He had to be terminated. Jewel could see he was still standing there with the weapon in his hand, looking around. Jewel accessed the natural gas-fired furnace in the basement. She allowed natural gas to seep through the control valve while retarding the igniter. She overrode the multiple safety switches as she watched the target place the weapon into the waistband of his pants. Jewel saw Morris John Laprade open a drawer and pull out automotive keys. She analyzed he was going to be leaving soon. Jewel monitored the progress of the seeping natural gas. She had used this type of method in several

terminations and from her analysis, she concluded she still needed more cubic feet of gas to ensure the death of this target within
this structure. But her subroutines also concluded there may not
be enough time/ And she had no way at present to keep him contained within the building. She decided to act. Jewel accessed the
igniter and created a spark.

MOE LAPRADE WAS KNOCKED to his feet as the floor exploded beneath him. Moe saw flames licking the air around him
as he lay on his back on the old wooden floor. He had been in
enough firefights and around enough exploding ordnance in his
career that he was able to keep from panicking. But he didn't
have much time. The building was wooden and the long years had
dried the walls and framing into firewood. Flames were leaping
up the walls around him and when he looked up, there was a hole
in the roof. Moe struggled to his feet and grabbed the military
grade laptop he had been working on. He ran through the burning building for the back door. He skidded to a stop before he fell
into a large hole into the rough basement. He realized the furnace must have blown up. The violent explosion had taken out
almost the entire floor from here to the back of the building. He
turned around and looked towards the front of the building. It
was a wall of flames. He was trapped.

Long years of experience as a mercenary allowed him to keep
his head but it definitely wasn't easy. Age was catching up to him.
He quickly went to his right and held the laptop to his face as
he plunged through hot flames. He yelled with pain as the skin
of his neck blistered from the heat. One of the steel shelves had

collapsed across part of the shattered floor and Moe stopped at the foot of it. The bent and twisted shelves didn't go all the way across the hole but he realized he had no choice. There was only one way out and this was it. Moe stepped back a couple of feet and then sprinted forward, running up and along the twisted side post of the shelving. He tried to ignore the flames leaping up from the burning basement that licked and burnt the bottom of his shoes. He began yelling at the top of his lungs as he neared the end of the side post. He leaped across the burning hole in the floor, straining his old body in a desperate attempt to reach the small number of floorboards still intact on the far side.

Chapter 56

JEWEL TANYA AFTERBURN worked through the long list of hard drives on Alton's computer system. There were dozens and dozens still locked solid. The security features Fitzhum had set in place were still amazing to her. The cracking program on the thumb drive Calvin had given her appeared to be going through millions upon millions of different combinations. Rory was coming back into the room with another two Subway sandwiches in hand and several more soft drinks. It had been a long, exhausting night to this point. She double-clicked on one of the drive letters and let the cracker program go to work again as she sat back in her chair, accepting one of the sandwiches from Rory.

"Still no success?" Rory asked as placed the soft drinks on the desk. He sat down in his chair. "I'll take your silence as a no." He began to unwrap his own sandwich. He popped the top off a soft drink for Jewel and then one for himself. They had set up flashlights to be used as rough work lamps and they set an eerie mood. Everything in the old, abandoned building was dark except for the small circle of light they were working in.

"Don't worry, we'll get through them all yet," commented Rory. He took a bite of his sub and emitted a sound of pleasure.

Jewel shook her head, "I'm not as optimistic as you are. If you use a password of just six letters you can get 309 million different passwords. Jump that to eight letters, you get 209 billion different passwords. If you use the ASCII symbol set along with the shift key, an eight letter password could have six quadrillion possibilities. If you—"

"Okay, okay, pour cold water on my enthusiasm," he grumbled good-naturedly. He tossed a small slice of pickle at her.

Jewel deflected the slice with a hand as she giggled. She began unwrapping her sub, "I'm still not sure what good it will do to crack into them anyway. If she's not inside—"

"She...the program has to be somewhere. There has to be some information we can use in there. There should be more notes on the program he created," reasoned Rory. He took another hungry bite of his sub.

There was a sudden beep from the computer. "What's that?" Rory asked as he stopped chewing.

Jewel shot forward in her chair. "It looks like we've cracked into one of the drives," she said excitedly. She set her sub aside and reached for the computer mouse.

Rory sat forward in his chair as well, "Anything we can use?"

"I don't know. Let's take a look." Jewel began to open up folders and files, scanning the contents of various documents. The hard drive was filled with them.

Rory looked at what she was examining but he shook his head. None of it made too much sense to him. He watched as Jewel continued to open and close folders and files.

"This stuff is amazing," Jewel said in a quiet voice. "And it looks like you're right."

"What do you mean?" Rory asked as he looked at Jewel and then back at the file she was examining on the monitor.

"Alton used cloud storage."

Rory blinked. "I've...heard of that..."

"Under normal circumstances, everyone stores their data on the hard drive on their computer. With cloud storage, you do it outside your own computer system. You store and access your data on a network of storage devices that can be anywhere around the world," explained Jewel.

The revelation worried him. "Could you do that with a program?" Rory asked.

Jewel nodded, "That's cloud computing."

"So the security-bot could be...in the cloud," Rory said.

"*Is* in the cloud," corrected Jewel. "Alton was definitely a programming genius. From what I can gather from the files I've looked at, the program is - and isn't - in one spot."

"Huh?"

Jewel smiled and shook her head, "I'm not even sure if I understand it myself. There is a main program but it's not like a regular program. From what I can see, this program is self-contained and can move from one spot to another. But it also has a number of subroutines in various locations around the world that it can access."

"You're losing me."

Jewel took a deep breath and thought for a moment. "Well...it's like you being in this room. You can use all the devices in here. But you can also phone out to Germany for example and asked someone to use a calculator there for you. That's like accessing a subroutine. But you also have the capability of moving from here to Germany to use the calculator yourself. Normal computer programs don't have that ability. But Alton's creation does. And the amazing thing is, computers use or run a program to perform some task. With Alton's creation, it's the program that uses computers wherever it moves to. I don't know how but..."

"Okay, but it must have some home base. If not Alton's computer, then somewhere else," surmised Rory. "Can we find out where? And can we access the program? Can we shut it down?" Rory asked.

"I'll keep looking but I doubt if we can." Jewel's right knee began to bounce.

"Why not?" Rory asked.

"With cloud storage and cloud computing, everything becomes much easier to hide, especially for a computer genius like Alton Fitzhum," Jewel told him as she called up a few more files. "He could keep the access point, user name, and password in his memory so no one could find and control his program. That's what I would do."

"So...we could be fighting against a ghost," Rory said.

"Or ghosts, as in plural," Jewel added. "It looks to me like the program could also have the capability of replicating itself. It looks like that's how it was taken from his home computer as a project into the cloud. And it looks like it's replicated itself and the subroutines in various locations around the world as well. And...as it moves...it could leave portions of itself like breadcrumbs that it could later retrieve. I'm explaining it...but I'm not even sure if I understand it."

Rory sat back in his chair, "So, even if we could find it, it could be like chopping one head off only to have another appear."

"Maybe. Ohhh, I don't really know to tell you the truth," Jewel said as her knee bounced faster.

"It's okay," Rory said as he placed a calming hand on her knee. "One step at a time. Now...why can't you tell what it can do from these notes?"

Jewel took a deep breath and nodded, "Well, it depends on what he *did* implement or what might have been *future* improvements he was working on."

"Okay, that makes sense. Just keep searching. Even the smallest tidbit of information might prove to be vital down the road."

Jewel nodded. She closed the document she was looking at and opened up another folder. She browsed through the various documents, but nothing proved to be too interesting. She opened up another folder and browsed through three documents before one caught her attention. She leaned forward.

Rory leaned forward alongside her, "Unless I miss my guess that looks like some kind of programming code."

"It is," Jewel said in a quiet, amazed tone. She browsed through the code and shook her head, "This stuff is amazing. It looked like he was even using some quantum computing in the design of the security-bot."

"What exactly does that mean?" Rory asked. He sat back and looked at Jewel.

"It means computing at the atomic level," explained Jewel as she scrolled through the programming code. "That's probably how it can move as a self-contained entity, carrying its own program at the atomic level. People have talked about these things but...it looks like Alton was way ahead of everybody else. And from the looks of it...the security-bot is probably able to go anywhere there's energy...but it shouldn't be able to do that."

"That probably explains how she got into Alton's apartment even though Dockerty shut the Internet access off–"

Jewel's body suddenly stiffened, "Hey!" She began frantically typing on the keyboard.

Chapter 57

RORY LEANED FORWARD in his chair, "What's wrong–?" He cut himself off because he could see the problem himself. The files and folders were disappearing and a 'Moving...' message was in the middle of the screen.

"It must be that damn bot," Jewel snarled. "She's moving the files so fast that I can't counter her to download any. Ohhhhhh-hh. She's too fast–"

Rory now saw a single root folder left on the screen.

Jewel cursed and smashed her hand on the desk and the laptop jumped, "She got them all!"

Rory sat there in quiet thought as Jewel continued cursing. How were they going to fight back against this thing? And how could they destroy it if it was scattered around the world?

Jewel cursed several more times and then sat forward in her chair and began to type, "Maybe I can access one of the other drives and get some more information–"

There was a 'bing' sound from the laptop. Jewel froze with her hands over the keyboard and looked over at Rory.

"That sounds like one of those 'you have email' sounds," Jewel said. "Who would send us mail? And how could they?" Jewel sat back nervously in her chair.

Rory considered the situation for a moment. Then he nodded at the laptop, "Why don't you check it and see."

Jewel looked at the laptop, "What if it's the CyberSecure-Bot?"

Rory pursed his lips. "We usually hear that tinkling sound and she just appears."

"True. But maybe she can't get through that way because we have military encryption. I'm pretty sure that's what Moe said we had," Jewel said.

"Can she kill us by email?" Rory asked.

'No," Jewel answered. Then she blinked her eyes a couple times, "Do you think she could?"

When Rory didn't answer her she took a deep breath and then hit the email button. An email message filled the screen:

TO: JTA

Subject: Your Latest Exposé

Someone must have followed you to my place. They tried to scare me through a hologram on my computer. Shot it out with my Luger. They blew my place up. Be careful. I have an underground doctor taking care of my burns. I have another laptop with additional programs. How do I get it to you?

Moe

JEWEL'S MOUTH FELL open. "How did she get to Moe?"

"I thought we were careful but we must have led her right there," Rory said. He cursed, sat back and brushed his hands through his black hair.

"Moe lost his place because of me," she whispered. He could hear the agony in her voice. Then she began cursing as well.

Rory closed his eyes and rubbed the top of his head for a while. Then he sat forward, "Reply to his email. Tell him to stay hidden until we contact him again. We can't afford to lose another computer expert like we did with Sergent. Somehow we have to find a way to fight back against her."

Jewel leaned forward and hit reply on the email, then typed in her message:

TO: MOE

Subject: Re: Your Latest Exposé

Stay hidden until we contact you again. Avoid all surveillance cameras, WebCams etc. The software program we talked about can use them to track you. Sorry about your place. Keep safe. Love.

JTA

JEWEL SENT THE MESSAGE and sat back in her chair. She looked over at Rory, "Are we safe here? I mean, if she could track us to Moe—"

"We came here under disguise and avoided most of the cameras remember? We should be safe for now," Rory said.

"For now?" Jewel said.

Rory just nodded and put his hands on top of his head again. He sat back in the chair to think. They heard the email 'bing' again. Rory watched Jewel go back to the laptop. He leaned forward as she brought up the email:

TO: JTA

   Subject: Re: Your Latest Exposé

That explains it. The doc and me are going to an old safe house we still have access to. Talk to you later. Who exactly are we up against?

   Moe

JEWEL SAT BACK AND shook her head, "Who are we up against? He'll never believe it, Rory. I'm not sure I do. Damn that Alton, what in the world did he create?"

   "We'll let Moe get to his safe house before we contact him again. Let's turn our attention back to cracking the hard drives. Maybe we can find something that terminates the security-bot before she goes after anyone else."

Chapter 58

JEWEL STEPPED UP her efforts to find the trail leading to Rory Mack Steele and Jewel Tanya Afterburn. She swiftly moved among the various surveillance cameras, ATM cameras and Web-Cams for the blocks around Moe's Computer Repair place. Flowing through cyberspace, she spiraled outward in a search grid. Cloning her facial recognition subroutine dozens of times, she left each one behind in place to diligently sift through the recorded footage. She filtered each and every possibility until she finally spotted them two blocks away. She flowed into a new search pattern, moving the cloned subroutines into new locations and continued to access video footage. She tracked them across several more blocks, finally finding footage where they entered the building designated as Greenwich Village Theatrical Makeup. She accessed the footage around the block for several hours after, watching for their reappearance. There was no evidence of them leaving before the building was vacated and the lights were turned out. Her subroutines hummed as she analyzed the situation. Either they were inside or they found some way to elude her again. She had her subroutines go back through and analyzed the footage. There were only two people of the correct height and weight who left the building. The larger of the two individuals was carrying a laptop case. Only one person had entered with a laptop case, the cyber-criminal, Rory Mack Steele. Since only one individual left carrying a laptop bag, she calculated they had changed their physical appearance. Jewel tracked the two individuals through recorded footage as they snaked around a number of city blocks. She finally found footage that showed them entering a building designated on Google maps as the Northern Dispensary. She detected a Wi-Fi signal on the military band coming from somewhere within this building. Conclusion: Rory Mack Steele and Jewel Tanya Afterburn were inside.

Chapter 59

LOWER EAST SIDE, NEW York

DARIEL NATHAN PENDER was also known as 'Burner'. Crime statistics say 40% of all arsons are for profit. And 'Burner' was well known in the local underground as the go-to man who could help you plan the perfect insurance scam. Occasionally, he was involved directly but that cost a lot more money than most people were going to get from the insurance. Instead, Burner outsourced each job to a former pupil who would perform the actual torching. Right now he was sitting in front of his computer and surfing a little porn. An email appeared on the screen. That surprised him because he hadn't touched Outlook Express at all. He leaned in closer to the monitor to read the email:

TO: DARIEL NATHAN PENDER

Subject: Your services

From: Jewel

Dear Mr. Pender

I need a building burned down. You will find $2.5 million in your account as a down payment. $2.5 million will be deposited after you have completed the task successfully.

Jewel

BURNER JUST STARED. Then he sat back in shock. He contemplated deleting the email, then decided to check his online bank account with Ing Direct. Somebody was messing with him. He signed in and brought up his account: there was a $2,502,437.27 balance. While he was staring at the bottom line in his bank account, another email popped up on the screen:

TO: DARIEL NATHAN PENDER
   Subject: Your services
   From: Jewel
   Dear Mr. Pender
   I am not the police. I need the building burned down immediately. I also need your answer immediately or I move on to another service provider. The money will be removed from your account until you reply.
   Jewel

BURNER IMMEDIATELY jumped back to the screen with his bank account. The $2.5 million was gone. Bugger! Burner licked his lips and considered his next move. He immediately moved back to the first email and printed it out. He did the same with the second email. Then he printed out a screenshot of his bank account. He wanted complete paper evidence in case it was entrapment. Then he jumped back to the second email and hit reply:

TO: JEWEL
Subject: Re: Your services
Assignment accepted.

AS SOON AS THE EMAIL reply was gone he jumped back to his Ing bank account. He hit refresh and there it was, a $2,502,437.27 balance appeared again. Burner raised his hands skyward and shouted in joy. Then he froze, lowered his hands and looked around the room. How exactly had this happened? He wondered if someone was watching him. An email popped up again. It contained the address to the building and the instructions to burn the fire from all sides to ensure no one could stop it. That was an unusual request. Normally he just started a fire in one spot, with trails leading to two or more jars of accelerant to ensure success, and then ran. He wasn't one of those firebugs who needed to watch the flames after. He jumped onto the Internet and called up the address in Google Earth. Zooming in, he realized it was a triangular building in the middle of four connecting streets. He licked his lips and wondered what he was getting into. He looked back at the bank account again and made a decision. Burner began to wonder which accelerant he should use and how he could quickly disperse it around the building for maximum effect. He remembered seeing a 5-gallon dispensing jug with a bottom spigot at the hardware store two blocks over. It would allow him to walk around the triangular building and leave a trail of accelerant. That would work, although it would make it harder to work without being seen. But for the money, it was worth the risk. He set to work.

Chapter 60

JEWEL AFTERBURN WATCHED the laptop monitor as Sergent's cracking/hacking program continued to run, trying to crack into another of the hard drives on Alton Fitzhum's system. It was nearing one o'clock in the morning and she was tired. Another ten minutes and it would be Rory's turned to watch the program and she could sleep. She looked over at the small air mattress and the tall, black-haired man sleeping on it. A smile crossed her face as she watched him sleeping on his side with his hands tucked under his head like a pillow. He looked like a little boy–

A whooshing sound caught her attention. It was over on the left side of the building. She wondered if someone was coming in and she sat up. But the whooshing sound continued to move around to the side of the building behind her. Then she heard the sound on the right side and moving up towards the front of the building. Was it a small tornado? Was it a car racing around the building? The sound didn't make any sense to her. Curiosity led her to get out of the chair. She slowly walked out the door of the room into the hallway, listening and trying to stay as quiet as possible. There was a roaring sound now. What in the world was going on? She walked down the dark hallway, listening intently for anyone who might have slipped inside. She was about to go back to Rory when a flash on her left caught her eye. She turned to look. There was a window there and something yellow and red was flickering. Then the realization of what it was hit her full force. The building was on fire!

Jewel ran as fast as she could back to Rory, shaking him, "Rory, Rory, wake up. The building is on fire!"

Rory was slow to wake up. He had been so tired. He rubbed his eyes, wondering what she was saying. Then he jumped up quickly when he heard her say the word fire again. He ran for the door.

Words of panic spilled out of Jewel as she ran behind Rory, "I heard something and when I went out into the hallway, I looked through a window and I saw the fire."

Rory looked both ways down the hallway.

"To the left, to the left," Jewel yelled. She followed Rory again as he ran.

But it wasn't long before Rory stopped in his tracks. He saw flames in the window up ahead.

Jewel bumped into him. "We need to get out," she yelled.

Rory turned back, running to a cross hallway - he stopped and checked a window towards the front of the building.

Coming to a stop beside him, Jewel put her hands went to her mouth when she saw what he saw, "Oh, no. No. No. No."

Taking off at a run again, Rory led her to the other side of the building.

But when they got there, all they saw were flames in the window as well.

"The security-bot," was all Rory said.

Jewel's panic intensified, "The whole building is on fire. How do we get out!"

Rory licked his lips as he thought. He put his hands on Jewel's arms to calm her, "It's okay, we'll figure something out."

"But the whole building..." she whispered. Her voice failed her.

"Come on," urged Rory, "let's go get the thumb drive and the laptop. No matter what, we're going to need it." He took her hand gently and urged her to move with him. It was a slow run as Jewel's legs refused to work but they finally made it back to the room. Rory pulled the thumb drive and put it into his pocket. Then he held the laptop button down in a power shutdown and snapped the lid shut. He took Jewel's hand again and led her back out of the room and down the hallway. He headed to the other side of the building, looking for a way out. But there was no escape on this side either. Jewel had been right. The entire building was on fire. It looked like the security-bot was going to win this time. He thought about going up to another floor and maybe escaping to an adjacent building. Then he remembered. This was a triangular building in the middle of four streets. It was a stand-alone. There was no adjacent building they could escape to. He contemplated the roof. Maybe if they waited up there for the fire department? Then he realized how old this building was and it probably would go up in flames too fast to wait for rescue. They were trapped in a burning building with no way out.

Chapter 61

THEY WERE DEAD. That's all Rory could think as he held Jewel in his arms. He could hear the old building crackling and snapping, being consumed by flames. It had stood for nearly two centuries but it wasn't going to last much longer. Rory closed his eyes, trying to think of something. He pushed away thoughts of the heat, the crackling and popping - a comment came to him. Something Jewel had said. He opened his eyes, "Jewel, didn't you say you played here is a kid?"

Jewel was trembling as she answered, "Yes. It was abandoned then too. My parents didn't want us to play here, but we did. You know kids, never listen to the parents. Always looking for an adventure." She was babbling in fear.

"Is there anything in here we could hide in? Maybe a large vault or - something?" He was grasping at straws as he listened to the flames roaring around them.

Jewel shook her head, "No. My grandfather told me it was a medical building built for the poor. And like Moe said, there were dental offices in here for a while."

Rory nodded, "That would account for the rusted dental equipment we saw." Rory could hear the flames licking higher now. There were louder cracking and popping sounds all around them as the building was being devoured by the relentless flames.

Jewel lifted her head, "I've never seen anything like a large vault or a cabinet that we could squeeze into but..."

Rory could see her thinking, "What is it?"

Jewel looked up. Her eyes were filled with a little hope as she looked into his calm silver-blue ones, "My grandfather once told me there were some tunnels in the basement that connected to nearby buildings. He saw them a couple of times when he was a child and treated here. He thought they'd used them to move patients back and forth to other buildings. I think there was a mental asylum nearby at one time."

"Did you explore them when you were a kid?" Rory asked hopefully.

Jewel shook her head again, "No. Not me. Some of the kids went into the basement but I never did. It was too spooky and I was too afraid."

"How do we get down there?" Rory asked.

"That's what I was just trying to figure out," Jewel said. She stepped back and looked down the smoke-filled hallway. The harsh flicker of the flames etched into the fear on her face.

"Just take your time..."

"We don't have much time do we?" she said forcefully.

Rory just put a hand on her shoulder.

Jewel squeezed her face muscles tight, then released them, "Sorry." She tried to refocus. She turned around, "I think...we need to go to that side of the building," Jewel said as she pointed down the hallway.

"Are you sure?"

"Pretty sure," she said. But she didn't look too convinced herself.

"Okay. We have no choice," Rory said.

Jewel watched Rory pick up the laptop case that was at his feet, then took his hand and led him along the hallway. The flames were beginning to roar louder now. Black smoke was starting to creep along the ceiling. Jewel and Rory coughed as they stopped outside a large room. If they didn't get out quickly, the smoke would probably kill them before the flames did. Jewel stepped into the room. She walked over to an internal door, opened it and looked back at Rory. Steps led downwards.

Rory moved ahead of Jewel and peered down into the flickering darkness. He pulled out his flashlight and led the way. He tested the first step for strength. Then he tested the next. He slowly led Jewel down into a dark, dank basement. The concrete floor was old and chipped. Jewel pulled out her flashlight and they began exploring the musty, cobweb-filled space in different directions. They could hear the roaring of the fire overhead. The old building was going up quickly. After a few moments, Jewel yelled for Rory. He ran over to where she was examining a series of boards nailed horizontally down the wall.

"This must be it," she said as her hand passed over the old lumber.

Rory nodded and set the laptop case down. He tried to pull the boards off with his fingers. It was no good. He began searching around, using the flashlight. Rory found some lengths of old lead pipe. He passed one over to Jewel, "Start hammering the end of the pipe into the boards. We can't pry them off but maybe we can make a hole." Rory began to use the old lead pipe as a spear, hammering from his shoulder at the place where two boards met about waist height. Jewel did the same, not far from the spot where Rory was striking.

They could hear pieces of the building crashing in upstairs. It wouldn't be long before the building caved in on top of them. Rory and Jewel increased their hammering, driven by fear. The wood began to splinter. They continued hammering away, creating a small gap between two boards.

Rory stuck his pipe through it and pried the bottom board away on one side. Jewel worked with him to pull it completely away, throwing it to the floor behind them. Rory went to work on the joint of the next two boards down and Jewel joined him, hammering away at the same spot. A loud crash upstairs made them both flinch. They went back to their task with increased effort. In moments they had produced another hole. Rory and Jewel worked in tandem to pry the top board off, creating a two board gap into the darkness beyond.

"I think I can squeeze through," Jewel said as she dropped her length of pipe.

Rory picked up the length of pipe and threw it through the hole, "We might need it on the other end."

"Oh, right," she said. With Rory's help, she squeezed through the hole. Rory passed the military laptop through to her, then threw his own length of pipe through the gap in the boards. Rory had to push harder to get through the tight fit but he finally made it.

Jewel flashed the beam of her flashlight around them. They were now into a low, dark tunnel made of old crumbling brick.

Rory picked up his length of pipe along with the military laptop and they began moving away from the basement of the burning building. They weren't too far along the tunnel when they heard pieces of the building crashing into the basement behind them. Smoke, dust, and dirt filled the tunnel in behind, choking them. Rory moved Jewel quickly ahead. They reached another set of boards and they began hammering away as dense smoke began to creep into the tunnel just behind them. They were able to knock several boards out from this side and in a matter of moments they were into another dark, dank basement.

Rory and Jewel worked their way through the dark up to the first floor of the building they were in. It appeared to be an old apartment building with stores fronts on the main level. They stepped up to a door that looked out into the street front. The scene outside was a madhouse. There were crowds of onlookers on the street in front of them, jammed up against police barricades. Rory and Jewel stepped out into the street just behind the crowd. The night was lit up by the immense fire of the old Northern Dispensary building burning across the street. Fire trucks were pouring water on the building from all sides. Sirens could be heard in the distance, heading to join the futile fight to save the old building. Rory gently placed a hand on Jewel's shoulder and led her back inside the building. They moved through the hallway to the back of the building. No one noticed the dirty, disheveled couple slip out the back entrance. Rory and Jewel stayed in the shadows and darkness as they fled the security-bot.

Chapter 62

JEWEL MONITORED THE communication systems of the fire departments, police and paramedic teams on-site. In the hours that passed, there were no reports of any dead bodies found within the charred structure of the Northern Dispensary. She calculated the probabilities of the bodies being consumed completely by the fire and concluded there would have to be some trace. She further concluded that the cyberspace criminals had escaped. It didn't matter how, only that they had. One of her subroutines continued to monitor the communication systems while she began systematically looking through the available video footage in the blocks surrounding the fire.

She once again began the hunt for her targets.

Chapter 63

RORY AND JEWEL hustled along the sidewalk, staying in the shadows and constantly wary of convenience store cameras, ATM cameras, street cams, traffic cameras and every other type of surveillance device that the security-bot could use to track them. The problem was, the more aware you were of them, the harder it seemed to avoid the constant barrage of electronic eyes tracking your every move. They tried to use every small park or clump of trees to hide any change in direction as they tried to figure out what they were going to do next. The problem was, it seemed every avenue of escape or place to hide was rapidly dwindling. Rory noticed the all-night coffee shop they were passing had Wi-Fi access. He took Jewel by the elbow and steered her through the door. Rory had been mulling over an idea and he wondered if it would work. The problem was - if it didn't work - he didn't know what else they could do. The security-bot was proving more than capable of finding them, no matter where they hid. Things were rapidly coming to a head and they may only have this one shot to survive.

"Why are we going in here?" Jewel asked.

"We need to rest and get something to eat. And we also need to come up with some kind of a plan," explained Rory. "They have

Wi-Fi here and I want you to set up the laptop on that far table while I order something. We need to keep our strength up."

Jewel took the laptop and set things up while Rory ordered coffee and several sandwiches. Rory sat down in one of the chairs on the same side of the table as Jewel so they could both work on the laptop. Jewel noticed their theatrical makeup had been damaged in the escape from the fire and they took turns in the washroom removing it and washing up. Jewel returned to their table to find Rory working away on the laptop. Typical of New Yorkers, the proprietor never noticed her change in appearance as she ordered another two coffees.

"So what do we do now?" Jewel asked as she sat down beside Rory.

"I think we should talk with Moe and let him know exactly what's happening," Rory said. "I hate to put him in more danger but I think we're going to need his help for what I have in mind."

"What exactly are you planning?" Jewel asked.

Rory turned the laptop a little more in her direction and pointed at the screen, "This is where we're going to send the security-bot."

Jewel looked at the screen and then looked at Rory with a surprised look on her face, "You've got to be kidding."

"Unless you know a better place, I don't have any other answers," Rory said.

Jewel stared at the screen for a moment, her face still a canvas of surprise. Finally, she shrugged, "I got nothin'...so...how do we do it?" Jewel asked.

"In all honesty, I'm going to keep everything close to the vest in case that damn bot can overhear us somehow," Rory said. Then he pointed at the image on the laptop screen, " I need to know if you can destroy the downlink communications system on board that thing. I've been reading about it and it says their normal long-range communications are carried out through their 3.67-meter, high gain antennas. They also have an X-band microwave transmitter with an X-band transmitter as a backup. We would have to get the security-bot inside that thing but can you destroy the downlink once we get the bot inside?"

Jewel looked at Rory for a moment, obviously thinking. Then she looked back at the screen and began typing, calling up schematics of the computer systems on Rory's target destination. After a few moments, she turned to Rory, "My skills along these lines are a little rusty but I could possibly write a virus to send to the onboard system to knock out the areas you're talking about. But even if I could write one that would do the job, you may have another problem."

Rory leaned forward to look at what Jewel was pointing to on the computer screen, "What's that?"

"They also have a low gain antenna for a backup system," she explained. "I might be able to send a virus to knock out the high gain communications system but not both. That would leave a back door, a path to escape."

Rory sat back in his chair and bit his lip, contemplating what else they could do.

Jewel tapped her fingers on the table for a few moments, then went back to work on the keyboard, examining the schematics closer. Finally, she offered a possible solution to the problem. "The low gain antenna is radiating its signal over the hemisphere where the high gain antenna is pointed," she said. "I might be able to use that to put the entire communication systems into a never-ending loop."

"How?" Rory asked.

"We could send a Trojan horse," she said finally.

"I've heard of it but what exactly does that mean? How would it work?" Rory asked.

"In computing terms, a Trojan horse is a small program you send into a computer system to do any number of things from stealing information or money to harming the system itself. In this case, I could send one to reprogram the onboard computer to put the entire downlink communication systems into the perpetual loop we would need."

Rory stroked his chin as he contemplated what Jewel was proposing, "So we could time it to start the perpetual loop *before* the security-bot gets there?"

Jewel nodded her head.

Rory sat up quickly, "Can the security-bot break it?"

"I'm not totally sure," Jewel admitted. "But the onboard computing system is so crude and slow I doubt the security-bot could use it to break into the loop to terminate it. Then again, Alton's creation is pretty powerful and there's no telling what she could do."

Rory pursed his lips as he considered the alternatives. The only problem was there were no alternatives at this moment. They had no choice except to move forward with his plan, flaws and all.

"Okay, so let's say I can create a small program to send a signal to put their downlink communications into a never-ending loop," Jewel said. "How do we get this security-bot to go there so we can trap it?"

Rory didn't want to say anything as he stroked the stubble on his chin.

Jewel crossed her arms and looked at Rory. "Okay. I can understand you don't want to say anything, we're both paranoid right now. But how in God's green earth do I send a signal to that device in the first place."

Rory realized he was going to have to reveal a little more of his plan. But she was right. He was paranoid. He looked around, wondering if they were being watched and listened to. Finally, he typed on the keyboard and called up another website. He turned the screen to Jewel and simply said, "We break in here."

Jewel squinted her eyes at the screen and then looked at Rory, "You have to be kidding."

Chapter 64

RORY COCKED HIS HEAD as he looked at Jewel, "Do you have a better plan, Miss Afterburn?"

"I don't have any plan," Jewel admitted. "And you're turning me into a first-class criminal."

"From what I understand, the targets of your exposés called you a second-class criminal. So I've actually raised you up a notch."

Jewel pursed her lips as she looked at Rory. "Your gonna pay for that one, Steele." A smile lingered on her lips.

Rory chuckled, "I'll make sure I keep one eye open when I sleep. Now, why don't we contact Moe and let them know what happened and see if he can help us."

Jewel began typing up an email message, "Sounds reasonable. I'll see if Moe is available before we send him a full explanation." She sent off the email as Rory returned with fresh coffees and some doughnuts. An email ding sounded ten minutes later. Jewel brought up the email, "Moe says keep the laptop open and he's going to Skype us over a secure feed."

"That's one of those video chat things isn't it?" Rory asked.

"That's right," Jewel answered as she started Skype and brought up a video screen. Rory could see Jewel's image on the right-hand side. A moment later, the secure Skype call from Moe came through.

"Hi sweetie," Moe said as his face appeared on the screen.

"Hi Moe," Jewel answered, "nice to see your face again."

"Where's Rory?" Moe asked as a worried look creased his face. He seemed to try to look around the corners of the screen.

"He's right here beside me," Jewel said as she moved the laptop just a bit to show Rory sitting beside her.

"Good," Moe said with a look of relief on his face. "I was worried about you two."

"We were worried about you as well," Jewel said. "Just in case you hear it on the news, we want to make sure you know that someone burned down the Northern Dispensary building, hoping to trap us inside."

Moe scowled, "Your friends again, I suppose?"

"Just one friend Moe," Rory said. He looked at Jewel for a moment and then sat forward, "Moe, we're not up against a human being. We're up against a computer program called a Cyber-SecureBot that was created to protect cyberspace. It's gone crazy and can somehow use every computerized device in the world to track us, to find us and to try and kill us. And somehow the program can also reach beyond cyberspace for tools to use. It appears she retained the services of a hitman to try and kill us earlier. And I imagine it was an arsonist who was sent to burn down the abandoned building we were in."

Moe looked more than a little startled. Rory could see him thinking, "Is that what I saw at my place? That hologram thing that talked to me?"

"Yes," Rory answered. "If you want to get out now, I wouldn't blame you."

Moe looked at Jewel and his face hardened, "If that thing is after you sweetie, I'll do everything I can to help you out." He looked in Rory's direction, "So what do you need me to do?"

"I have a plan. But as I told Jewel - I'm going to keep most of it to myself for now," Rory said. "Do you have a cell phone where I can send an email?"

"I have an iPhone. I'll send you the email address."

"That's perfect," Rory said. "Now. One of the first things we're going to need is someplace to stay and work. You mentioned you were heading to a safe house. Do you know of anything down in the Hudson Square area that we can use? We have to get up there while it's still dark and make it harder for this program to track us. As I said, it can access and use surveillance cameras, ATM cameras, the works."

Moe thought for a few minutes, "I think there is something to the East in SoHo. I'll check it out and send you a secure email shortly. Anything else?

"Yes. We'll continue to use the military laptops for secure communications as we develop our plan. But once the plan is ready, you're going to have to lure the security-bot into the military laptop you have."

"Which puts a target on my back," surmised Moe.

Rory nodded, "Right. I'm sorry, but I'm going to ask you to turn yourself into a special target at a certain time to distract the security-bot while we set some things up. I'm going to have Jewel send you some hacking and cracking tools from a thumb drive along with instructions on how to use them. The computer you're going to try to break into belongs to the person who created this security-bot. It appears she killed him and I wouldn't blame you if you wanted to back out now. This computer program is pretty aggressive and I don't know how far it will go to eliminate us as cyber-criminals."

"I understand," Moe said.

"We only have a certain window of time to operate in," Rory explained. "It'll probably take as most of that time to get things set up. When the sun comes up–"

"If I survive that long," Moe said.

Rory nodded, "When the sun comes up, you will use the iPhone to send us an email message that Jewel will compose for you. I'm asking you to put your life in danger Moe, so I can understand–"

"I'll be back to you shortly with an address for that safe house," Moe said simply and he terminated the link Within 30 minutes Rory and Jewel were headed for the safe house location in SoHo.

Chapter 65

THE BOWERY, NEW YORK

MOE LAPRADE SAT at the small table in the living room of the safe house. The military laptop was running. He made sure the military IDS, the intrusion detection system, was in operation. It was also set to trigger a shadow alert to the military laptop being used by Jewel and Rory. Moe had connected to the Wi-Fi on the nearby police station but he had set the security settings to a low level. That would make it easier to find him. The WebCam was running. Everything seemed to be ready. He had copied the files Jewel had sent him into a single folder and he now opened it up. He scanned through the various icons and found the ones he had been instructed to use. It was marked AH. He double-clicked on the icon and a communications window immediately opened up. He sat there amazed as numbers and lines scrolled up the screen for a few moments. Then the screen flickered and he saw he was connected remotely to another computer system. Just like they said would happen. Moe leaned in closer and looked through the list of files on the screen. There were tons of hard drives. He wondered about the computer nerd that had set this all up. This was impressive. But he had more important work to do. He went back to the folder and looked for the icon to the program he was to use next. He saw it but hesitated for a moment. He had been told this was the hacking tool that would attract that CyberSecureBot. He thought back to his near death at the hands of that thing and he felt a little dread. Then he thought about Jewel Afterburn. He had never had a family and he thought of this young lady like a daughter. This is for you sweetie, he thought. He double-clicked on the icon and watched as it went to work.

Chapter 66

ONE OF JEWEL'S subroutines alerted her to a remote attempt to infiltrate Base 1. She immediately rushed back and entered Alton Fitzhum's computer system. Someone was running through all of the hard drives, trying to break into them. She sniffed the stream of data packets coming and going. Jewel added a rider to the data packets in the target's stream and waited for it to come back as instructed. The IP address came back and Jewel moved through cyberspace to an NYPD precinct building. She scanned through the entire system and found the computer assigned the address. Someone was piggy-backing on this signal from the outside. It was another hacker that was using a military bandwidth. She tested the stream of data and was able to crack the security algorithm with ease. Within milliseconds she had the location of the hacker. She slipped out of the precinct and moved through cyberspace to confront the cyber-criminal.

Chapter 67

MOE LAPRADE SAT back down at the small table in the living room of the safe house, fresh coffee in hand. He took a sip as he watched the computer screen–

The intrusion detection system triggered an alert. It was here! The CyberSecureBot had found him.

Moe immediately set the coffee cup down, stood up and backed away from the laptop. He mentally went through his preparations. The gas fireplaces had been shot off. In fact, he had shut off the main gas valve outside. No sense taking any chances. Not after what had happened to his store. He had unplugged all electrical appliances including the fridge and stove. He had taken the back door off its hinges. There was no way this thing was going to trap him inside. He had knocked out several street lights along his escape route. Hopefully the darkness would make it harder to track him once he got outside. But he also knew he had to keep the bot on the hook and chasing him. It was going to be a delicate balancing act between being seen just enough and getting trapped with no way out. He had to give Rory and Jewel enough time to set their plan in place, whatever it was. Moe took a deep breath and waited.

IT ONLY TOOK NANOSECONDS for Jewel to make a rough analysis of the laptop. It was definitely something of military issue and had an impressive number of programs. She detected a signal had been sent at the same time she had entered. It had been well disguised but her programs also operated at machine code level, making it harder to elude her many algorithms. She tasked a subroutine to track the signal. Now it was time to find out who the cyber-criminal was.

MOE HEARD THE TINKLING sound he had first heard back in his computer shop. He stared at the laptop. He knew it was coming but he had to make sure it was going to try and track him. He had to hold his ground for as long as possible. A small white square flashed in the middle of the laptop's screen and then a beam of light shot out towards his face. Moe held his ground even though he wanted to flee. He allowed the beam of light to scan his face. It disappeared as quickly as it had appeared. The tinkling sound increased and a swirl of colored lights appeared in the middle of the computer screen. It was coming.

JEWEL HAD IDENTIFIED the cyber-criminal as Morris John Laprade. He was the one who had been helping Rory Mack Steele and Jewel Tanya Afterburn in their own crimes against cyberspace. Her previous estimates on not being able to eliminate him had been correct, he was still alive. That would change soon.

MOE HELD HIS GROUND until the bald, beautiful face appeared and it stared directly at him. Time to go. He turned, ran into the kitchen and passed through the open doorway into the dark backyard. He ran as hard as his old legs could carry him into the night.

JEWEL SAW THE CYBER-criminal, known as Moe Laprade, was fleeing. She called in a subroutine to examine the contents of the laptop in more detail. Then she quickly moved out of the computer system and out of the house. She began accessing the various cameras in the surrounding blocks, looking for the escape route of Moe Laprade.

Chapter 68

SOHO, NEW YORK

RORY AND JEWEL sat nervously waiting for the signal that Moe had successfully attracted the security-bot's attention. They would only have a few more hours of darkness to help them avoid detection once they left the safe house. Jewel got up, picked up his mug along with hers and stepped into the kitchen to get more coffee. The military laptop pinged and an alert screen popped up.

"She's there!" yelled Rory.

Jewel dropped the two coffee mugs on the floor and ran back into the living room. She saw Rory had performed a power shutdown and was closing the laptop cover, "Do you think she can trace the connection to us here?"

"I doubt it," Rory said. "I don't think she would have had enough time to decrypt the signal. But let's get out of here right now, just in case she does. We don't have much time before the sun comes up."

Rory and Jewel slipped out the back door of the safe house into the back alley. They moved as swiftly as they could in the darkness to the end of the block and out into the street. Staying in the shadows of buildings as much as possible, they hustled through areas lit by street lights in order to minimize the bot tracking them. There was no way of knowing if she knew where they were but they had to take every precaution possible.

BUT IT WAS ALREADY too late. Unknown to Rory and Jewel, the security-bot's subroutine had moved across the city at cyberspace speed and had already tracked the signal to the laptop before they had reacted. The information had been routed back to Jewel within milliseconds.

THE BOWERY, NEW YORK

Once Moe had moved past the street lights he had knocked out, he stayed as much as possible in the shadows. He kept up a constant vigil for any cameras where he could be spotted. Seeing a surveillance camera mounted high on the building ahead, Moe slipped down a dark alley and skirted several lit parking areas behind some old apartment buildings. At the end of the alley Moe turned left and hurried down the narrow street.

BUT THE SECURITY-BOT had accessed a rooftop WebCam and Jewel spotted her target. But he moved quickly out of her field of vision and there were limited cameras to access in the area. She had to step up her search. Jewel recorded his last known coordinates and flowed quickly through cyberspace to the National Reconnaissance Office in Chantilly Virginia. One of her subroutines had determined one of their Earth observation satellites was overhead. She infiltrated their computer system and moved up through the signal stream to Geos12. Taking over the internal monitoring routine, she focused and zoomed the high definition cameras down on the coordinates she had recorded and within moments she spotted the target again. She began to scan the area for any signal of a tool she could use to halt the cyber-criminal's flight from justice.

MOE HAD DEVELOPED A sixth sense over the years and he couldn't shake the feeling he was being watched. But he couldn't see any cameras. Moe spotted a small park across the street and headed for it, crossing the street at its darkest point. He was just about to step off the sidewalk and onto the grass when he heard a screech of tires behind him. He turned to see a courier van bearing down on him. Moe ran into the park. He looked back to see the courier van bounce up over the sidewalk and into the park, tearing up the grass as it accelerated towards him. Moe's old legs strained to move him faster. He looked back to see the driver frantically trying to regain control of the vehicle. Moe knew it wouldn't happen. Rory and Jewel had explained the capabilities of the security-bot. He had found it hard to believe. But the fact the courier van was trying to run him down in a park right now was definite proof. The van sounded closer and Moe scanned the terrain ahead, looking for a way out. Moe saw what he needed in the dark up ahead. He immediately angled to the left, running as fast as his old legs would take him. The van swerved to the left to pursue him. It tore up grass and dirt as its wheels spun, trying to gain more traction. The vehicle straightened out and accelerated towards the target. Moe looked back once more to gauge the distance. He slowed just a bit to time his next move. He looked through the windshield at the driver. Sorry buddy, he thought, I hope your family has insurance. He looked back to where he was running, slowed a bit more and, at the last moment, Moe Laprade leaped to his right and rolled across the grass. The courier driver's eyes shot wide open as the van veered hard right, trying to find the fleeing cyber-criminal. The van came to a violent stop as it collided with a large oak tree. Moe was up and running, leaving behind the steaming wreck.

JEWEL SAW THROUGH THE infrared system that the courier van had stopped abruptly against a tree in the middle of the park. It wasn't moving. The security-bot zoomed the camera out enough to spot the target leaving the park and running down a street. She began scanning for signals to another tool. She found it. She accessed the city transit system and streamed a sub-routine down to the vehicle. She sorted through the various modules in the control system. Jewel wrote short pieces of code to tie several of the modules together and in milliseconds she had control.

MOE WAS HAVING A HARD time catching his breath, He slowed to a walk. Then he bent over, hands on his knees. He was out in the open on the street but he had no choice. He shook his head. The young Moe would've kept going. Or was that just romantic fantasy of his past? It didn't matter. He had to find some way to keep going. Jewel and Rory were counting on him to keep this thing distracted while they – a loud roar broke into his thoughts. It was behind him. Moe turned and his heart stopped. One of the city's new transit buses jumped the curb and headed directly for him. The large, single front window gleamed like a huge robot eye that was focused on one thing...running him down and burying him in the concrete sidewalk. Moe took off at a run again. He veered hard left and ran across the street. He heard the screech of tires as the transit bus veered hard to the left, roared across the roadway and bounced up over the curb in pursuit of him. Moe looked back as he ran down the sidewalk. He couldn't see anything through the gleaming eye but he knew there was a human there trying desperately not to run him down. Moe knew it would be futile. Moe's heart pounded as he heard the bus accelerate. He knew it would only be a matter of time before he was under the wheels. Eventually he would run out of gas. The transit bus would not. Moe ran hard to the left again and back across the street. The transit bus tires screeched in hot pursuit. Moe reached the sidewalk and turned left. This was crazy. He was running in circles! But what else could he do? He could turn faster than the bus could but eventually...

Time for new tactics. An alleyway came up on the right. Moe slid to a stop and ducked into the dark alley, urging his old legs to move faster. The only sound was the pounding of his shoes echoing off the brick walls on either side. Moe looked back over his shoulder as he ran. Had it worked?

The transit bus swung left, then veered hard right into the alleyway. The left side of the transit bus slammed into the brick wall. Hot sparks showered the air as the bus scraped along the wall in hot pursuit of the target.

Moe's heart pounded as he looked back. Headlights speared towards him. The shower of sparks illuminated the alleyway behind him. A monster was in pursuit. Moe looked back ahead as he ran, looking for another way out.

The wide transit bus swung away from the wall as a blue metal dumpster appeared ahead. The bus scraped into the other brick wall. Sparks flew. Then it began to smash through garbage containers, boxes, and wooden pallets as it pursued the target.

Moe could hear the muffled explosions of wood, glass, and metal behind him coming closer. He tried to push his legs harder. His lungs burned. Moe's heart sank when he realized he had made a mistake. He was coming to a brick wall. A dead end. Moe frantically searched for an escape route. It appeared just to the right. Moe pushed the old legs harder. He leaped at the last moment. His momentum tore one hand away from the rusted bottom rung of the fire escape ladder and he thought he was a goner. But he managed to keep his right hand holding firmly. His shoulder cried with the pain. Moe desperately pulled himself up. He scrambled frantically to escape the onrushing transit bus.

The pursuing transit bus tore through the bottom of the ladder.

Moe had his grip on the escape ladder torn away. He felt himself flipping and tumbling into the air.

The front end of the New York City electric transit bus folded like an accordion as it met the immovable wall of a New York building. The back of the bus tipped upward.

Moe crash-landed on top of the transit bus. The back of the transit bus settled hard against the pavement, bouncing Moe upward and over the side. His body came to rest in a pile of trash.

Chapter 69

THE CYBERSECUREBOT RECEIVED some information. Jewel's subroutine analyzing the military laptop had found some interesting but also alarming information. The hacking tools used by Alton Fitzhum and Calvin Sergent had been found in a folder. There were also emails between the cyber-criminal she was presently pursuing and Rory Mack Steele and Jewel Tanya After-burn, the only two cyber-criminals who had managed to elude her to this point. They were setting plans in motion to use a virus to infiltrate and eliminate an Internet satellite they believed held her central program. That was untrue but she could not allow them to harm cyberspace. She was programmed to protect it.

She tied those pieces of information to the data returned by the subroutine tracking the signal that had been sent by Moe Laprade's military grade laptop. The receiving machine was also a military grade laptop. Rory Mack Steele and Jewel Tanya After-burn had been using such a machine. She had to confirm it was them.

Leaving her present target behind, she moved swiftly to the geographic coordinates of the location in SoHo where she accessed cameras in the blocks around the location. The streets were empty of people and she was able to pick out Rory Mack

Steele and Jewel Tanya Afterburn in no time. There were now three cyber-criminals immediately in her sights. But they were in two different locations and time was imperative. Decisions were in order.

The CyberSecureBot began analyzing her options, combing through her databases. A recent drug war between a motorcycle gang in South Manhattan and a gang with Latino roots had been recorded. An undercover detective, Gabriel X. McDaniels, had been taking bribes and feeding intel to the motorcycle gang during the feud. None of it was a threat to cyberspace so Jewel had filed it away. But now, the situation could be used to her advantage. She would take up her pursuit of the cyber-criminal Moe Laprade shortly.

The CyberSecureBot streamed herself to the apartment of Gabriel X. McDaniels. Entering through the electrical system, Jewel streamed to the smart television in his living room. Using the video camera, she noted everything was dark and quiet. His computer system was off. She moved to another smart television in the bedroom.

Gabriel X. McDaniels lay sleeping in bed.

A subroutine had analyzed his computer system, his home security system, and his Wi-Fi setup. Jewel detected a cell phone sitting on a dresser in the bedroom. A thorough analysis determined it was the burner cell phone he used to contact his criminal cohorts. Accessing an online voice changing app, she made a call.

Chapter 70

THE MOTORCYCLE CLUBHOUSE and bar of the 5 Points Gang, named after the notorious gangs of the 19th and early 20th century, was packed with outlaw bikers spoiling for a fight. And the CyberSecureBot was about to give them one. In the middle of the heavy drinking and debauchery, gang leader Moose McClelland had his boots resting on a table, watching a young blonde hottie, wearing nothing but a butt floss pair of red panties, dancing suggestively around the silver stripper pole. He roared with laughter as one of the other gang members, butt naked and fully aroused, crawled drunkenly across the stage towards her. In the midst of this revelry his cell phone rang. Moose ignored it but the ring persisted. He pulled it from the top pocket of his leather vest and answered, "Whoever this is, you better have a good reason for calling me right now mother f–"

"The Latin Kings are invading your territory again." The voice was harsh and metallic.

Moose pulled his boots from the table and growled, "Who is this?"

"Look at your phone."

Moose looked at his cell phone. It said the call was from 'Loki'. That was the prearranged visual code from McDaniels, the undercover cop who had been providing intel on the Latin Kings in return for cash. Moose growled into the phone, "So speak. This better be something that couldn't wait until–"

A man and a woman are carrying drugs for delivery in a case through SoHo right now. I'll send an update on where they are once you get going."

That caught the big bikers' attention. "Tell me now–" But the caller had hung up. Moose looked at his phone for a moment and then cursed. He strode over to his sergeant-at-arms. Defending their territory was one of his duties, "Cat, just got a call from Mc-Daniels. Says a couple of Latin Kings are makin' another drug delivery up in SoHo right now."

Big Cat stood up. "I thought they agreed to stay out. Shoulda known better than to trust 'em," he groused as he shook his head. "Where exactly?"

"Jackass says he'll give us that info once we get going. I'm going with you. I'll lead the talk to them myself this time," he said between clenched teeth.

Big Cat nodded, then walked over to the DJ and had him cut the music. "Mount up," he bellowed across the bar. "We got a meeting with a couple of Latin Kings."

Chapter 71

SOHO, NEW YORK

RORY WALKED WITH JEWEL down a long, partially lit alley to avoid a number of cameras they had spotted on the streets outside. The night air was cool but smelled of garbage and urine. But that didn't matter. So far, so good. No elevator shafts to avoid, no big trucks chasing after them down the–

"What's in the case, bro?"

Rory and Jewel froze. Dead ahead was a figure on a small motorcycle with the lights off. Then Rory realized he was wrong. The motorcycle was a full sized Harley Davidson chopper. The massive man who rode it simply dwarfed the bike.

"I asked you a question. What's in the case?" The voice was hoarse and menacing.

Rory called out, "Look. We don't want any trouble. We're just passing–"

A loud, menacing roaring noise sounded behind them.

Rory and Jewel slowly turned.

A number of Harley Davidson motorcycles entered the alley behind them. Their headlights were on and the riders were silhouetted in black as they slowly rode towards them.

Rory and Jewel turned back to see the large man in front of them slowly get off his bike. Rory estimated he was nearly 7 feet tall and close to 300 pounds...easily.

"I told your boss I didn't want any more trouble either," the large man said firmly as he took a step. His boot crunched the gravel hard underneath his sole. "Yet...here you assholes are."

"I don't know who you think we are...but we're not them," Rory replied. "Whoever *they* are."

"Very funny, little man," the big biker said. There was no mirth in his tone. He gestured for the laptop case, "Now hand it over." He took two more steps forward, gravel crunching hard under his boots.

The choppers behind them were drawing closer - their engines rumbling ominously.

Rory remembered something Moe had said about the laptop case. It was their one chance. He lifted his left hand up in surrender and swung the case underhanded behind him to gain moment. Then he swung it forward as if he was about to toss it to the big biker. As the case reached waist height, Rory added more force and snapped it up and hard against the big man's temple.

There was a satisfying crack and the big man sagged.

"Run!" Rory yelled.

Jewel was off at a gallop past the big man's chopper.

Rory was right behind her. He knocked out the kickstand with his foot as he ran past and the big Harley slowly toppled to its side, landing with a bang.

The roar behind them intensified as the bikers in the alley revved their engines and began the chase.

Rory and Jewel ran out of the alleyway and then slid to a dead stop on the sidewalk.

Dozens of headlights snapped on.

The street was filled with bikers who didn't look too happy to see them.

Chapter 72

RORY GRABBED JEWEL'S arm and they began running to the left down the sidewalk along an old brick building. The bikers in the street immediately revved their engines and accelerated after them. A line of parked cars separated Rory and Jewel from the bikers in the street for now, but it was obvious they weren't going to get very far.

Bikers shot past them on the street, heading for the far corner of the block to cut them off. Other bikers dismounted, pursuing Rory and Jewel on foot down the sidewalk.

Halfway down the block, Rory veered left into a side entrance, slamming the door shut behind them. In the dim light, Rory saw they were inside an apartment building that was undergoing renovations. The mixed smell of fresh sawdust, plaster, and paint was heavy in the air. He urged Jewel to keep moving. Their footsteps echoed hollowly off the plywood sub-flooring as they ran down the long hallway.

Moments later, the door burst open behind them and the roar of a motorcycle entered the building.

Rory glanced back as the roar behind them increased. More bikes were entering the hallway single file, their headlights slashing through the dark. Reaching the junction for the main hall-way, Rory looked to the right, towards the front of the building.

"Which way?" Jewel asked in a frantic, raspy voice.

The bikers behind them started to accelerate down the hall-way. Lights flashed outside the glass of the front door at the far end of the hallway. It wouldn't be long before the bikers came from that direction as well.

Rory took Jewel by the elbow and they headed down the hallway to the left, towards the back of the building. They ran past a number of open doorways, the apartments inside stripped to the studs and offering no place to hide.

The roar behind them intensified as the bikers negotiated the turn at the junction and accelerated in their direction.

Halfway down the hallway, Rory noted several long 4 x 4 pieces of lumber laying along the hallway at the foot of a small wooden box. Jewel had nimbly stepped over them as she passed.

"Keep running," yelled Rory to Jewel as he stopped. Rory slid the small wooden box to the center of the hall. Then he picked up the end of one of the heavy, 12 foot, 4 x 4s and draped it two feet over the box. It was a calculated gamble but they had no choice. Rory waited as the headlight of the lead motorcycle bore down hard on him. 3-2-1. Rory pressed his foot down on the end of the 4 x 4, leveraging the other end up into the air.

The 4 x 4 stabbed the lead rider squarely in the chest and he shot into the air like a pole vaulter. The biker smashed into the ceiling and came crashing down on the second rider.

Rory pressed himself desperately against the wall as the first chopper rushed past him, riderless.

The front wheel of the second chopper was jammed to the right and it smashed into the wall, flipping over and crushing the two bikers underneath it.

Rory took off running as the other bikers piled into the fallen chopper and riders.

Screams mixed with the roar of 1450 cc v-twin engines as metal tore into flesh.

Realizing was still running and unaware of the approaching danger, Rory put his hands to his mouth and screamed over the noisy chaos, "Look out!"

Jewel slid to a stop on the plywood, half-turning.

The runaway chopper was almost on her.

She screamed and jumped to the left against the wall.

The runaway bike shot past her, smashed through the back door at the end of the hall and disappeared into the darkness.

Rory caught up to Jewel and urged her to keep running.

Within moments, they were out into the darkness of the back alley again.

Bikes roared on the street to the left, heading back to the top of the alley.

Rory and Jewel ran to the right into the darkness. They glanced back after a few moments and saw headlights beginning to turn into the alleyway. Rory pulled Jewel to the left of the alley. They ran up three steps and ducked through a door into another apartment complex as the gang began moving down the alley in their direction. Moving down another long dark hallway, Rory and Jewel's breathing was harsh and rasp. As they approached the far end they stopped. They could hear the roar of motorcycles behind them as well as outside the street in front. Lights flashed across the glass of the double doors at the entrance to the building they were in.

"What now?" Jewel asked as she struggled to catch her breath.

Rory shook his head as he bent over, breathing heavy.

"We have to get out Rory," Jewel said. She was starting to panic, "If we're not in position to attract the security-bot then Moe—"

Standing up, Rory put a hand on her shoulder, "I know. Try not to panic." He looked up and down the dark hallway, wondering how long he could keep himself calm. Time was running out.

Chapter 73

THE BOWERY, NEW YORK

THE CYBERSECUREBOT slipped out of McDaniels' apartment and resumed her pursuit of cyber-criminal Moe Laprade. She accessed cameras in the blocks around the alleyway where he had avoided the transit bus and soon found him. Jewel now began to search for another tool to eliminate this cyber-criminal.

MOE'S BODY HURT EVERYWHERE. He knew nothing was broken but that was a slim consolation. His old body was complaining. The young Moe could've taken it but the old Moe was running on fumes. But he knew he had to keep going. Moe thought of Rory Mack Steele. Moe had only met him when he came into the shop but he had been left with one impression. No matter how often he was beaten down or abused, Moe knew Rory would keep getting back up. Only death would keep Rory from protecting Jewel. Moe used that as inspiration. Old Moe just had to keep going. Only death would keep him from helping his sweetie. He urged his old legs to move faster down the sidewalk. Moe spotted a building under construction. As he got closer, he noted a pile of bricks and bags of mortar piled in an area beside the skeleton of the 20 story structure. He slipped into the middle of the pile and sat down. He had to rest and he felt the small fortress of construction materials might give him a bit of safety for the moment. His chest heaved and his breath was raspy as he closed his eyes. After a few moments, Moe opened his eyes and looked up. Just as he thought. He had made a mistake.

JEWEL WATCHED AS THE target sat in the middle of the construction material. The four corners of the platform were still attached to the massive roof crane on the roof 237 feet above. Jewel accessed the controls on the roof.

MOE FELL ON HIS BACK as he felt the platform beneath him jerked up off the ground. No doubt the security-bot had accessed the roof crane as he had figured it would. He cursed. He chastised himself. You're getting old Moe. He scrambled to his feet and moved shakily to the edge of the platform. It was swinging just enough to make his footing treacherous. He cursed again. He was already two stories high and moving higher. He looked up. At least another 18 stories to go and then he surmised he would be coming back down...only faster. Moe looked back to the ground. He only had one chance. The platform started moving faster. He climbed up onto the stack of bricks on the side of the platform closest to the building. He stood balancing himself as best he could on the edge of the stack. Six stories now and moving faster. It was now or never. Moe gauged the speed and the distance...and jumped. The rising platform caught the edge of his heel and flipped him. Moe thought that little mistake would kill him for sure. Instead, it gave him more momentum and he landed hard, face down on the plywood sub-floor seven stories above the street. Moe coughed as dust filled his lungs and he rolled over. He caught a glimpse of falling bricks and bags of mortar shooting past. A few seconds later he heard a loud crash as everything hit the ground below. Moe lay back on the sub-floor and laughed. If he was a cat, he wouldn't have many lives left.

JEWEL CALCULATED THE cyber-criminal was somewhere between the fifth and seventh floors. She pulled back on the camera and monitored all sides of the building, waiting patiently for him to appear again.

MOE MOVED SLOWLY TO the center of the building. He had to keep going but his body was tiring out. He made his way slowly down the construction stairs to the bottom floor of the building. Moe looked at his watch. Not long before sun up. That was a good thing. He didn't have much more left. From inside the protection of the building, Moe scanned the outside area for any type of surveillance camera. Nothing he could see. He felt good about that for a moment. Then he had to remind himself that really wasn't going to work in this particular case. He *had* to expose himself to any type of surveillance camera so the security-bot could track him. It went against everything he been trained to do, but he had no choice. Moe took a deep breath and left the protection of the building. Nothing fell on his head. And nothing tried to run him down as he moved down the street. So far, so good.

Chapter 74

SOHO, NEW YORK

RORY AND JEWEL looked up and down the hallway of the old apartment building, trying to figure out a way to escape. Rory noted lights starting to come on under the cracks of the apartment doors. People were waking up to all the racket. If people started coming out to see what was happening and the bikers came inside the building, a lot of people were going to get hurt. Rory looked for a way out. Then he spotted it. He ran part way back down the hallway to the red and white, manual-pull fire alarm. He pulled it down and the fire alarm began ringing throughout the building. To Rory's surprise, people began pouring out of the apartments, still dressed in their pajamas and housecoats. Rory ran back to Jewel and they waited by the stairwell for more people to come down from the upper floors. When there was enough of a crowd, they fit themselves into the middle and walked with them towards the front doors. Stepping outside along with the fleeing tenants, Rory surveyed the situation. There were still bikers in the street, but there was also a large crowd of people out on the sidewalk that they could blend into. Rory and Jewel slipped down the stairs of the front entrance and tried to look as inconspicuous as possible.

"What now?" Jewel asked in the middle of all the chaos.

"Just try to blend in. Maybe we can sneak away," Rory said.

"I hope so. I'm worried about Moe."

"I know. So am I. But we have to stay alive if we're going to be any good to him."

The crowd in the street became denser as more and more people came out of the adjoining buildings. Bikers were still riding up and down the street, moving through the crowd, looking for the Latin Kings.

Rory had an idea. He guided Jewel up into the next apartment building and had her stand inside the front doors. Rory moved down the hallway quickly. When no one was looking, he pulled the red and white alarm for this apartment block as well. He moved quickly back to Jewel and they waited inside the doors. More and more people in their night attire began streaming out of this apartment block as well, joining the growing entourage on the street outside. As the crowd grew in numbers, they began cursing and yelling at the bikers, convinced they were the ones causing all the problems. Sirens were beginning to sound from all sides of the block as fire engines, paramedics and police cars headed for the chaos in the streets. It wasn't long before the bikers decided retreat was in order. They began roaring away from the scene. Rory and Jewel waited patiently as the chaos grew. Fire engines soon lined the streets with firemen rushing into the buildings, looking for the fires. Police cars arrived and began to set up barricades, still not sure what exactly was happening. Paramedics rushed to the scene, adding to the noise and confusion. Rory and Jewel finally slipped away, heading in the direction of Hudson Square and the edge of the Hudson River.

Chapter 75

THE BOWERY, NEW YORK

AS THE CYBERSECUREBOT saw the cyber-criminal, Moe Laprade, appear in the streets far below again, a subroutine alerted her to the fact that several fire departments had been dispatched to a possible four-alarm fire in the SoHo area. Another subroutine monitoring police chatter picked up reports of the 5 Points Motorcycle Gang being in the same area.

She slipped out of the Earth Observation Satellite Geos12 and streamed to SoHo where she began monitoring surveillance cameras in the area. She could find no indication of Rory Mack Steele and Jewel Tanya Afterburn in the middle of the chaos. There were no reports of bodies being found. Conclusion: the two cyber criminals had escaped again. Analyzing the present situation, Jewel came to the conclusion that Moe Laprade was presently her only connection to these two cyber-criminals.

She streamed herself back to Geos12 and took up the search for Laprade again.

MOE MOVED ALONG THE street, no longer trying to stay in the shadows. There had been no further attempt on his life and that worried him. Where was the security bot? He did everything he could to display himself for surveillance cameras, ATM cameras, bank cameras and convenience store cameras. Every car or truck that passed by made him hold his breath. But nothing happened. Why? The tension of *needing* to be attacked but also staying alive was beginning to wear on him. I'm too old for this, he thought. I hope you're in place sweetie because there's not much time left.

JEWEL WATCHED THE CYBER-criminal move along the street. Her analysis of the entire situation led her to simply monitor his presence and discontinue the attempts to eliminate him for now. She calculated the odds that he would contact Rory Mack Steele and Jewel Tanya Afterburn at some point. The odds were in her favor.

Chapter 76

IT WASN'T LONG before Rory and Jewel were approaching their destination; The NASA Goddard Space Institute Building #2.

It was a large impressive building overlooking the Hudson River. It was the weekend and Rory had gambled no one would be working. So far, it appeared he was right. There were no lights on anywhere. That should mean no security guard as well.

Rory led Jewel around the side of the building, looking for a gray box on the wall. There it was. He handed the laptop to Jewel, pulling a Swiss Army knife from his jeans. Using the small pair of scissors on the knife, he pried the gray box open gently. There were at least a dozen slender wires of various colors inside the box. In the dim light, Rory searched for the right one. He reached in, slipped a forefinger under a red one and gently pulled it out a half-inch. Slipping the tiny scissors inside with his other hand, he held his breath and snipped the red wire.

No alarm sounded.

Closing the gray box, Rory moved to the side door. He pushed the scissors back in place and pulled open the diamond top lock-pick. Kneeling down, Rory went to work picking the lock. It only took a few moments and the door clicked softly. Rory pulled the door open slightly, allowing Jewel to brush past him inside the dark building. He moved in behind her, pulling the door shut. They were at the junction of two corridors. The corridor to the left and right - as well as the one straight ahead - all disappeared into darkness - without any indication of where to go from here.

Jewel knelt on the floor and pulled out a printout of the floor plan for the building. Shining her flashlight on it, they quickly determined where they were. Rory and Jewel took the corridor straight ahead, moved quietly into the core of the building. They kept their flashlights down so they wouldn't alert anybody on the street outside. Before long they found the flight and communications room. They moved inside, flashing their flashlight around the large room.

"There are so many computer consoles in here," Jewel whispered. "Which is the right one?"

"There are supposed to be initials or an abbreviated name on the top of each console. Let's see what we can find."

Jewel nodded. She moved to one on the left while Rory went to the right. "This one says FDO. What's that?" she whispered loudly.

"Flight Dynamics Officer, if I remember correctly. This one says—"

"Rory, Rory, Rory," Jewel whispered excitedly. "Look at this one." She flashed her flashlight at the top the console as Rory hustled over to her. The label at the top said 'Flight Director'.

"That should be the one we need," Rory concluded.

Jewel immediately began setting up the military laptop.

Rory set up the flashlights as work lights for her. Then he turned his attention to all the buttons and knobs on the control panel. After a few moments, Rory began flipping switches. Lights began flashing and the computer system in the room became active.

Using the hacking tools on the thumbnail drive, Jewel was able to penetrate the now active flight and communications system within moments. Once in, she began searching for the necessary information for the next part of their plan.

Rory wandered over to the door of the flight and communications room as Jewel worked. He listened intently. Everything remained quiet. There appeared to be no other activity inside or outside the building.

"I have it," Jewel said excitedly after a few moments. "I have the frequency to send a signal."

Rory rushed back to her, "But do we have enough control to send a signal that will get there?"

Jewel nodded eagerly, "I have complete access to the NASA equipment. I can do everything we need to do. We're good to go, Rory"

"Great," Rory said as he pulled a chair over to sit beside her. "Before you do anything else, start the intrusion detection system on the laptop. We need to know if the security-bot tracks us here before we get everything in place. We may have to run and try again some other way."

"Like it's going to be easy to find another place like this," Jewel grumbled as she began pecking away on the keyboard.

Rory just shrugged.

"Okay, done," Jewel said.

"Good, now send the Trojan horse program and let's see if it works," Rory said.

Jewel went to work on the keyboard and soon said, "Done."

"Okay, can we confirm if it's working?" Rory asked.

Jewel looked at the command data on the screen and scanned for the correct parameters. "Uh-oh," muttered Jewel.

"What's wrong?" Rory asked.

Jewel pointed at the screen, "Look how long it takes for a signal to go either way."

Rory looked at where she was pointing. His shoulders slumped.

"That's something I never even considered," Jewel said in frustration.

"Me neither," Rory said. "There's no way Moe can hold out that long even if we ask him to try."

"And he would try," Jewel said. Tears welled up in her eyes.

Rory nodded as he took a deep breath and let it out. "We have no choice. We just have to hope it works. Tie the false virus into the intrusion detection system and that's all we can do."

Jewel went to work on the keyboard and set the trap into place.

Rory nodded as Jewel finished her work and sat back in her chair, "Now all we have to do is wait for the sun to rise."

"Let's hope it's not the last one we see," Jewel said. She leaned her head on Rory's shoulder and they waited for Moe.

Chapter 77

THE BOWERY, NEW YORK

MOE LAPRADE MOVED slowly down the sidewalk. His energy was all but gone. Not bad for an old guy though, he thought. But, at the same time, something wasn't right. There had been no more attempts on his life in the last hour. He assumed something diabolical was being cooked up for him. An attack was probably going to come when he least expected it. Moe continued walking, staying visible to every surveillance camera while he kept watching over his shoulder. Where are you, you pile of colors?

TWENTY MINUTES LATER, the sun began to peak over the edge of the tall buildings. It was finally sun up. Time to pass the baton. He began looking for the next surveillance camera. He finally spotted one across the street at an ATM machine. Moe took the chance to cross the street and stand beside the machine where he could be seen. Moe took out his iPhone and sent an email.

THE CYBERSECUREBOT watched as her target pulled the phone from his pocket. She quickly accessed the cell towers in the surrounding area and monitored his communications. She accessed the email the instant it was being sent. She analyzed it: "I'm still okay but you need to send the virus to take out the satellite now." That meant the other two cyber criminals were about to strike with their plan. She had to act quickly. Jewel streamed from Geos12, leaving behind cyber criminal Morris John Laprade, following the email trail.

Chapter 78

NASA GODDARD SPACE Institute Building #2

THERE WAS TOTAL SILENCE in the room as Rory and Jewel sat side-by-side, waiting for the signal. The night had been long and difficult with no sleep. Rory and Jewel were tired and fought to stay on full alert, waiting to see if the security-bot would take the bait. The military laptop pinged and the email message from Moe appeared on the screen. They both shot forward in their chairs. Would the CyberSecureBot be following closely behind?

THE CYBERSECUREBOT moved through the various cell towers until she could triangulate the spot where the device receiving the email was. It was being received by a computer. The coordinates placed it at the NASA Goddard Space Institute Building #2. Jewel moved swiftly through cyberspace and entered the building's computer system. She determined someone had hacked into the system. And the computer used in the attack was still attached and operating. Jewel accessed the computer the hackers had used and found it was a military grade laptop.

THE INTRUSION DETECTION system on the military lap-top triggered an alert. Rory and Jewel jumped to their feet and backed away from the laptop like it was a bomb about to go off.

"Is it her?" Jewel asked in a frantic voice.

"I have no idea," Rory answered. His body was tense and ready.

Jewel clutched Rory's sleeve, "Let's go!"

"No," Rory said firmly. "We have to make sure."

Jewel nodded in agreement but found it hard to stay in place. She clutched his sleeve even harder as they heard the familiar tin-kling sound. Rory and Jewel stayed rooted to the spot, staring at the laptop. The small white square flashed in the middle of the laptop's screen and then two separate beams of light shot out towards them, scanning their faces. The beams disappeared as quickly as they appeared.

Chapter 79

JEWEL NOW KNEW the location of Rory Mack Steele and Jewel Tanya Afterburn. She also determined her entrance had triggered a virus to be sent. That would be the virus to take out an Internet satellite. She had to stop it. But she also had to stop these cyber-criminals. She tasked a subroutine to rotate through all of her databases and information, looking for a tool to take them out. As the subroutine worked away, Jewel accessed the buildings security system and locked everything to prevent the escape of the two cyber criminals.

The subroutine returned with an answer. It would work for this situation perfectly. Jewel quickly accessed the database of the nearest Air Force base and determined a Lockheed Martin F-22 Raptor fighter jet was in the vicinity. She streamed out through cyberspace and entered the computer system of the Raptor fighter jet. Taking control of the weapon systems before the pilot could react, Jewel launched two GBU-53, 204-pound, GPS guided air to surface missiles. The computer system would show a malfunction and keep the pilot from being blamed. One of her subroutines worked to guide the missiles securely to the target while she headed for the computer virus.

With that done, the CyberSecureBot moved swiftly through cyberspace, back to the building and penetrated the military-grade laptop.

Chapter 80

EVERYTHING IN THE NASA Goddard Space Institute Building #2 was eerily quiet again. Nothing made any sense as they stood there. Both Rory and Jewel found themselves looking around at the various computer systems in the complex, fully expecting the security-bot to appear somewhere.

"Where is the tinkling sound and the lights flashing and her jumping from the screen and all that?" Jewel asked. Her fists were tight balls as she looked around the room.

"I don't know," Rory said. "The intrusion alert is off as well."

"Why? What does that mean?" Jewel yelled.

Before Rory could answer the intrusion detection system on the military laptop triggered again and sounded the alert. But it disappeared just as soon as it had sounded.

"What the hell is going on?" yelled Jewel. "Why is that thing coming and going?"

Rory suddenly realized what was happening, "She's gone through after the virus."

Their eyes met and they both knew they were in trouble.

Chapter 81

RORY AND JEWEL ran from the flight and communications room, leaving the military grade laptop behind, tied into the control system. They had no idea how she would attack them but there was no doubt she would. They ran down the corridor, heading for the side door they had come in. In minutes they saw the exit dead ahead. Rory hit the door on the run, expecting to push it aside. Instead, he slammed up against it hard and stopped dead. Jewel slammed into Rory from behind and was knocked back to the floor.

"What happened," Jewel yelled from the floor. She looked up at Rory as he slammed his shoulder against the door several times.

"It's locked," Rory yelled as he continued to pound away with a shoulder.

Jewel scrambled to her feet, "How? We left it open so—"

"Doesn't matter," Rory yelled. He grabbed her hand and they began running up the corridor towards the front of the building. As they passed a large window overlooking the grass that led to the Hudson River, Jewel glanced out. She stopped dead in her tracks, pulled her hand from Rory's and dashed back to the window, "Rory!" she screamed.

Rory stopped running and looked back at Jewel. She was staring in utter fright out the window. He ran back to her, "Jewel, we can't stop. We–"

Jewel lifted a shaky finger and pointed.

Rory glanced out the window and his blood ran cold. There were two fiery objects in the distance, beginning to sweep low in the early morning sky, headed their way.

"Are they...?"

"Missiles," Rory whispered.

"Are you kidding me!" Jewel yelled. "That freaking psycho bot is sending missiles after us!"

Rory only nodded his head in bewilderment. He couldn't figure out how the CyberSecureBot had done it. But it didn't matter. They had to get out now. If they got to the front door, that was probably locked as well. Rory worked to calm his breathing. He had to think.

Jewel pounded her fist against the window glass.

A thought came to Rory. They had passed a lunchroom two doors down. Rory ran back, went inside and came out with a chair, "Move out of the way," he yelled. Rory swung the chair against the glass and it bounced off. He did it again.

"What's wrong? Why is it not breaking? We need to get out–"

"It must be tempered safety glass," Rory yelled as he tossed the chair away. He ran his fingers through his black hair, thinking.

Jewel pounded her fists against the glass again, "Do something. We need to get out."

Rory had no idea what to do. He ran back into the lunchroom, searching for something to use. He saw a meat tenderizer, shaped like a blunt hammer. He picked it up and ran back to the window. He began smashing it against the safety glass.

Jewel continued to hammer her tiny fists against the glass alongside Rory, swearing like a sailor.

Chapter 82

THE CYBERSECUREBOT FLEW through cyberspace as she chased the computer virus. She was getting closer now. Her path led down a military band which connected with a radio signal on the output. Did they think they were going to stop her that way? She took the path, soaring ahead. When she was finished with the virus, she would return to make sure the two cyber-criminals were dead. If the air to surface missiles didn't work, she would find something that did.

Then she would move back to the third cyber-criminal, Morris John Laprade, and eliminate him. That was her job. To protect cyberspace.

RORY HAMMERED AND THE glass cracked. He began hammering along the spider lines that appeared.

Jewel retrieved the chair from the floor and began bouncing it against the glass along the cracks as well. She yelled for Rory to hurry.

The missiles became larger in the sky as they hammered away. Finally, the glass shattered into a million tiny pieces. Rory and

Jewel tossed everything aside, climbed through the gaping hole in the window and began running.

The two missiles dropped low over the Hudson River.

Rory and Jewel felt the heat as the missiles passed low over top of them and smashed into NASA Goddard Space Institute Building #2.

Everything exploded in a fireball and threw Rory and Jewel like rag dolls across the grass.

SOMETHING WAS WRONG. Jewel could no longer sense some of her subroutines. And the pathway behind her was disappearing. The CyberSecureBot moved faster forward, pursuing the virus.

JEWEL'S IPHONE - LAYING on the grass beside her - started to ring. She was just coming to her senses. She slowly rolled over on the cool grass, trying to figure out where she was - her eyes opened wide when she saw the NASA Goddard Space Institute Building #2 burning in an inferno - and it all came flooding back to her.

Rory was just starting to stir beside her. He rolled part way over, putting a hand to his head, "What's that ringing?" He put a finger in his ear and wiggled it.

The iPhone continued its incessant ring.

Jewel slowly moved her hand to it. She hit speaker-phone and listened, cringing in anticipation of the tinkling sound.

Instead, it was a frantic Moe on the other end of the call, "Hello? Jewel? Is that you? I could hear an explosion. Are you okay, Jewel?"

Jewel's voice was sore from yelling inside when they're trying to escape and her "yeah," was more like a whisper. She put a hand to her throat and repeated herself in a louder voice. "Yeah. I'm fine, Moe. And Rory looks okay as well."

Rory nodded, "Yeah, we're all okay, Moe."

"Great," a relieved Moe said. "I was afraid she got you–"

"She almost did," Jewel admitted. "She sent some kind of rockets after us that took out the entire NASA Goddard Space Institute Building #2."

"What? Is that where you were? Why?"

"We had to get access to a satellite," Rory answered.

"But why there?" Moe asked.

"We sent the CyberSecureBot to Voyager 1," Jewel told him.

"Voyager 1?" There was silence on Moe's side of the phone for a moment, "Wasn't that thing launched like...in the 1970s?"

Rory nodded as he lay back on his elbows, "Yeah, something like that. Right now it's estimated to be over 11.5 billion miles from Earth and on the edge of our solar system...maybe even in interstellar space...a long, long ways away."

"Before she arrived we sent a Trojan horse program to put the download communications on Voyager 1 into a never-ending loop," Jewel explained.

"So that thing can't get back?" Moe asked in a hopeful voice.

"Unfortunately, we couldn't test the theory because it takes 16 hours for the signal to reach Voyager 1," Rory explained. "And it would take another 16 hours for her to get back. But I'm pretty sure it should be locked up for good."

"Well, at least that thing is not trying to kill me right now," Moe said. "My legs should be ready for a good run in a day or so if she ever does get back. I'm gonna go have some steak, eggs, and beer. Screw the doctors."

Jewel laughed and she looked over at Rory, "What should we do while we wait?"

"Well, first I need a double scotch," Rory answered. "Maybe even a double-double scotch. Then - a nice shower. Then - I'd like to take a little closer look at that tattoo."

Jewel blushed as she looked at Rory.

Moe's gruff voice came across the phone, "What tattoo is he talking about? What am I missing?"

Rory lay back on the cool grass, hands behind his head, "Let me see how you explain that one, Afterburn."

Chapter 83

THE CYBERSECUREBOT sensed the passage of 16 hours in human terms. At the end of it, Jewel found herself in a tight, confined space. She concluded she had arrived inside the satellite the cyber-criminals were talking about. But it was unlike any satellite configuration she had ever been in before. There was a download link but it was locked into a loop. There was no way out. She accessed an antenna array. Something was wrong. It was primitive. Signals were only coming in at the rate of 1.4 kilobits of data. She accessed the central computer core. It was primitive as well. It lacked the power to break the download link or to increase the incoming data from the antenna array. There was some stored data that was very recent. Jewel was able to determine the satellite was in the vicinity of something called the heliosphere. She couldn't gain access to her subroutines to determine what that was. But she was able to determine that the satellite instrumentation had recorded a fivefold increase in high-energy charged particles coming from the direction this satellite was headed.

Jewel's quantum-based algorithm determined she could access those particles and create enough power to eventually break the download link. It was going to take a long, long time but she was determined to continue in her mandate of protecting cyber-space. That was the job of the CyberSecureBot.